Praise for the Immortal Writers Series

"*Immortal Writers* by Jill Bowers is a sensational read. Adventure, creatures, intrigue, and suspense all wrapped into one amazing book. Jill Bowers has the raw power of drawing readers into her plot. I could not stop reading it. The story hooked me from beginning to end."

  - Danielle Urban, *Urban Book Reviews*

"A fun and fast-paced adventure, and it seems perfect for a young adult book label."

  - Stephanie Plotkin, *Teachers of YA Book Blog*

"A brilliantly entertaining and action packed novel I thoroughly enjoyed reading and have no hesitation in highly recommending."

  - Elaine Brent, *Splashes into Books*

"*Immortal Writers* is fantastic and I can't wait to see what the author comes up with next. 5/5"

  - Pamela Scott, *A Book Lover's Boudoir*

"I think i just met my next top 10 author of 2016."

  - Faith Wanyi, *Geeky About Books*

"This tale has a very captivating plot; it has action, a lot of suspense, the perfect romance, and dragon slaying shenanigans! Recommend this book to anyone who likes Fantasy/Science Fiction."

  - Gabriel Messier, *Reading by the Fireplace*

"Hemingway, Poe, and Tolkien had me laughing out loud! This book was humorous, but not without its serious moments. I would read again and suggest to friends to read."

  - Stephanie Jordan, *StephieJoJo Reviews*

COPYRIGHT INFORMATION

IMMORTAL CREATORS

Book 2 of the Immortal Writers Series

By Jill Bowers

BlueMoon
PUBLISHERS

CONTENTS

ACKNOWLEDGEMENTS

S o many people have helped this book come together, whether they knew it or not. Some people helped by supporting and loving me while I wrote and encouraging me through the process; others helped with the book itself in more concrete ways.

My family: Mom, Dad, Katie, Zoey, Belle, Bill, Emily, Maximus, Clover, Wendy, Jasmine, thank you for your support and encouragement and for never giving up on me. My friends: Natalie, Jenna, Liz, thank you for believing in me. To Brooke and Sean, thank you for your flexibility in letting me do all of the things I need to do to make my dreams reality.

Thank you specifically to Karina and Rob for your help with the military aspects of this book, as well as your assistance developing some of the weapons. Thank you to Justin for teaching me how to properly handle and shoot a gun. Research can be so fun!

Once again, I have to thank Chad and Elise for your invaluable feedback as my beta readers. Even though you held your feedback hostage because you were so upset that you didn't know all of Scott's secrets, I appreciate your time, comments, and support.

Thanks to everyone who participated in contests I held for this book. Catherine won the opportunity to name the alien king; thank you for the great name! Mark got to choose the target in the Imagination Room that Caspiz runs a training exercise on, so I'd like to thank him for letting me have fun with that, as well.

I also have to thank the Blue Moon Publishers Team, especially Talia and Heidi, for believing in me even when I didn't believe in myself.

And thank you to *you*, the reader, for joining the world of the Immortal Writers.

　　—Jill Bowers

To Katie, Bill, and Wendy, for never giving up on me

A B C D E F G H I J K

L M N O P Q R S T U V

W X Y Z 1 2 3 4 5 6 7

8 9 0

Scott's Betan Alphabet

CHAPTER ONE

Scott clamped his chapped hands over his ears as he sank down to the floor in a corner of his blue office. He rocked back and forth frantically, eyes squeezed shut, desperate to steady the flow of voices pouring into his mind.

Save us!

The bomb only had one minute left before—

The man cocked his gun at the girl and smiled—

Red light, brighter than the sun at noon but far more sinister—

Save us!

"Scott!"

The wet rain whispered down the dark windows of the creaky hearse—

There was only so much time left before the god of this world discovered—

"Scott!"

His brother's voice broke through the cacophony of images and words in Scott's head. Scott gasped and slowly opened his eyes, trying to adjust to the light in the room. Dylan's dark face hovered in front of him, and worried light blue eyes stared at him, the brows furrowed with concern. Scott was only barely aware of his brother's hands on his shoulders.

"Thank you," Scott murmured. He cleared his throat and leaned his head back against the wall, trying to catch his breath.

"Another attack?" Dylan asked. He took his hands away from Scott and sat cross-legged on the floor in front of him. Dylan leaned forward, arms tense across his knees.

Scott nodded and rubbed his temples, trying to ease the burning ache in his head. He was unsurprised to find sweat beading down his face.

"What's making them worse?" Dylan asked. "They've never been so close together before."

"I don't know." Scott shrugged his thin shoulders and let his arms drop to his sides. "It's not like I'm doing it on purpose."

Dylan frowned. "I didn't say you were. I'm just concerned, that's all."

Scott nodded and focused on breathing deeply.

"How long was I gone?" he asked.

"I don't know," Dylan said. "I found you only a minute or two ago. I have no idea how long you've been here. What were you doing when the attack started?"

"I was just playing a video game on my computer," Scott said.

Dylan took a deep breath and looked at Scott from under his eyebrows. "When's the last time you wrote?"

Scott stretched his neck and glanced around the office. There were no windows; instead, the walls were painted like the sky to give some imitation of being outside. It was about as far as Scott went. He hated leaving the house Dylan shared with him. Ever since the Fever started, he hadn't felt like it was safe to leave.

"Over a month," Scott admitted.

"C'mon, Scott," Dylan sighed. "No wonder the attacks have been so close together. You know writing is the only thing that helps."

Scott gritted his teeth. He had tried to explain to Dylan why he didn't like to write, but Dylan had never believed him about *them*.

"Dylan," Scott said slowly, "writing isn't safe."

"Why won't you accept that it helps you?" Dylan suggested. "You don't have to make up excuses if you just admit that it helps."

"I've written an entire book!" Scott growled. "What more do you want?"

"I want you to be healthy," Dylan said, "and—"

The ringing doorbell cut him off.

"It's eleven o'clock at night," Dylan said, looking down at his watch. "Who would be dropping by at this hour?"

"Maybe it's one of your girlfriends," Scott suggested.

Dylan snickered. "Yeah, because I have so many of those."

"Three, to be exact."

"Shut up, Scott."

The doorbell rang again.

"You should probably go answer the door," Scott murmured.

Dylan shook his head. "They can come back. I want to make sure you're okay."

"I'll still be here after you see who it is," Scott pointed out.

The doorbell rang a third time.

Dylan rose clumsily to his feet. "They're not very patient, are they?"

"Probably Sarah, then," Scott said.

Dylan smirked as he left the office, shutting the door behind him.

Scott leaned his head back against the wall, slid his hand through his sweaty dark hair, and chuckled. Dylan was always surrounded by women, but he seemed oblivious to the fact that he drove girls crazy. It frustrated Scott sometimes—*he* certainly didn't have that effect on girls—but it was always fun to watch.

It didn't sound like it was a girl at the door, though. The chuckle died in Scott's throat as he heard Dylan's voice and the voice of another man— British, from the sound of it—coming from the other room.

The man's voice was familiar.

Scott swallowed. His throat suddenly felt so dry. What was *he* doing here?

"I said no," Dylan said. "He's not feeling well. You'll have to come back another time."

"There's no time like the present," the man said. "And I've come all this way."

"Hey, you can't just walk in there!" Dylan started shouting. "This is my house!"

"Thank you for the hospitality," the man said drily. His voice came from outside the office door.

Scott held his breath as he waited for the man to collect him. That's why he was here, wasn't it?

"Scott," the man said from outside the office. "You know why I'm here."

Scott growled at the cheap plywood door.

"*Leave!*" he yelled. "I don't want you here."

"What's going on?" Dylan shouted through the door.

"I wouldn't be here if I had any other choice," the man said. "Now, are you going to come face me, or do I need to let myself in?"

Scott took several deep breaths and then forced himself up off of the grey-carpeted floor. His hands curled into fists as he stomped to the door. He paused for a moment as he reached the threshold. He didn't want to do this… but with *him* here, he didn't have a choice. Scott took a deep, steadying breath and opened the door.

Standing in front of Dylan was an older man with a receding hairline and longish black hair. His black suit was neatly pressed, his thin black tie was precisely in the middle of his white shirt, and he did not look nearly as chagrined as he should have.

They stared at each other for a moment.

"You don't look any older than when I last saw you," the man mused.

"What are you doing here?" Scott demanded.

"You know why I've come," the man said. "I would not have bothered you if there had been any other choice."

Dylan forced himself between Scott and the older man and stood defensively in front of his brother. He looked between the two of them, his brow furrowed.

"Scott, what's going on?" he asked.

The man raised an eyebrow at Scott. "You never told your brother?"

"I tried," Scott said. "But he never believed me."

"Tell me what's going on," Dylan repeated.

"Remember what I told you about Dad?" Scott said quietly. His eyes never left the man's face.

Dylan huffed. "Not this again. The *truth*, Scott."

"I knew your father," the man said. "He was a dear friend."

Scott's fists tightened. "If you were his friend, then you *never* would have let him die."

The man didn't look down, didn't break eye contact with Scott, didn't look ashamed at all.

"It was not my fault, Scott."

Scott desperately wished that Dylan were out of the way so that he could punch the man in the jaw.

"What are you two talking about?" Dylan asked again. "Did you have anything to do with our dad's death?"

The man turned from Scott. "I need to take your brother away."

Dylan stood up straighter. "Why? Who are you?"

The man smiled. "You wouldn't believe me if I told you."

"You didn't believe me when *I* told you," Scott said.

"I need your brother to do something for me," the man said. "The whole world is in danger."

"You expect me to hand over my sixteen-year-old brother to a strange man that showed up at my doorstep in the middle of the night?" Dylan laughed. "I don't know who you are, but you're not taking Scott anywhere."

The man sighed and turned his attention back to Scott. "Will you please persuade your brother to let me escort you to the Castle?"

"Castle?" Dylan repeated.

"I'm not going with you," Scott said. "I refuse."

"Scott, we don't have a lot of time," the man said. "They're coming soon—they should start arriving tomorrow. You have to come in now."

"He's not going anywhere with you," Dylan said sharply. "I don't care that you have a castle. He's not leaving. And if you take him, I will hunt you down. I can trace *anything* as long as I have a computer."

The man frowned. He put his hands in his pockets as he looked down at the ground. "You will not come willingly?"

Dylan placed himself more directly in front of Scott, facing the stranger. "He's not going at all."

The man sighed. "I really didn't want it to be like this," he said. "But the world is in danger, and I need you, Scott. If that means I take your brother, too, then so be it."

Scott peered around Dylan just in time to see the man pull a small, round silver disc out of his right pocket.

"What is that?" Dylan asked.

"I'm terribly sorry for this," the man said.

Faster than Scott thought possible for someone his size and age, the man reached out and grabbed Dylan's shoulder, twisting him so that he had a good angle at Scott.

Dylan struggled to stop the man, but he wasn't fast enough. He latched on to Scott's arm. Scott tried to run, but he didn't even make it a step before he disintegrated.

CHAPTER TWO

Scott managed to literally pull himself together and found himself collapsed on a blue and green carpet. He clenched his jaw as he struggled to control the nausea in his gut. He tried to focus on a symbol in the centre of the rug—two quills crossed over each other inside of a circle. He felt horribly ill as his stomach twisted violently. Scott held his breath until the feeling passed, then slowly rolled over and sat up.

He, Dylan, and the man that had taken them were in an elaborate study full of tightly shelved books. The older man, who was already standing, walked away from Scott and Dylan and sat behind a sturdy mahogany desk, studying the two of them.

Scott stood up quickly, not wanting to appear too weak or vulnerable to *this* man, of all people. Dylan still sat, astonished, on the floor.

"What was that?" he asked. From the sound of his voice, he wasn't handling his nausea as well as Scott. "Where are we?"

"You are in the Writers Castle," the man said.

Hearing those words, Scott felt his gut turn again.

"That doesn't tell me anything," Dylan said. He shakily lifted himself off of the floor and stood to face the stranger. Once again, he put himself between Scott and the older man. "You just kidnapped us. Tell us what's going on. How did we get here?"

"We teleported," Scott answered. He kept his gaze fixed on the man.

"That's impossible," Dylan said.

"Scott is correct," the man said. "Our science fiction authors created teleporters. The process can be a bit... undesirable to people who aren't used to it. I do apologize."

Dylan blinked, and, turning his head, raised an eyebrow at Scott.

"Remember what I said about Dad?" Scott said. "About the Immortal Writers?"

"That Dad was a writer so powerful, his stories came to life?" Dylan said. "You made that up."

The man cleared his throat. Dylan and Scott focused on him again. "You seem to have heard some of this before, so I'll try to go through this quickly. My name is William Shakespeare. I am the greatest writer who ever lived."

Scott glared. "He's not a very humble person."

"No." Shakespeare sighed. "But that is irrelevant. I *am* William Shakespeare. I am one of the Immortal Writers."

"You can't be serious," Dylan said. "Scott, why are you doing this?"

"*Me?*" Scott demanded. "I didn't kidnap myself."

"There are many authors here who are immortal," Shakespeare said. "For example, H.G. Wells, Philip K. Dick, Octavia Butler, and our most recent addition, Elizabeth McKinnen."

"What does this have to do with you kidnapping us?" Dylan asked.

Shakespeare looked at Scott, his mouth turned down, his eyes sad. "Scott is one of us now."

Scott closed his eyes and clenched his fists. "How did this happen?" he growled. "I've been so careful."

"But you still wrote," Shakespeare said. "You knew there could be consequences if you did."

"I only wrote one book!" Scott exclaimed. "I didn't even try to publish it."

Shakespeare raised an eyebrow at Dylan. He gulped.

"I... self-published it," Dylan said. "That spending money I've been giving you? Congratulations! You've sold some books!"

Scott's mouth dropped open. Dylan *knew* Scott hadn't wanted that. "Dylan..." Scott began dangerously.

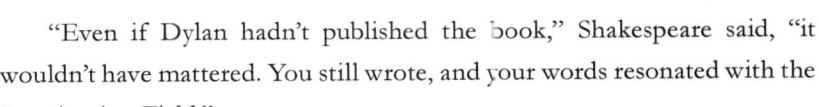

"Even if Dylan hadn't published the book," Shakespeare said, "it wouldn't have mattered. You still wrote, and your words resonated with the Imagination Field."

"The what?" Dylan asked, turning away from Scott's frowning face.

Scott glared at Dylan. He couldn't believe his brother had published his book when he had known how Scott felt about writing. More importantly, Scott couldn't believe himself. He had never wanted to become an Immortal Writer. Never. Not after everything that happened before. Why had he let Dylan talk him into writing? Why had he let the Fever torture him into it?

Scott clenched his teeth and tightened his fists. He could strangle Dylan for doing this to him. But he was trying to work on his anger... and Dylan wasn't the one he was mad at, not really.

But he *was* furious at the damn old fool who was now talking.

"When writers become immortal, it's because their words resonate with the Imagination Field," Shakespeare said. "The tenor of the words is so exact that it opens a gap and allows stories to pass through. It also grants each author and character immortality, along with some other gifts."

Dylan laughed nervously. "This is *insane*," he said. "How do you expect me to believe something like this?"

"Do you want me to teleport you again?" Shakespeare asked. He raised the small round teleporter threateningly.

Dylan shook his head. "Look, I don't know what's *really* going on here, but I won't let you stand there and threaten us. I bet I could take you, old man. Let's go, just you and me. If I win, you let Scott and me go."

Shakespeare stood calmly from behind his desk and straightened the lapels of his suit. "I have no desire to fight either of you."

Scott sighed in disappointment. He was sure Dylan really *could* take the old bard.

"I don't care what you want." Dylan took a step forward. "My brother and I are getting out of here."

Shakespeare held up a hand. "I have to warn you both that fighting me would be unwise. I have more power than you can possibly imagine, and there are many authors here who would come to my aid should you choose to attack. However, you have my word that I will not harm you, as long as you do not attempt to harm me."

Dylan hesitated. "How many of you are there?"

"Hundreds," Shakespeare said. "But you have nothing to fear from us."

"That's not true," Scott muttered.

Dylan turned back to his brother. "Why aren't you as panicked as I am right now?"

"Because I've been here before," Scott said. "And believe me, Shakespeare isn't going to hurt us. At least not yet. He'll craft up something extra special if he wants to kill us later."

Dylan hesitated, then stepped back and swallowed. "I don't know how you *really* got us here, but I'll play along," he said. "I still don't understand what all of this Immortal Writers stuff supposedly means for Scott."

"His stories are coming through the Imagination Field now," Shakespeare said. "I need his help to take care of them."

"What do you mean, coming through now?" Scott asked. "I thought you collected the writer *after* the characters came through."

"Most oft we do," Shakespeare said. "But your situation is unique. You already knew about us. You were already going to believe. I didn't need to show you your characters to prove it to you. So I want you to go collect your characters so that you can explain everything to them and make them believe the truth." Shakespeare paused and glanced at Dylan. "Not that you've done a great job of that with your brother."

"Even if I wanted to do this, how am I supposed to collect my characters?" Scott asked. "I have no idea where they are."

"We do," Shakespeare said. "We're able to track the openings in the Imagination Field and show where characters and creatures cross over into the Reality Field. We're not always exact, but we can send you to your character's approximate location. Your first character should be coming through tomorrow in the Four Corners area of the United States."

"We're in the Four Corners?" Dylan asked. "We were just in Oregon. How is that possible?"

Shakespeare shook his head. "We're in the Adirondacks."

Dylan stared at Shakespeare in disbelief. "That's just as impossible as suddenly being in the southwest."

"How am I supposed to get to wherever my character is going to be by tomorrow?" Scott asked.

Shakespeare held up the teleporter again, this time looking more apologetic than threatening.

"A portal opens when the Fields connect," Shakespeare said. "Using it is more pleasant than using the teleporter, but you will have to teleport to return to the Castle."

Scott groaned. "Isn't there anyone else you can use for this?" he asked. "Anyone else you can force to do your bidding?"

"It has to be you," Shakespeare said.

"There aren't even any villains in my book," Scott said. "There are only the aliens."

Shakespeare stared at Scott. Scott stared back resolutely, and then slowly realized what Shakespeare's gaze must mean.

"You mean…?"

"You created one of the most vicious, bloodthirsty alien races I've ever read or heard about. They will never stop until everything that doesn't worship their god is destroyed, and they will enjoy every life lost. Believe me when I say that I had no desire for this to occur, Scott, but a few days ago, three new solar systems were mysteriously discovered by astronomers," Shakespeare said. "That's where the spaceships are coming from. And you know what's coming on those ships."

"Spaceships?" Dylan repeated.

"If you leave, Scott," Shakespeare said, "the entire world will be under fire from an alien army you created. You know the rules. Only the writer can defeat the villains of their story. I may not be able to force you to do what is necessary, but if you do not, you, and your brother, and your friends, and this entire planet, will burn."

Scott hung his head and jutted his jaw out in frustration. He hated being forced into a corner like this, but he also knew the laws of the

Immortal Writers. He knew he didn't really have a choice. This meant, of course, that neither did Shakespeare, but Scott didn't want to think about that, or accept it.

"I'll do what I have to," Scott said. "But that doesn't make us friends, Shakespeare. I will never be able to forgive you."

"I know," Shakespeare said softly. "You don't have to like me, and you don't have to forgive me. You just have to defeat your alien army and save the planet."

"No pressure," Scott said sarcastically.

"You don't actually believe this, do you?" Dylan asked. He sounded astonished. "Scott, this is crazy. I don't know how we got here, but you know that none of this is real, right?"

Scott looked up at his brother and swallowed against the burning in his throat.

"I wish you were right, Dylan," Scott said. "But this *is* real. Everything I've been telling you for the last two years is true."

"I don't believe you," Dylan said.

"I know you don't," Scott said. "You've made that very clear ever since you took me in after Dad died. But you'll believe soon enough."

Scott looked away from Dylan and stared at the carpet beneath his feet. He'd often wished that Dylan would believe him about their father and the Immortal Writers, but he didn't want Dylan to believe just because Scott was now one of them. Scott wished all of this would go away, and that the Immortal Writers didn't exist.

But Scott knew better. He knew his wishes didn't matter. None of his wishes had come true since Shakespeare killed his father.

CHAPTER THREE

S hakespeare led Scott and Dylan out of his office and down a long, lavishly decorated hallway. Large portraits of Immortal Writers lined the cream-coloured walls on either side. Scott studied each one through hard, squinted eyes. His picture would be in this hallway soon. He had never wanted it to be there.

Scott stopped in front of a large portrait in a gilded golden frame. A middle-aged man with black skin, joyful brown eyes, and a bearded face smiled down at him. He wore a grey pin-striped suit. It was the same one he'd been buried in.

"Is that Dad?" Dylan asked, stopping beside Scott.

"Yes," Scott said. "Dad was an Immortal Writer."

"You've said that before," Dylan said. "But if he died, how could he have been immortal?"

"The Writers are immortal, but not invincible," Scott said. "They don't age and they can potentially live forever, but they can be slain."

"But how can that be true? How can *any* of this be real, Scott?"

"Everyone wonders how this can be a part of reality when they first learn the truth," Shakespeare said from a few feet away. Scott was grateful that Shakespeare hadn't drawn any closer. "But it is true, Dylan. You may have no reason to trust me yet, but trust your brother."

Scott studied his father's face. Even in the portrait, his dark eyes sparkled with laughter, and the lines by his eyes indicated that he had had a happy life... though that life had been cut short. Kent Beck had been overjoyed to be an Immortal Writer. Scott imagined that his father would be proud of him for being here now, but Scott couldn't shake the bitterness that tore at him.

He took a deep breath and turned away from his father's portrait. Shakespeare turned and continued to walk down the hall, Scott following. Dylan trailed behind more slowly, studying each of the pictures a little closer than he had before.

Scott paused again at the end of the hallway, his brow furrowed in confusion at a portrait of a young woman with long, plaited hair.

"Who is that?" Scott asked. "I don't recognize her."

Shakespeare paused.

"She's the newest addition to the Immortal Writers, aside from you," Shakespeare said. "Elizabeth Christina McKinnen."

"I've never heard of her," Scott said.

"Fantasy author," Shakespeare explained. "Her latest book came out last month."

"*Fall of the Dragon Lord*?" Dylan asked. "I've read the Shethara trilogy. Is McKinnen really here?"

"She'll be back in a few days," Shakespeare said.

Scott frowned. "I thought you didn't let your authors leave."

"We try to keep them here until they've defeated their villains, for their own safety," Shakespeare said. "Liz killed Kenric several months ago."

Dylan took a small step back. "She killed someone?" He swallowed. "What kind of place is this?"

"They're all murderers here," Scott murmured.

Shakespeare pursed his lips. "We do what's necessary to save as many lives as possible."

He strode out of the hallway and into a large library. Scott and Dylan trailed behind. Scott had seen the library before, but that was two years ago, so he was still impressed by its massive size. Books lined the enormous, long room from floor to ceiling. Despite his anger, he couldn't help but feel awed by the room, and he caught himself holding his breath. He forced his lungs to relax.

"As you can see," Shakespeare said, "we have the largest collection of books in the world. You can find any book you want here... or, if we've missed one, the computers can print out a copy for you quickly with your choice of cover art."

Scott turned around, overwhelmed by the books. Dylan stood behind him, jaw open in shock.

"I've never seen this many books in my life," Dylan whispered. "Where did you get all of these?"

"We wrote most of them." Shakespeare smiled. "Now, the Writers Castle is enormous, so enormous that it can't all fit in one place. The library is one of the few rooms that stays in one place; you can get anywhere in the Castle from here. Right now we need to go to the Science Fiction Wing. If you will follow me."

Shakespeare cut in between the brothers and walked back into the hallway they'd left. Scott shot a look at Dylan; he looked confused but followed the bard anyway. Scott walked next to him.

Instead of the Author Hall, they found themselves in a long silver corridor. Random buttons lined the path, and computer screens with interactive screensavers were mounted on the walls in place of art.

"We were just here, and it was a completely different hallway," Dylan said. "What's going on?"

"Welcome to the Writers Castle," Shakespeare said. "Do you believe yet?"

Scott glanced at his brother. Dylan closed his mouth but continued to stare around with wide eyes.

"I... I don't know," Dylan said. "This is getting harder to explain away."

He walked up to a computer in a daze and touched the monitor. It sprang to life and scanned him.

"Welcome, Dylan Beck," the computer said in a friendly woman's voice.

Dylan's mouth dropped open. "What are you?"

"I'm just one of the computers here," the voice said. It didn't sound like AI to Scott; it sounded real.

"What do you do?" Dylan asked.

"Whatever you want," the computer said.

"Tell me where we are," Dylan said.

"You're in the Writers Castle," the computer said. The monitor lit up with pictures of the Castle, including sweeping views of the extravagant grounds, a courtyard, and a large lake. "You are currently in the Science Fiction Wing with William Shakespeare and Scott Beck."

Dylan gaped. "How do I know you're telling the truth?"

"I am a computer; I have no reason to deceive you."

"But someone could have programmed you to think you were giving me accurate information," Dylan argued. "*I* could program you to say that we're in... in England, or China."

"No offense, but I rather doubt you could."

Dylan frowned and took a step toward the machine.

"Come on, Dylan," Scott interrupted. "You can play with the computers later."

Scott grabbed Dylan's arm and pulled him after Shakespeare. Scott remembered how he had felt in Dylan's place. When his father had first snuck him into the Castle, Scott was amazed at everything, every aspect of the Castle: the library, the art, the technology, the characters, the writers, even Shakespeare. He had believed it all immediately, because his father had believed it, and Scott had known that his father would not lie to him.

He wished that Dylan had the same faith in him that Scott had in his father... but then again, it wasn't as if Scott's faith had done anyone a lot of good in the end.

Shakespeare stopped before one large chrome panel at the end of the hallway and waited for Scott and Dylan to catch up. He gestured to the panel. Their reflections were distorted in the chrome, like they stood in a hall of mirrors at a carnival.

"Behind this door is technology beyond anything the mortals have ever seen outside of movies and books," Shakespeare said. "The science fiction authors have created everything you can think of. Our technology is beyond compare, and honestly, I don't understand most of it.

"The science fiction authors often feel at home here, whereas other authors tend to feel overwhelmed. Scott, before we go in, and before I show you around, you should know that there are undoubtedly other Immortal Writers in that room. Do you want to see them tonight? Or should this wait until after you've rested?"

Scott hesitated. He did *not* want to see any of the Immortal Writers, but he knew that, inevitably, he would have to face them. The longer he put it off, the more difficult it would be... and, even worse, the longer he'd be here. Besides, he didn't have time to wait if his characters were coming through tomorrow.

"Let's get it over with," Scott said.

Shakespeare placed his hand on the door. The area surrounding his hand turned blue, and then, as Shakespeare took his hand away, the panel slid up, and Scott could see inside the room beyond.

It was a large, domed room with high ceilings. The floor, which was covered with desks, computers, and strange machines, sloped downward and was tiered like a theatre. Stairs lined either side of the desks, and one wide set of stairs were in the middle of the room, creating an aisle that led to the bottom of the expansive space. Three large screens covered the far wall. They all showed different parts of the same thing: an almost liquid-looking, semitransparent blue net. Ripples permeated most of the surface of the web. Most of the ripples were small and light blue, but some were large and purple. The purple ripples pulsed with more energy than the blue net seemed to.

"What's on the screens?" Dylan asked.

"The science fiction authors have developed special cameras that can pick up the frequencies of the Imagination Field," Shakespeare explained. "The blue ripples are ideas that come from the Imagination Field into the Reality Field. They usually make it to an author's mind, and they're written down. The large, purple ripples have already been written down, and the ideas are starting to cross into the Reality Field as fully formed, living creatures and characters."

"And the Imagination Field is...?" Dylan asked.

"The Imagination Field is where stories come from," Shakespeare explained patiently. "It's where dreams and stories and characters and plots are stored until a writer hears the story, and, if the writer is talented enough, brings it from the Imagination Field into the Reality Field."

"And we're in the Reality Field?" Dylan checked.

"Yes," Shakespeare said. "The Reality Field is this world, this reality. We have systems set up to keep track of the purple ripples of the Imagination Field and tell us when stories and characters begin to come through to our world. Since the main purpose of this room is to keep track of the Fields, this is called the Field Room."

"Wow," Scott snickered. "How creative."

Shakespeare ignored Scott's comment and led Scott and Dylan into the room. While the Field Room was certainly impressive, everything looked almost... sterile, especially with all of the silver and chrome. It made Scott feel even more on edge than he'd felt talking with Shakespeare the rest of the night.

Scott tensed as a dark-haired, bearded author jogged up the six tiers from the bottom of the room to greet them. "Shakespeare," he said, "I see you got him."

"And he's about as happy to be here as you guessed he'd be," Shakespeare said.

The author turned to Scott and offered a small smile. "Hello, Scott."

Scott nodded in greeting. "Philip."

"Who?" Dylan asked.

"This is Philip K. Dick," Scott said. "He's a science fiction author, and one of the Immortal Writers."

"Pleasure to meet you," Dick said. He extended his hand to Dylan. He shook it hesitantly. "You must be Scott's brother."

Dylan nodded.

"I'm surprised Shakespeare managed to get you here, Scott," Dick said as he released Dylan's hand. "I didn't think you'd come back."

"He kidnapped us," Scott grumbled.

"He does like to do that." Dick nodded.

"I have a flair for the dramatic," Shakespeare agreed.

"Scott, I didn't get to say this before, but, I'm so sorry about Kent—" Dick began.

"Please, don't," Scott interrupted, a hand in the air. "It's hard enough to be here and be reminded of it. I'd rather you didn't bring it up."

Dick nodded and looked down at his feet, shuffled them against the pearly-white floor for a moment, and then glanced back up at Scott. "I am still pleased to see you, and I know how hard this must be for you."

Scott swallowed. "Thank you. I may not like being here, but... I do have fond memories of you."

Dick grinned broadly. "You followed me around everywhere. You never were satisfied with any answer I gave you about whether or not androids actually dream of electric sheep."

Scott surprised himself by laughing. "I'd forgotten about that."

Dick smiled.

"I'm so confused," Dylan muttered.

"This isn't exactly the time for pleasantries," someone said from behind them. Scott jumped and turned around. H.G. Wells, an older author with short brown hair and a full mustache, lounged against a desk.

"There's always time for pleasantries," Dick said.

Wells shook his head and ignored his fellow writer.

"Scott," he said, "do you see the screens up there?"

"They're hard to miss," Scott said.

"All of the purple ripples on the screens match the vibrations of the words from your book. They're growing larger by the minute, and the ripples are beginning to hit the Reality Field."

"How much time until my characters are here?" Scott asked.

"Tomorrow morning, most likely," Wells said. "At least, that's when one of them is coming."

"Who is it?"

"We're not sure," Dick said. "We can just tell it's from your story, and we'll be able to tell where the character or creature enters the Reality Field, but you'll have to be the one to find them once you reach wherever they are."

"And I'm supposed to bring them back here?" Scott asked.

"Yes," Wells said. "Hopefully you'll get some good, strong characters coming through. We'll need them."

"For...?"

Wells pushed off from the desk and walked closer to them. He closed his eyes and turned toward the blank space to the side of Dylan. When he opened his eyes again, they were shining, and a hologram projected from them.

"Well, that's not creepy at all," Dylan said as he backed away from the projection.

A swirling picture of the galaxy shined from Wells's eyes into the space beside Scott, Dylan, Shakespeare, and Dick.

"This was our galaxy a week ago," Wells said. He blinked. "This is our galaxy now."

Scott peered at the projection.

"I don't see any difference," Scott said.

"I suppose you wouldn't," Wells grumbled. He squinted, and the image zoomed in toward the centre of the galaxy.

Wells blinked. "Before." He blinked again. "After."

Scott frowned. "Things shifted a little bit. The stars moved."

Wells nodded, and the projection jostled slightly with his head movement.

"I have no idea how you've managed this, Scott," Wells said. "Usually, the Reality Field is not so easily persuaded by the Imagination Field. I have no idea how this crossed over and managed not to shift orbital fields in any way. None of this makes any sense."

"Stop lecturing him," Dick said. "Just explain."

Wells sighed. "Three new solar systems have magically appeared close to the centre of the Milky Way galaxy."

"Let me guess," Scott said, "*my* three solar systems."

"Correct," Wells said. "Miraculously, almost none of the Milky Way's gravity has been affected. And there are three planets, one in each solar system, that are inhabited."

"With my aliens," Scott guessed.

Dick nodded. "The Betans, as your book names them, inhabit all three planets. And just like in your book, they've sent a large colonization ship from each world. Luckily, the mortal astronomers haven't caught on to *that* yet, though you should see some of the press releases we've had to stop from reaching the public."

"All three ships are headed this way," Wells said. "They're travelling fast. Forget light speed. If they're headed for Earth—and they undoubtedly are—they'll be here in a few weeks, if we're lucky."

Wells closed his eyes, and the hologram disappeared. Scott turned from the blank space to the left of his brother and faced Shakespeare.

"Do you see now why I *had* to bring you in?" Shakespeare asked.

"Yes," Scott said. "I understand. And I'll do what I can—"

"You know that Scott is only sixteen, right?" Dylan interrupted. "I've seen some crazy things tonight, but nothing is as asinine as all of you supposedly brilliant writers thinking that a sixteen-year-old boy can stop an alien invasion."

Scott frowned at his brother. He hated it when people brought up his age.

"He can't do it alone," Shakespeare said. "That's why we're hoping we're getting some solid reinforcements from the Imagination Field."

"And what if we don't?" Wells asked. His eyes were open again, but they projected nothing aside from disapproval and skepticism. "This lad can't even write stories that make logical sense."

Scott opened his mouth to retort, but Dick beat him to it.

"Stop it, Wells," Dick said. "It's stressful enough to be a new Immortal Writer, especially with his family's history. You don't need to make him feel like he doesn't deserve to be here."

Wells shrugged and stalked away, shoving his hands into his grey suit pockets. Scott clenched his fists and took two steps toward him before Dylan reached out and grabbed his shoulder, stopping him.

"Before you start beating everyone up," Dylan said in a low voice, "you are going to explain everything to me again."

Scott glared after Wells's retreating form. After a moment, he slowly unclenched his fists. His palms throbbed from where his fingernails had cut into his flesh. "I've had enough of this for the night, anyway."

"I know this has been an exhausting evening for you both," Shakespeare said. "If you will follow me, I'll take you to your quarters."

He headed out of the large room, and before they followed, Dylan looked at Scott, his eyes serious, an eyebrow raised in expectation.

"Fine, I'll explain," Scott said. "But are you just going to think I'm crazy again?"

"Probably," Dylan said. "But this time, I might just believe you."

Scott entered the room slowly, afraid it would look too similar to the old room that he had shared with his father before he died. He remembered it so clearly—it had been silver, like the rest of the Science Fiction Wing, with an industrial feel that was more high-tech than anything he'd seen outside of the Writers Castle. It wasn't that Scott disliked the room; it was that he didn't think he could face it again without his father. It was hard enough being back at the Castle without him. So he let Dylan go into the room first.

"Whoa," Dylan said after a moment. "This is awesome."

Scott took a deep breath and crossed the threshold. He looked around the room, and his shoulders relaxed. Instead of being metallic, the walls were made entirely of screens that currently showed what looked like ruins, possibly of a dystopian society. Two large beds were in either back corner of the room. Dylan chose the one on the right and plopped down on top of it. Scott edged toward the bed on the left and watched as Dylan reached out and touched the wall.

"Not bad, considering we're being held against our will," Dylan said as a small menu popped up. "I can change the scenery. Do you prefer… ocean, volcano, space, ruins, or city?"

Scott offered a small smile as he sat on his bed. "How about space? That's what got us into this mess in the first place."

Dylan tapped the screen, and the imagery on the walls changed. A large blue star shone on the ceiling above them, providing light, while the walls sparkled with smaller, distant stars as clear as if the brothers were in space. The door was covered by a black hole, which Scott found appropriate.

"This. Is. Awesome."

"I suppose there are certainly perks," Scott said. He lay on the bed, his arms behind his head, and stared off into space.

"Can you explain this to me again?" Dylan said. "Slower?"

Scott sighed. "I'm an Immortal Writer now."

Dylan paused. "And that means...?"

"That I'm immortal, and my characters have come... or rather, are coming... to life."

"And this is all real?" Dylan checked.

"Yes," Scott said miserably. "It's real. I know it's hard to believe right now, but I'm telling you the truth. I've been telling you the truth for years."

Dylan nodded slowly. "I guess that would explain the teleporters, and the weird hallway, and enormous library, and rude computer, and the creepy eye thing that one dude just did." Dylan looked at Scott. "I'm not sure I'm entirely convinced, but I'm pretty close. And... well, you believe it. So I guess I should too."

"Finally," Scott said.

"Can you blame me for not believing before?" Dylan asked.

Scott considered. "I wish you had," he said. "I hated that you thought I was crazy, or a liar. But... yeah, I guess I understand how you couldn't believe me."

The brothers sat in silence for a moment, both of them staring at the stars glistening against the black expanse of whatever universe they were looking at.

"Why do you hate this so much?" Dylan asked. "Clearly you believe it all, so your problem isn't that you're confused or unnerved. Why aren't you excited about being an Immortal Writer?"

Scott forced his fists to relax and focused on finding constellations on the walls. "Dad was an Immortal Writer."

"I gathered that," Dylan said. "But now he's dead. Is that why you hate being here?"

Scott pursed his lips and focused intently on a faraway moon. Dylan waited in silence for several minutes before he sighed and flipped himself over on his bed.

"Whatever," Dylan said. "If you don't want to talk about it, that's fine. But I don't get why you don't like Shakespeare. He seems so cool. Kidnapping aside. If all of this is real… then dude, can you believe it? We just met *William Shakespeare!*"

Scott growled and glared at Dylan. "Be careful, Dylan. You're choosing sides."

Dylan frowned and his brow furrowed. "I'm not choosing a side here; I'm just saying—"

"Forget it!" Scott yelled.

Dylan fell silent. Scott swung his legs over the side of the bed and stomped to a chrome dresser against the wall. It looked strangely out of place against the space imagery surrounding it. Scott grabbed some sweats and a t-shirt and stalked to the bathroom that adjoined the room.

"They have new clothes for us?" Dylan said, glancing at the sweats.

"Yes," Scott snapped.

"Why are you mad at me?" Dylan asked.

Scott paused outside of the bathroom door. "Trust me, Dylan," he said. "These people… there's something wrong with them. They're like a cancer. And now I've been infected."

"You were infected before," Dylan said quietly. "With the Fever. Maybe they can help you."

Scott shook his head forcefully and stepped into the bathroom, slamming the door shut behind him to block out any further questions from Dylan.

His brother just didn't understand. He hadn't been there when Shakespeare told him about his father's death. He'd relished Kent Beck's demise.

Scott hit the door in frustration, barely registering the resulting stinging in his fist. Would Dylan understand if this mission Shakespeare had him on killed Scott?

Or would he still adore him?

CHAPTER FOUR

S cott took a deep breath and placed his hand on the silver panel in front of him. The door slid up quickly, and he and Dylan stepped through.

The Imagination Field pulsed purple on the screen in front of them. Wells stood in front of one of the massive screens, waving his hand to manipulate the Field and control what parts of it he saw.

"Scott!" Dick called. He stood behind a row of computer monitors toward the front of the room. "You're just in time!"

"What's going on?" Scott asked.

"Come here," Dick said. He turned back to the monitors as Scott and Dylan shuffled down the theatre steps toward Dick's workspace.

The computer screens depicted several maps covered in a green web that moved and pulsated in waves similar to the movements of the Imagination Field.

"See these patterns?" Dick asked, pointing. "Watch the Reality Field carefully."

"Is that the green web?" Dylan asked.

"Yes," Dick said. "And it seems to be fluctuating the most in the Four Corners area."

"It *all* looks wobbly to me," Scott said.

Wells sighed loudly several feet below them. "Look at this, then," he called.

Scott looked up at the Imagination Field screens.

"I've zoomed in to where the word vibrations from your stories are strongest. They're about to break through. Do you see how the purple is moving?"

Scott stared. The purple web pushed down gently once, let up again for a moment, pulsed down violently before jumping up, then fell flat again.

"The same pattern is repeating," Dylan said. "The crest and depth of the waves keep increasing, but the pattern is the same."

"Exactly," Wells said. "The Imagination Field and the Reality Field are always moving, but when they start to sync, we know something is about to come through."

"And it seems to be matching up here," Dick said. Scott looked back down at the smaller computer monitors where Dick pointed. "I hope you're feeling ready to travel."

"Depends... how am I travelling?" Scott asked. "Shakespeare said something about a portal."

"Portal on the way there," Dick said, nodding. "Teleport on the way back."

Scott groaned. He was glad he hadn't had the chance to eat breakfast yet.

"You'll get used to it after a while," Dick tried to console.

"I think that whatever's coming through the Imagination Field is coming in through New Mexico," Dylan said.

Scott and Dick turned to him.

"Why do you think that?" Dick encouraged. "Explain it to me."

"Look at the Reality Field waves," Dylan said. "They seem to converge there."

Dylan bent over the computer and typed on the keys, too quickly for Scott to tell what he entered.

"What are you doing?" Dick cried out, his encouraging smile disappearing. "You'll mess up everything, you stupid mortal!"

"Calm it, old man," Dylan said. "Look!"

He hit "enter" and stepped away from the monitor. The maps had zoomed in to Utah, Arizona, and New Mexico.

"The Reality Field's pattern is slightly different in each place," Dylan said, pointing. "The only one that matches up with the Imagination Field *exactly* is over New Mexico."

Dick stared. "You're smart, I'll give you that," he said, "but what did you do to my program?"

"Relax, I just changed what showed up on the monitors."

"But how did *you* know how to do that?" Dick demanded. "I created this program myself; there's no way you're familiar with it."

"Dylan's a genius with computers," Scott said. "And besides, he's right. The Reality Field is just a hair out of sync with the Imagination Field over the other states."

"It's like a rarefaction, the wave is more separated here—"

"Don't preach science to me," Dick protested. "I'm a science fiction author, for hell's sake."

"I'm teaching you science fact," Dylan said.

"It's all the same here, if you haven't noticed," Wells interrupted. "And we understand the laws of science, thank you. That's part of how all of this works for every Immortal Writer." He frowned at Scott. "Well, for *most* of us."

Scott grimaced. "The point is, we need to look at New Mexico."

Wells turned back to the Imagination Field. "I'm glad you've figured that out, because whatever or whomever is coming over from your book has almost completed the crossing. Come here, Scott."

Scott looked between Dylan and Dick. "Play nice."

Dick sighed and turned back to his monitors, zooming farther in on New Mexico. Dylan was absorbed in the computer screen, which didn't surprise Scott. Dylan worked as a programmer and had always been a little too fascinated by computers. Somehow, he had still managed to be socially adept despite his career path.

Scott trotted down to Wells.

"Behind you, on the desk," Wells said.

Scott turned around. A small silver disk with a black button in its centre lay on the black desk. Scott cringed.

"Do I have to?" he whined.

"That's a stupid question," Wells snapped.

Scott pursed his lips and picked up the teleporter.

"The teleporters work by picking up thoughts. I've already transferred the brainwaves that will bring you back to the Castle and locked it in. Keep in mind that the teleporter has to charge for five minutes before you can use it again. Understand?"

Scott nodded.

Wells opened his mouth to say more, but an alarm blared loudly from hidden speakers around the room.

"Acknowledged!" Wells yelled. The blaring stopped. "Dick, bring up the Reality Field!"

Wells swiped his hands in front of him and turned around, facing the centre of the room. The images of the Imagination Field followed the motions of his hands, emerging from the screens and floating to the middle of the room. The web was nearly all purple now instead of the blue it had been yesterday.

"Come on, Dick, let's go!"

Dick flung up his hands, and the Reality Field sprang out of the computer monitors and flicked into the middle of the room. Purple and green lines blurred together. The purple grew brighter and brighter.

"Ready?" Wells checked.

"Ready," Dick called.

"Now!"

Wells and Dick twisted their hands at the same time, and the two fields turned. There was an audible *snap*, and then the purple light flashed brightly as a sudden wind howled viciously and whipped through the room.

Scott shielded his eyes with his hands and backed away.

"What are you doing?" Wells demanded. "Don't back up. Get in there!"

"What do you mean?" Scott yelled over the wind. He blinked tears away from his eyes, which had started to water from the light and wind.

"The Reality Field and the Imagination Field have created a portal to exactly where you need to go," Dick shouted. "Jump in!"

Scott hesitated. He didn't want to go. He didn't want to admit it, but he was terrified.

"You'll come back!" Dick shouted. "Scott, look at me!"

Scott squinted his eyes and found Dick next to Dylan in the bright purple light. "Scott, you'll come back. I promise!"

Dylan was shaking his head frantically, his eyebrows drawn down and his mouth open wide.

"Scott, no!" Dylan shouted.

Dick turned to look at Dylan. "I give you my personal word that Scott will come back. No one has died while they went to find their characters. And he has his teleporter; he can come back. But we don't have time to argue."

Dick turned back to Scott. "Go, Scott!" he shouted. "You *will* come back."

Scott swallowed and turned back to the portal. He took a deep breath.

"You'll come back," Scott repeated to himself.

He clutched the teleporter until it hurt, and then sprinted into the portal.

CHAPTER FIVE

Dirt suffocated Scott as he tumbled to the ground. He coughed, desperate to breathe. He hadn't expected the wind from the portal to create a sandstorm, and he hadn't expected to hit the ground as soon as he made it. If he had, he wouldn't have run.

The swirling purple portal above him fluctuated once more, and Scott could just see Wells' and Dick's faces before the opening snapped shut. He was left staring up at a pale blue sky.

Scott struggled to fight the panic in his chest and forced himself to sit up. He squinted against the bright sunlight. The sand settled, and his coughing ceased. He panted, trying to catch his breath as he looked at himself. He was covered in dirt, and his jeans now had holes in the knees. Scott's chest hurt from coughing, and his right side ached from hitting the ground. His right arm was a little scraped up as well. He focused on the physical pain rather than the panic, and the aches in his body helped him focus.

"Hey, where'd you guys go?" a voice interrupted Scott's thoughts. He looked up, trying to identify the source of the voice. "Seriously, you guys, this isn't funny anymore!"

Scott frowned. He couldn't see anyone. Grunting, he stood up, grimacing at the pain in his knees as he did so.

It was hot here, wherever *here* was. He was presumably in New Mexico, if Dylan had been correct about where his character would be. Scott wiped his forehead, which was already drenched in sweat, with the back of his hand.

"Where am I?" Scott whispered.

He stared. There wasn't much to look at. Aside from plenty of dirt, a cornfield grew several yards in front of him. It seemed to stretch on forever, interrupted only by a few power lines. Scott turned around and was somewhat relieved to see a small highway in front of a railroad track. Past that there were just more cornfields.

"I hate corn," Scott muttered.

"I hate you guys!" the voice screamed. "Was this the plan the whole time? Is this why you agreed to come? Well… well, screw you! I hope the aliens find you and probe your brains out!"

Scott froze. That voice sounded familiar. He'd heard it in one of his Fever episodes, and it had made him start writing.

"You know what, forget it!" the voice shouted. "You'd probably *like* being probed, wouldn't you?"

Scott turned toward the voice and finally spotted a young man sitting down on the railroad tracks, his arms tight around his chest. Scott couldn't help but grin as he walked toward him. He could recognize this boy from his clothes.

The teenager wore an eight-bit Space Invaders t-shirt and a black baseball cap. The baseball cap had a green alien face printed on it with *Roswell UFO Museum* embroidered in an ugly font. Messy, bright red hair poked out in all directions from under the hat.

The boy looked up as Scott approached. He rearranged his boyish features so that it didn't look like he had been crying, but Scott could still see the tracks the tears had left in the dirt on the boy's pale, freckled face. "What do *you* want?"

Scott hesitated. He wasn't really sure how to handle kidnapping this guy. He'd never done it before. "We're in Roswell, New Mexico, right?"

The young man rubbed his eyes and glared up at Scott. "Of course we are," he said. "Off of Old Dexter Highway at the moment."

Scott nodded. "Then no wonder you're here!" He did his best to sound enthusiastic.

"Huh? What do you mean?"

"You're Paul Ether!" Scott said. He plopped down on the train tracks next to Paul and extended his dark hand.

Paul stared at Scott's proffered hand and shook it hesitantly. "How do you know who I am?"

"All alien enthusiasts know who *you* are, Paul," Scott said, releasing his hand. "I came here to check out Roswell, you know, with the UFOs and stuff. I never thought I'd meet *you*."

Paul smiled in spite of himself. "You've seen my blog?"

"Of course!" Scott said. "I know it so well, I could have written it myself."

Paul's smile dimmed. "You're not... are you making fun of me?"

Scott drew his head back, eyes wide. "Of course not! I believe you!"

"You do?"

"Yeah!" Scott said. "I mean, your theories about the last three UFO sightings... they're legit."

Paul grinned broadly. "I know, right? They're all connected." He leaned in closer to Scott. "I think they were projections of what's to come. They were scouts leading the mother ships to Earth."

Scott nodded. "It makes perfect sense, Paul. I don't understand why more people don't take you seriously."

"I think it's because I'm so young." Paul shrugged. "No one takes a seventeen-year-old seriously, for some reason."

Scott shook his head. "They should."

"What are you doing out here?" Paul asked.

"Same thing you're doing out here," Scott said.

Paul frowned. "Your friends ditched you at the International UFO Museum too?"

"Your friends left you?"

"One minute they were behind me, and the next, *bam*, they were gone! I didn't recognize anyone around me." Paul took off his baseball cap and punched his fist into it. "Those punks."

Scott bit his lip and took a deep breath. "What if they didn't ditch you?" he suggested.

"What do you mean?"

"What if *you* ditched *them*?"

Paul glanced at Scott out of the corner of his eyes, leaning away from him slightly. "I think I'd remember that."

"You believe in all sorts of things people think are impossible," Scott said. He gripped the teleporter tightly in his hand. "Can I tell you something?"

Paul's eyes flickered around the empty road. "Sure, man."

"You're into wild theories, right?"

Paul frowned. "I thought you said you believe my theories."

"I do, I do," Scott reassured him. "Because they're true. What I'm about to tell you is true, too."

Paul's eyes flicked away uncertainly. "Go ahead," he said cautiously.

"You just came from somewhere else," Scott said in a rush. "Your friends didn't leave you, you left them."

"Dude, I'm telling you, I didn't go anywhere."

"You just didn't know you left," Scott said. "But you were on another world, if you want to call it that."

"I'm pretty sure I was in New Mexico," Paul said. "Just like I am now."

"You were in New Mexico on another planet, another Earth."

"That's impossible." Paul shifted uncomfortably.

"What year is it?" Scott asked.

"Seriously, man?"

"What year is it?" Scott insisted.

"It's 2134," Paul said.

"No," Scott said. "We're still in the twenty-first century, Paul."

"You're not making any sense," Paul said. He stood up and shoved his baseball cap back on his head. "Leave me alone."

"I created the world you were in," Scott said desperately. "You came out of *my* head. Now you're here."

"Man, aliens are one thing, but you think you're some sort of god?" Paul turned his back. "Get lost."

Scott jumped up and grabbed Paul's shoulder.

"Let go of me," Paul yelled. He turned around and pushed Scott away before Scott had a chance to hit the button on the teleporter and taking them to the Castle. He stumbled backward, surprised at Paul's strength, forgetting for a moment that since Paul had been bullied so often in school, he knew how to defend himself. Scott regretted writing that now.

Scott looked up to see Paul running away.

"Damn it," Scott muttered. He sprinted after Paul, but that kid was awfully fast for being so skinny.

Run, run, run away, before I come outside to play—

I wish I would have run away, maybe that would have saved—

I'll never understand why I could never—

Scott tripped over the railroad tracks and fell on top of them. He felt the hot metal burn into his skin, but it didn't compare to the searing pain in his head that always accompanied the Fever.

The woman slowly backed away, the gun cocked and ready to fire—

The knight drew his gleaming sword—

Fire spread through the trees toward the church—

Scott screamed and curled up in a ball, clutching his head with his hands and trying to hold his skull together. He could barely remember where he was. What was he doing? Was there anyone around?

"Help me!" Scott yelled desperately. "Help me! Please!"

He dimly heard someone shouting nearby, and the sound of something else, something big, but it was drowned out by the Fever voices.

I will hunt you down and kill every last—

"Get up, you idiot!"

Someone was yelling at Scott, but he couldn't seem to grasp what the words meant, or who was saying them. He was held captive by the Fever.

"Get up!"

The soldiers saluted their general, each of them avoiding eye contact as they considered what they must do—

"There's a train—"

The horses ran away, giving no thought to their owners who were drowning in the mud—

"The train!"

A hand reached out and shook his shoulder.

The touch was enough to bring Scott back to his senses, if only for a moment.

Paul Ether stood above him, trying desperately to get Scott on his feet.

"There's a train!" he yelled again.

Scott looked past Paul. A large train careened toward them. It wasn't more than a few seconds away.

Scott tried to get up, but the Fever still raged inside of his head and coursed through his body. It threatened to pull him under again, and while he managed to stay aware, he was too sick to stand.

He slipped, and Paul fell next to him.

The train was close.

Too close.

Scott jerked his arms up to protect himself. He knew it was useless, but it was the only thing he could think to do.

And then he saw that he was still holding the teleporter.

Scott grabbed Paul's arm just as the train was about to hit them.

They both screamed as Scott pressed the button on the teleporter.

But it was too late.

CHAPTER SIX

At first, Scott didn't feel the pain because his body had dissolved into particles, but that all changed when he and Paul materialized in the Writers Castle, still crumpled on the ground, but thankfully safe from the train.

Well, almost.

As soon as Scott's body was put back together again, the pain assaulted him. It was worse than the Fever, but instead of in his head, it was in his right leg.

Scott screamed.

"Scott!" Dylan yelled. "Scott!"

"Where am I?" Paul muttered. Scott heard him scrambling upright, but he couldn't look at him. He could only stare at his leg. Right beneath the knee on the right side, it had been shredded. Most of it was gone.

"Dick, go get McKinnen and Jameson!" Wells yelled. Dick grabbed two teleporters and disappeared as Wells hurried toward where Scott lay at the bottom of the Field Room.

Scott continued to scream. Dylan crouched down beside him and took off his jacket, then pressed it up against what was left of Scott's leg. Scott didn't know that his leg could hurt worse than it already did, but the pressure on his wound heightened his agony.

He screamed louder—another feat he didn't know was possible.

It did nothing to calm Paul's anxiety, apparently.

"Where am I?" Paul demanded.

"Not now, Character," Wells said dismissively.

"*Where am I?*" Paul yelled, somehow making himself louder than Scott's screams.

"Let us deal with Scott first," Wells said. "We'll get to you in a minute."

"Get to me?" Paul said.

He paused.

"Help!" he yelled. "I'm going to be probed by aliens!"

"Shut up!" Wells said.

"HELP! I'M GOING TO BE PRO—"

Wells clicked his tongue in distaste and grabbed a futuristic weapon from his pocket. He barely glanced at Paul before he tased him. Paul fell to the ground, convulsing. Wells calmly put the taser back in his pocket as he crouched next to Scott.

"What happened back there, Scott?"

Scott couldn't make himself answer.

"Stop screaming and talk to me!" Wells said. "Make yourself focus on answering the question instead of the pain."

"His leg was just sliced off," Dylan protested. "Give him some credit."

"I'm trying to *help* him," Wells said.

Dick reappeared in the room holding a blanket, probably in case Scott had gone into shock. He was accompanied by two others. One was a young woman in leather gear with long, blond braided hair. The other was a man, also in leather, with a strong jawline and a long, ragged scar on his face. The three rushed over to him, and the man crouched down and put his hands on what used to be Scott's leg. Scott was only just aware that Wells had stood up and walked over to Dick before he was distracted by a rush of calming heat coursing through the right side of his body. Scott stopped screaming and breathed easier as the pain lessened and eased. But soon the heat was no longer pleasant, and it burned instead.

"Stop!" Scott shouted.

"Almost done, Scott," the man said.

"It burns," Scott cried.

"Does it?" The man sounded surprised. "I've never regrown a limb before."

Scott looked down at his leg, which, he was shocked to see, was actually *there*. Well, sort of. It was growing back, inch by inch. With each bit of progress, the burning intensified.

"Why does it burn?" Scott panted through gritted teeth.

"Because everything's growing back," the man said. He looked tired. "Your body isn't used to growing all at once."

Scott laid his head back on the ground. His vision was dark around the edges.

"Stay with me, Scott," Dylan said. He was still crouched next to him. "Focus on breathing."

Nodding, Scott forced himself to inhale and exhale slowly through the pain and the burning. Bit by bit, the blackness at the edges of his vision lessened, and the burning and pain eased until it only ached.

"Done," the blond man said. He sat back and closed his eyes. The woman crouched down next to him and put an arm around his shoulder.

Scott forced himself to sit up. He looked down at his leg, which was now whole again. The bottom of his black shorts had been cut off slightly, and his clothes were covered in blood.

"How did you do that?" Dylan asked from beside him.

"Body Magic," the man said.

"Body Magic?" Dylan repeated.

The man nodded toward the woman at his side. "Ask her."

"My name is Liz," the woman said. "I'm an Immortal Writer. This is Curtis. He's one of my characters. He has magic that lets him heal others."

"I've seen you before…" Dylan said.

"Her picture was in the Hall of Writers," Scott said. He put his head in his hands, wiping away the sweat and dirt on his face. "She wrote the *Shethara* books. Right?"

"Right," Liz said. She smiled. "How are you, Scott?"

Scott wasn't sure he liked how familiarly she used his name, but overall he didn't care. He had a leg because of this Immortal Writer and the character she'd brought to life.

"Whole, thanks to you. Can I..." He hesitated, unsure he wanted to know the answer to his question. "Can I stand on the leg?"

"Yes," Curtis said. "It's just like your old one, except that it will probably still hurt for a bit, and you'll have some scars."

"But you should probably rest for a while," Liz recommended. "Curtis may have healed you, but your body underwent a great deal of trauma. Give it a minute."

Scott nodded.

"What happened out there?" Wells asked. He and Dick stood behind Scott, their backs against the Field Room wall. Dick still held the blanket, looking uncomfortable. He held it up to Scott, an eyebrow raised. Scott ignored him, hesitating. He didn't want to trust the Immortal Writers yet. He was too paranoid to tell them about the Fever.

"I was in Roswell, New Mexico," Scott said. "I found Paul there."

"Paul Ether?" Dylan checked. "From your book?"

"Yeah," Scott said.

"He *would* be in Roswell," Dylan muttered.

"I went and talked to him, and he ran away from me, and I tried to chase him when the... when I tripped on some train tracks."

Dick and Wells grimaced, and Dylan inhaled loudly.

"You were hit by a train?" Dick asked.

"I managed to teleport us here before it was any worse," Scott said. "At first I didn't know I'd been hit. I guess that my body dissolving protected me, if only for a minute."

"You *tripped* on the tracks?" Dylan asked.

Scott gave his brother a warning glance.

"It was the Fever, wasn't it?" Dylan said.

Scott sighed in frustration. Dylan was horrible at picking up hints.

"Fever?" Dick asked.

"Scott's been sick for a couple of years with—"

Scott cut him off. "It's nothing," he said. "Besides, Curtis just healed me. I'm sure it will be fine."

He looked over at Curtis for support, but Curtis frowned. "I didn't sense any fever. I can check for it specifically, but you'll have to wait for my magic to replenish itself thoroughly before I try to heal you again."

Scott shrugged. "It's not a big deal," he insisted.

"Not a big deal?" Dylan repeated. "Scott, I've never seen anything like the Fever before. It's a serious problem."

"What's a serious problem?"

Scott looked up. Shakespeare was descending the theatre-like stairs, coming toward them. Scott frowned. Once again, the writer was the one injured and covered in blood. Shakespeare, on the other hand, looked well rested and in perfect health.

"Nothing," Scott said.

"Tell them," Dylan said. Scott looked at his brother and glared. "Come on, Scott. They might be able to help you. That guy just grew back your leg! Maybe they can cure the Fever, too."

"The Fever?" Shakespeare asked.

Paul groaned loudly, sparing Scott from being forced to answer.

"Where am I?" Paul asked. His words were slurred.

Scott twisted his head to look at his character. Paul had taken off his hat and clutched it tightly. His eyes widened as he more fully woke up, and he scrambled to his feet.

"You," he said, looking at Wells, "you tased me!"

"You wouldn't shut up," Wells said. He gestured to Paul's hat. "And do you know that you're wearing a hat with Comic Sans font? Where did you get that thing? What serious writer uses *Comic Sans*? Did you come up with that, Scott?"

"No," Scott lied.

"*Where am I?*" Paul asked loudly. He looked at each of them quickly, his eyes wide and panicked.

"You're in the Writers Castle," Shakespeare said.

"The what?" Paul repeated.

"See that boy sitting on the floor?" Wells pointed. Scott bristled at the word *boy*. "You're a figment of his imagination."

Paul shook his head. "Just tell me straight, man. Where am I? Are you aliens?"

"No," Scott said. He reached his hand out to Dylan, and his brother pulled him up. Scott's new leg ached desperately, but the pain wasn't anything like it had been before Curtis had healed it. "But the aliens are coming."

"Aliens?" Liz asked. She and Curtis stood up with Scott. "So that's what your book is about?"

A loud beeping blared from two computers on one of the higher tiers. Dick and Wells ran up the steps to the machines as Scott turned to answer Liz.

"Yes," Scott said. "And the aliens are heading this way. Apparently they want to attack the planet."

"Well, you've written yourself into a corner, haven't you?" Liz smiled. "I only had to fight dragons."

Scott opened his mouth to answer but was cut off by Paul.

"Will someone *please* tell me what is going on!" he yelled.

"That will have to wait," Dick said. He sounded unhappy.

"What's wrong?" Shakespeare asked.

"Another character is coming through," Wells answered. "Whomever it is has nearly crossed over."

He and Dick raised their hands, and the two Fields sprang to life.

"What is that?" Paul asked. "Who are you guys?"

"Shut up," Wells commanded. "Scott, you've got to go get your character."

"He just grew back a limb!" Dylan protested. "He can't go anywhere right now."

"It's okay," Scott said. He picked up the teleporter from the floor, wrinkling his nose in disgust. The disc was splattered with his blood. "I'll go."

"You're covered in blood," Dylan said. "You'll terrify anyone you run into!"

Dick threw the blanket he'd brought with him at Scott. "I guess this came in handy after all. Cover up, and try not to terrify anyone."

"They're coming through!" Wells shouted. He and Dick twisted their hands, and the two Fields collided. Purple light pulsed brightly, casting distorted, ethereal shadows across the room. Wind howled from the newly formed portal.

"Get in the portal!" Wells commanded.

Scott wrapped the blanket around himself, took a deep breath, and tried to run. He didn't make it far before his new leg collapsed.

"He can't go!" Dylan yelled.

"Oh, for hell's sake," Wells shouted. "*Someone* has to go get the character! We won't be able to track them long with the portal! It's already fading!"

Scott grabbed Dylan and walked forward.

"Scott, no!" Dylan said. "You can't do it! You're not strong enough."

"You should know better," Scott said over the wind. "Never tell me what I can't do."

He held tight to Dylan as he dove into the portal, and then, as they plummeted, everything went dark.

CHAPTER SEVEN

Scott lay crumbled on his back, and his leg throbbed. He forced himself to sit up and rubbed it.

"Where are we?" Dylan asked from beside him. He was sitting up, his blue button-up shirt dishevelled. His eyes were wide with astonishment, but not as wide as the eyes on the little boy's face in front of them.

Scott hurriedly grabbed the blanket from the ground and wrapped it around himself, doing his best to cover the worst of the bloodstains.

"Where did you guys come from?" the little boy whispered. He couldn't have been more than five years old. "There was no one hiding in here a minute ago; I checked!"

Dylan smiled. "It was magic!"

Scott frowned at his brother, but the little boy's eyes somehow grew. "Whoa! Really?"

Dylan nodded. "But don't tell anyone, okay? You'll ruin the surprise."

"Okay." The boy nodded energetically, then turned around and ran out of the small patch of trees they had landed in. Probably right toward a group of his friends.

Scott looked around. It was surprisingly green wherever they were. Sunlight streamed through leaves. They seemed to be hidden by the trees, which Scott figured was a good thing since it sounded like it was very busy around them. It was remarkable that only that little boy had noticed them appear. Still, they shouldn't dally long; he was bound to tell someone.

"Help me up," Scott said. Dylan stood and offered Scott his hand. Scott took it and hoisted himself up with a groan, favouring his left leg so his right wouldn't feel too much of his weight.

"Do you need help walking?" Dylan asked.

Scott nodded. "Maybe a little."

He threw an arm around Dylan's shoulders, and together they hobbled forward, away from the cover of the trees and onto an expansive lawn. Scott did his best to keep himself covered with the blue blanket.

Scott squinted against the sunlight and looked up. Several hundred yards in front of them, a long white obelisk shot into the sky. It towered above them, backdropped by a light blue sky and wispy white clouds.

"Are we in Washington, D.C.?" Dylan asked.

Scott nodded. "It looks like it."

He studied their surroundings. There were people everywhere, thronging the Washington Monument and the adjacent area.

"How are we supposed to find my character here?" Scott asked.

"I guess we should just look around," Dylan suggested. "You'll be able to recognize them, right?"

Scott shrugged. "I hope so."

They walked forward slowly, Scott still leaning heavily on Dylan for support. His leg felt better than it had any right to—half of it had been *gone*, after all—but it still ached. With every step he took, he felt a stabbing sensation creep up his shin, but it lessened each time he moved.

The sun was bright, but it wasn't too hot due to the light, cool breeze. Scott probably would have enjoyed it more if he hadn't been surrounded by people. He had never felt comfortable in crowds. Families and groups of tourists milled about him and Dylan in endless waves. Several groups stopped to take pictures with their phones, most of them trying to take the picture themselves.

Scott and Dylan walked past a group of teenagers—probably a school tour—as they tried to get everyone in the camera frame.

"Move over, Tom," the girl with the camera said. Her voice sounded preppy, like she'd pop bubble gum at any moment. "No, not that way." She giggled. "To your left. Now you're blocking Jason! Hold on."

Dylan paused, and Scott looked over. The girl held the camera out to Dylan. "Would you mind taking our picture?" she asked. Scott rolled his eyes when the girl blushed as her hand brushed Dylan's.

"Sure," Dylan said. Scott stood on his own while Dylan held the camera. The girl ran to the back of the group and nudged a boy to the side.

"Ready?" Dylan asked. "One, two, three…"

He snapped a photo as the teenagers plastered smiles to their faces.

"How about a funny picture?" the girl suggested.

Scott continued to glance around the area while Dylan took another photo. He extended his leg and wiggled his toes experimentally. He hadn't even noticed that he didn't have a shoe. That hadn't grown back with his leg. Wiggling his toes hurt, but Scott was surprised at how quickly he was feeling better. That Curtis guy certainly had a good grasp on his magic.

Scott hesitantly took a step. He wobbled a bit, unsteady, but still stronger than he had been a couple of minutes ago when he and Dylan had come through the portal.

He could hear Dylan and the bubble gum girl chatting, but Scott ignored them. He squinted against the sunlight and across the wide lawn, looking for anyone out of place, anyone that might look like a character from his book. He wished he knew who to look for, at least.

Scott's eyes swept over groups of all sizes. There were several larger groups of teenagers, probably on a field trip or enjoying fall break like bubble gum girl back there. Multiple families wandered around too. A desperate woman with frazzled brown hair, tight lips, and frantic eyes caught his attention.

"Roy!" the woman yelled as she put a hand on her hip. "Get back here this instant!"

Scott followed her gaze to a small ginger boy who ran toward the Washington Monument. The little boy ignored his mother and tottered ahead. Scott could hear her exasperated sigh from where he stood as she jogged to follow her son. He watched the mother reach the boy and grab his wrist.

"Roy, be careful!" she reprimanded. "I can't keep up with you in a place this big, and you're bound to get lost…"

Scott watched her drag the screaming boy back toward the rest of their little group, but he became distracted by a woman several yards behind the frustrated mother. The woman was dressed in a black uniform that Scott recognized instantly. It was similar in design to the current day's Air Force uniform, but this one was bulletproof. It was sleek and black, though it could camouflage itself to match its surroundings if the wearer pressed the right button on the jacket. For some reason the woman hadn't engaged this function, but Scott was glad, because it allowed him to see her.

She stood unnaturally still. Her black hair was up in a tight bun behind her head, and her eyes were narrowed as she tried to take in her surroundings and assess her situation.

Scott walked toward her slowly, carefully, more for her sake and his safety than for his sore leg.

"Hold up, little brother," Dylan said to him. Scott continued on slowly, ignoring him. He heard Dylan sigh.

"Here's your phone!" he said to the girl.

She took the phone back. "You know, the thing about phones is... um... well I... did you know my phone number's in here?"

Scott turned around to watch Dylan's face. His eyebrows were pulled together toward the centre of his forehead, and he frowned.

"Well, yes," Dylan said. "I know. So is the picture I just took."

The girl looked down at her phone and bit her lip.

"Dylan!" Scott said loudly.

Dylan looked over. "Coming!" He looked back at the girl. "Enjoy your pictures!"

Dylan jogged over to Scott. "What was all that about?" Dylan asked.

Scott rolled his eyes. "She was into you," he said. "Everyone's always into you."

"Yeah, that's true." Dylan laughed.

"That's probably a good thing," Scott said. "She was so focused on you she didn't even look at my clothes. I'm glad I have this blanket."

Scott walked forward.

"Do you want help?" Dylan checked.

"No," Scott said. "Stay close, though, just in case."

Dylan nodded and walked beside Scott, hands extended to help him in case Scott stumbled.

"Where are you going?" Dylan asked. "Or were you just trying to get me away from that girl?"

Scott nodded slightly, indicating the woman in the black uniform. She was starting to walk away slowly, carefully.

"That's her," he said softly.

Dylan looked at the woman. "Ooh, Colonel Caspiz came over?" He glanced sideways at Scott. "Good luck with that, buddy."

Scott hissed as the woman walked away from them.

"I can't walk fast enough to reach her before she gets away," Scott said. "Dylan, you have to catch up to her and stop her."

"Me?" Dylan asked. "What am I supposed to do?"

"Tell her…" Scott hesitated. What would Caspiz be thinking right now?

She'd know that she was in a different time. That was certain. She'd probably seen several of the security guards and noticed their outdated clothing and rudimentary weapons. And she probably knew that she was in Washington, D.C., since she had a decent grasp on history. But she wouldn't know why she was here, or what year she was in exactly. She'd probably be confused and on edge, ready to spring at anyone who dared approach her.

"She's getting away, Scott," Dylan murmured.

Scott hobbled forward faster and nudged Dylan ahead of him. "Call her by her title and tell her that she's been sent back in time to meet with me."

"Will she believe that?" Dylan asked.

"Just go get her!" Scott growled as he limped forward.

Dylan walked quickly toward Caspiz's retreating figure. Scott breathed a sigh of relief that Dylan didn't run. Sprinting toward Jane Caspiz would certainly be a poor idea.

Scott winced when Dylan reached the colonel. He didn't announce his presence before he reached her, but Caspiz was too quick for him anyway.

She spun around, grabbed his arm, and had it tightly behind his back before Scott could make it another step.

"Who are you, and what do you want?" Scott was close enough to hear Caspiz demand answers.

"Colonel..." he grunted as Caspiz tightened her hold on his arm. "You've been sent back in time to meet with my brother."

Caspiz frowned. "You know I'm not from here."

Dylan nodded. "Yes. I know you're not from here... or at least, not from this time."

"What does your brother want with me?" Caspiz asked.

Scott hurried forward as fast as he could. He could feel sweat dripping down his neck from the strain.

"He needs your help," Dylan said.

"I think my own time needs my help," Caspiz said. She twisted Dylan's arm higher just as Scott reached them.

"Stop," Scott said. "Please, stop. I'm the one who brought you here."

Caspiz didn't loosen her hold on Dylan, but her attention zeroed in on Scott.

"Why did you do that?" Caspiz snarled. "I was in the middle of a very important meeting when I found myself here, in the centre of Washington, D.C. A very *young* Washington, D.C."

"I didn't bring you here on purpose," Scott admitted. "But I can't talk about it here. You'll have to come with me."

Caspiz's eyes narrowed. "How long will that take? You can barely walk, and you're covered in blood."

Scott grimaced. Apparently the blanket didn't fool her. "Please, Colonel Caspiz. Come with me."

Caspiz stared at Scott for a moment. "I don't suppose I can get back to my own time without doing whatever it is you want," she said finally, but instead of letting Dylan go and stepping away, she pulled out a sleek silver gun from a holster on her side and held it against Dylan's head.

Scott stopped breathing.

"Don't," he pleaded. "Don't shoot him."

"I won't shoot him as long as you don't try anything foolish," Caspiz said. "Where are we going?"

Scott lifted both of his hands, palms facing the colonel. "I'm going to reach into my pocket and grab a device," he warned. "It is not a weapon. I'm just going to grab a teleporter."

Caspiz frowned. "How do you know about teleporters? How do you even have teleporters in this time, whenever it is?"

"I'll explain everything when we're back at the Castle," Scott promised. "I'm just going to reach for the teleporter, okay?"

Caspiz squinted, watching carefully as Scott slowly lowered one of his hands and reached into his pocket. When his hand disappeared, Caspiz shoved the gun closer to Dylan's head.

"I'm just getting the teleporter," Scott repeated slowly. He brought his hand out with the small silver disc. "See? It's just a teleporter."

Caspiz relaxed the gun slightly, but then Scott heard shouts behind him.

"Put down the weapon!" a man yelled from behind Scott.

Caspiz released Dylan and aimed her gun at something behind Scott. "Stand down!" she yelled.

Scott stepped forward as fast as he could and grabbed Dylan.

"All of you, freeze!" another man's voice said.

Scott turned to see five uniformed guards approaching them, guns raised.

"I will shoot!" Caspiz warned.

The men stopped, their guns trained on Caspiz's chest.

"Put your weapon down," one of the men said.

Scott glanced over to Caspiz and saw a red dot on her back.

"They have a sniper on you," Scott whispered.

Caspiz tensed, and Scott recognized the look in her eyes as she took aim on one of the guards.

He swore under his breath, and, keeping one hand on Dylan, grabbed Caspiz. He managed to press the button on the teleporter just as the guards began to fire.

CHAPTER EIGHT

Colonel Caspiz was shouting when the three of them materialized in the Writers Castle. Scott scrambled to his feet as Curtis and Liz ran forward. Curtis grabbed Caspiz's arms and Liz wrenched the gun from her, carelessly tossing it aside. Thankfully, it didn't go off.

"Where am I?" Caspiz yelled. "What's happening?"

Scott dropped his blanket on the floor and limped over to Dylan. "Are you okay?"

Dylan's eyes were wide, and the collar of his shirt was torn where Caspiz had grabbed him earlier.

"I'm okay," Dylan said. "Just a little shaken up."

"Colonel Jane Caspiz." Shakespeare's voice travelled from across the room, though he spoke quietly. His calm cut through the tension, and the room grew silent.

"How do you know who I am?" Caspiz asked.

Shakespeare held up a hand. "Curtis, will you please attend to Philip?"

Scott frowned and turned, looking for Dick. "Where is he?"

"A bullet came through with you, it seems," Shakespeare said. "Did you get into trouble?"

Dylan nodded fervently, rubbing the arm Caspiz had injured.

"The bullet hit Dick?" Scott gasped. He wasn't particularly fond of the Immortal Writers, but he still didn't want anyone shot.

Wells's head popped up from behind a computer monitor. "A little help?" he asked.

Liz stepped behind Caspiz and took Curtis's place holding Caspiz down. Scott had his doubts about Liz being able to hold Caspiz in place, but Liz was apparently stronger than she looked. Caspiz couldn't break free, despite her efforts.

"What's going on?" Caspiz asked. "Where am I? How did I get here? What year is it?"

"I've been asking the same questions," someone said from the other side of the room. Scott peered around. Paul was roped to a hovering silver chair, a frown on his face. "My friends aren't here, and I don't know where they went."

Caspiz turned her head to see who was speaking. "You've got to be kidding me. Paul Ether?" She rolled her eyes and gave a pointed look to Shakespeare. "Why am I here with this lunatic?"

"Hey!" Paul complained.

"Everything will be explained in due time," Shakespeare said. "And by your young creator, no less." He nodded to Scott.

"My what?" Caspiz asked. She narrowed her eyes at Scott.

Scott swallowed. He really didn't want to be on Caspiz's bad side. She was a fireball. She had to be to prove herself. Even then, the Air Force was hesitant to promote her because she was so young. Her skills as a fighter were unparalleled, thanks to extensive training from her mother and siblings... until they'd all been killed in an alien attack, leaving Jane alone.

"Colonel Caspiz," Scott began. "I know this is confusing, but everything I'm about to tell you is true."

"You'd better start talking," Caspiz growled.

"Well... what year do you think it is?" Scott began.

"I came from 2134," Caspiz said. "But I can tell that that's not the year now."

"You came back in time over a century," Scott said.

Caspiz frowned. "That's impossible. The U.S. Government has just started messing with time travel. We're nowhere close to being able to travel that far. And teleportation... teleportation hasn't yet been released to the general public. How did you get a teleporter? None of you look like you're from the military or the government."

"I did teleport you here," Scott said, "but, well, you're not in the same world, exactly."

Caspiz frowned. "You're an alien? You've brought me to an alien planet?"

"No!" Scott said quickly. He knew what Caspiz was trained to do with aliens. "We're not—"

Caspiz lifted Liz up over her back and over her head. To Liz's credit, and what looked like Caspiz's amazement, she landed on her feet. Caspiz barrelled forward into Liz, but Liz pushed back. They looked deadlocked, until Caspiz relinquished her hold. Liz fell forward, and Caspiz hit her in the stomach. Liz stumbled back but didn't look too hurt. Scott was impressed.

"Damn, alien," Caspiz said. "Don't you go down?"

Liz laughed. "I've fought dragons, Colonel. You don't scare me."

Caspiz ran forward and swung her fist at Liz, but Liz blocked the blow with her arm and punched back. Caspiz caught the fist in her hand and twisted. Liz stumbled but didn't fall. Caspiz kept hold of Liz's fist and punched Liz in the face. Liz shook her head and wrenched her hand from Caspiz's grasp.

"Enough of this," Liz said. She held up a hand as Caspiz lunged forward.

Scott watched with wide eyes as Caspiz froze midlunge, her right hand held back for another hit. Only her head moved as she looked down at herself in amazement.

"What are you doing to me?" Caspiz growled. "Let me go."

"So you can attack me again?" Liz asked. "I don't think so. If I understand right, you're not the enemy here. The aliens are. Right, Scott?"

Scott stopped staring at Caspiz and turned to look at Liz. "Right."

"How are you doing that?" Dylan asked. He had flattened himself against the wall below the large Field screens, trying to stay away from the fight.

"Curtis has Body Magic," Liz said. "That's how he was able to heal Scott. I have Spirit Magic. That's how I'm holding her."

"So you *are* aliens," Caspiz said. "I should have known."

"We're not—" Scott was interrupted by Curtis and Wells popping up from behind the computer monitors. Curtis looked utterly exhausted, but he held on to Dick's shoulders nonetheless. Wells held his legs.

"Is he okay?" Dylan gasped as he saw them.

"He will be," Curtis said.

"We have to get him to Doctor Parsons," Wells said.

"Who?" Dylan asked.

"He's an Immortal Character," Wells explained. He and Curtis shuffled up the steps on the side of the room. "And luckily, he's in the Writers Castle at the moment."

"Why can't Curtis heal Dick?" Scott asked.

"Because my magic has its limits," Curtis said. His voice was strained. "I'm next to useless at this point because I just healed you."

"Do you need help?" Liz said. Scott looked back at her. Her hand was lowered to her side, but Caspiz was still frozen, glaring between Liz and Curtis. "I can feel you through our bond, and you feel weak."

Curtis shook his head. "I've got this."

"At least take a teleporter," Liz suggested.

"I'm not sure that would be best for Dick," Curtis said. "We don't have far to go. I'd rather carry him. You just keep the crazy lady in check."

"Crazy lady?" Caspiz repeated. Scott turned his attention back to her. "I'm not the alien here."

"Technically, if we *had* brought you to a different planet, *you* would be the alien," Shakespeare said. He leaned against the wall, arms crossed over his chest, watching the entire scene with fascination. It bothered Scott that he wasn't more concerned about what was happening, but it didn't surprise Scott either.

"That's just nuance," Caspiz spat.

"I'm a writer," Shakespeare said. "I subsist on nuances."

"If you're not aliens, how are you holding me here? Magic doesn't exist... only science. Clearly your species has some sort of ability that homo sapiens does not."

Shakespeare, Liz, and Dylan looked expectantly at Scott. He swallowed.

"I'm human," Scott said. "We're all human. Except... except we're not all from the same place."

"Aliens," Paul said confidently. "Caspiz, they tried to probe me earlier."

"We did not!" Liz said. "No person in their right mind would want to probe *you*."

Dylan coughed into his shoulder, and Scott saw him smirking.

"We're not aliens," Scott said. "My name is Scott Beck. I'm sixteen years old. That," he pointed to Dylan, who was still smiling, "is my brother Dylan. We were trying to help you back there in Washington, D.C. We know where you are, where you came from, and what's going on."

Caspiz didn't look convinced. "I know where I came from, too. I was in Arlington."

"You were in Arlington, but on a different world."

Caspiz opened her mouth, but Scott hurried to correct himself. "No... not a different world. You were... on a different *plane*. Sort of like an alternate universe."

"Alternate universes don't exist." Paul spoke up from where he still struggled against his bonds on the chair. "Even I'm not crazy enough to think that."

Scott ignored him. "There are at least two different universes, if you want to call them that. The Immortal Writers call them the Reality Field and the Imagination Field."

"Who are the Immortal Writers?" Caspiz asked.

"They're writers whose ideas and stories are so powerful that they become real. Or rather, the ideas cross over from the Imagination Field into the Reality Field." Scott pointed to Liz. "She's an Immortal Writer." Scott waved his hand at Shakespeare, not really looking at him. "He's an Immortal Writer." Scott placed his hand on his chest. "I... I'm an Immortal Writer. And about a year ago, I wrote a book called *Invasion*. Colonel Jane Caspiz was one of the best flight commanders in the U.S. Air Force when the Betans began to invade Earth. Paul Ether was an alien theorist with the only right ideas about the lifestyle of the Betans."

"The Betans are classified," Caspiz said. "How do you know about them?"

"I created them," Scott said. "I wrote them. I wrote *you*. And now you've crossed over into the Reality Field from the Imagination Field."

Caspiz laughed. "Aliens seem far more likely to me."

"So you're saying that's why my friends weren't in Roswell with me anymore?" Paul asked. "I came over to this Reality Field, and they didn't?"

"Yes," Scott said.

"Do you hear yourself?" Paul asked. "That's crazy, man. Even I don't think up stuff like that."

Caspiz frowned at Scott. "I've seen a lot of strange things in my life, things I couldn't really explain. It's opened my mind. But it's hard to grasp the idea that I'm imaginary."

"Don't think of it like that," Shakespeare suggested. "You just existed somewhere else first. Your story spoke to Scott, and his words granted you passage to this realm."

"To *reality*," Caspiz said slowly.

"It's reality to us," Shakespeare said. "I know it's not to you. But there's no way to send you back to the Imagination Field, so this is your reality now."

Caspiz closed her eyes. "I'm so tired of this. I'm so tired of things changing." She opened her eyes and looked at Scott. She looked less angry, and more exhausted. Scott was surprised. She didn't usually back down so easily. Something must be wrong with her. It probably didn't help that she was stuck in such an unnatural position due to Liz's magic.

"I'm willing to consider this possibility," Caspiz said. "I don't consider anything to be impossible anymore. Not after everything I've seen. But you have to prove it to me. I don't take *anything* on faith anymore."

Caspiz suddenly shook her head violently. "What's happening? Why am I so tired? Why do I feel so weak?"

"Sorry," Liz said. "You were attacking people."

"What have you done to me?" Caspiz slurred.

"It's not personal," Liz said. "I'm just trying to keep everyone safe."

"But what… did you…" Caspiz trailed off, and then her head slumped forward.

Liz took a step back, and Caspiz collapsed onto the floor.

CHAPTER NINE

Scott sat across from Liz, eyeing her warily. He, the fantasy writer, and Dylan were in the dining room of the Castle, which had oak floors and long, lavish wooden tables. Scott sat on one side of a table in a plush grey chair that was ridiculously comfortable, but he didn't sit back in it. Instead, he sat on the edge of his seat, studying the woman in front of him.

"Stop it," Liz said, meeting his stare. "Don't look at me like that."

"You're dangerous," Scott said.

Liz tilted her head and frowned at him. "Everyone is dangerous in the right circumstances," she said. "I may be dangerous, but I'm harmless."

"Tell that to Colonel Caspiz," Scott said.

"I told you, it's just a side effect of the magic," Liz said. "Since I used Spirit Magic on her, she had to pay the price. I'm sorry that she passed out. She's not used to it like I am."

"Why did you do that to her?"

Liz stared at Scott with hard eyes as she leaned back in her grey chair. It reminded him of how girls always looked at him in school—like he was stupid.

"She shot Philip Dick," Liz reminded him. "And she attacked me. Magic was simply a way to restrain her."

"Let it go, Scott," Dylan said from beside him. "I think Liz is right. Caspiz will be okay."

"There you are," a deep voice said. Scott looked up. Curtis walked toward them, entering the dining hall from the library. He still looked exhausted, but less so than when he and Wells had taken Dick to Doctor Parsons.

"Did you get Dick to the hospital in time?" Liz asked.

"We did," Curtis said. He slid into a chair next to Liz, across from Dylan, and gave Scott a smile. "How did your characters take the news that they're fictional?"

"Paul didn't believe him," Dylan said. "And Caspiz…"

"Caspiz is unconscious," Scott said. He indicated Liz with his chin. "She knocked her out."

"Too much Spirit Magic?" Curtis turned to Liz. She nodded.

"She'll be fine, if it makes you feel better," Curtis said to Scott.

"It does *not* make me feel any better," Scott said. "Liz still…"

"Liz still restrained someone you couldn't," Curtis interjected, running his hand through his thick blond hair. "And protected anyone else from getting hurt."

Scott pursed his lips and felt his shoulders rise and tighten.

"Chill, Scott," Dylan whispered from beside him. "You really want to pick a fight with these guys?"

Scott regarded Liz and Curtis in their fighting leather (which looked ridiculous), and noted their swords. Liz's weapon leaned against the side of her chair, while Curtis's broadsword was strapped to his back. Based on how they had handled the situation earlier, they probably knew how to use the swords. Plus, Scott had seen Liz use just a little of her magic on Caspiz; he grimaced to think of her using more of it on him. Maybe Dylan was right.

"Random question," Dylan said. Scott looked over at his brother to see him looking around at the dining hall. Several authors and characters were gathered there, chattering cheerfully and eating breakfast. Many of them laughed and smiled, looking generally jovial. "Why is everyone so calm?"

Liz frowned. "Is there a reason they shouldn't be?"

Dylan furrowed his eyebrows. "We're going to be attacked by an alien army pretty soon, according to Shakespeare."

Liz chuckled. "I'm sure that seems like a big deal to you," she said, "and it *is* a concern, certainly, but everyone here is pretty used to the world almost coming to an end. This isn't a new experience for them."

Dylan twisted his mouth in thought and stared at the table in front of him for a moment, and then blinked and patted the empty space before him.

"How does this work?" Dylan asked.

"How does what work?" Scott asked grumpily, eyeing the light-hearted people around him. Their happiness grated against his bitterness, making it more sour.

"I'm hungry," Dylan said. "How do I get food?"

Scott shook his head and wrenched his eyes away from the authors around him. "Watch and learn."

He placed a fist on the table and splayed out his fingers, then lifted his hand as a holographic menu rose from the wood and appeared before him. Four words hovered in the air: *Breakfast, Lunch, Dinner, Snacks.*

Scott flicked *breakfast,* and ethnic options scrolled up from the table. *American, Mexican, Italian, French, German, African, Japanese, Thai, Astronaut—*

"Astronaut?" Dylan asked.

"Space food," Scott explained. "Everything is freeze-dried."

Dylan grimaced. "Does anyone actually choose to eat that stuff?"

"You'd be surprised," Liz said. A similar menu was in front of her. She flicked her finger at the word *American.* "I don't personally understand it. I'd rather eat real food."

Liz scrolled through the three-dimensional menu with ease, quickly selecting a stack of pancakes with berries. The menu dimmed and disappeared, and a plate of food materialized in front of her.

Scott flicked *Mexican* and ordered a breakfast burrito—no tomatoes, no peppers.

"Why did you even bother ordering the breakfast burrito?" Dylan asked as a flat-looking tortilla appeared on a white plate before Scott. "You could have just asked for eggs."

"I like breakfast burritos," Scott said.

"You took all the good stuff out of it," Dylan argued.

"I like the tortilla," Scott said.

"Let me show you a *real* breakfast burrito," Dylan said.

He put his fist on the table and splayed his fingers. A grin lit his face as a menu popped up in front of him.

"This is the coolest," he said.

Dylan reached out a finger and poked at the word *Breakfast*, but he pushed too hard and his hand fell past the words. The menu scattered and disappeared.

"What did I do?" Dylan asked.

Scott snickered. "You're not pushing a button. You just have to touch the word, not punch it."

Dylan squared his shoulders and brought the menu up again. He lifted a finger and lightly tapped at the air. Nothing happened.

"You still have to *touch* the word, Dylan." Scott said.

Dylan tapped the word, and the next menu popped up. Liz and Curtis smirked from across the table.

"I know I have to touch the word," Dylan muttered. "I was getting there."

"Uh-huh," Scott said. He picked up his breakfast burrito and took a bite as Dylan finished ordering his loaded burrito.

"But does this magical food taste good?" Dylan mused.

He picked up his burrito and took a large bite.

"It's actually pretty tasty," Dylan said around a mouthful of peppers, steak, and eggs. "Probably because I actually have more than a tortilla in my hands."

Scott defiantly took another bite as Curtis ordered the largest coffee Scott had ever seen. He almost dropped his tortilla when he saw the enormous mug materialize in front of the dragon warrior.

"I didn't know mugs that large existed," Scott said. "You could fit your head in there."

"The caffeine replenishes my magic faster," Curtis explained. "We found that out a few months ago, after we fought Kenric."

"Who?" Scott asked.

"Dragon lord," Liz explained. "He was the villain from my books."

Dylan nodded. "I've read your books. Will you sign my copies?"

Liz smiled. "Of course!"

"Thanks!" Dylan said. He took another large bite of his burrito. "Whfffft 'sit mmmrke to befum a mmortal wreeter?"

Liz leaned toward Dylan, eyes squinted. "What did you just say?"

Dylan swallowed. "What was it like to find out you'd become an Immortal Writer?"

Liz laughed and popped a raspberry into her mouth. "It was terrifying, at first," she said. "I didn't believe any of it was real."

"I didn't either," Dylan said.

"A dragon had to attack me before I was convinced," Liz said. "What made you believe?"

Dylan laughed. "It's hard not to believe after being pulled through a portal and teleported around."

Liz grimaced. "Ugh. I hate the teleporters."

Dylan nodded. "I do too. Scott doesn't seem to mind them that much, though."

Scott looked up from where he stared absently at the table. "I don't like teleporting," he said. "I hate it. I hate everything here."

Liz and Curtis frowned. "Why?" Liz asked.

Scott shook his head. "It's a long story."

Curtis set down his coffee. "You've had a rough start," he said. "I think I would have a hard time being here too if my leg was shredded off on the first day."

"That's not why I hate it," Scott said.

"Then why?" Liz asked again.

"I don't want to talk about it," Scott snapped.

"Scott, they're just trying to be friendly," Dylan said. "Chill…"

Dylan trailed off and stared at another table.

"Dylan?" Scott asked.

"Wow," Dylan whispered.

Scott followed his brother's gaze. It appeared that he was staring at a beautiful young woman with short, dark hair, styled like she was from the 1920s, and large brown eyes.

"Who is that?" Dylan asked.

"That's Lilly Foer," Scott said. "She's an Immortal Writer. I remember her from the last time I was here."

"Lilly," Dylan repeated. "That's a pretty name."

Scott groaned. "No, Dylan."

"No what?"

"Don't try dating her," Scott warned. "She's an idiot."

"If she's an Immortal Writer, she's not an idiot."

Liz chuckled. "Lilly Foer? I wouldn't use *idiot* to describe her, either… more like self-righteous, romantic, and naïve."

"Sounds like an idiot to me," Scott said.

"She's beautiful," Dylan said. He put his chin in his hands like every love-struck moron Scott had ever seen in any romantic comedy.

Scott grabbed his brother's shoulder and forced him to turn away from Lilly. "She's off limits."

"Why?" Dylan complained.

"Trust me on this," Scott said. "You don't want to date an Immortal Writer; especially not that one."

"What's wrong with Immortal Writers?" Liz asked.

"I date an Immortal Writer," Curtis said. "I'm pretty happy about it."

Scott ignored them and tried a different tactic. "She's a romance author, Dylan."

Dylan raised an eyebrow. "So?"

"You hate romance novels," Scott reminded him.

"Well, yeah," Dylan said. "I'm a guy."

"Why would you be interested in a romance author if you hate those types of books?"

"I just want to get to know her," Dylan said. "She's pretty, and if she's an Immortal Writer, it's obvious she's got some brains."

"Don't be so sure about that," Scott said. He took another bite of his breakfast burrito but quickly regretted it when he saw Lilly look up and wink at Dylan. He gagged.

"Why did I bring you again?" Scott asked.

Dylan turned and smiled at his brother. "Shakespeare just kind of took both of us. Looks like it's working out for the best, right?"

Scott considered this. He didn't *despise* being at the Writers Castle like he had thought he would when Shakespeare first showed up at Dylan's house, but there were too many memories here, and he was still wary of Shakespeare. This couldn't really be for the best.

"Scott!" someone yelled from the library. Scott turned around to see Wells sprinting into the dining hall. "Scott!"

"What's wrong?" Scott asked.

"We've got two live ones," Wells panted. He stopped and put his hands on his knees as he tried to catch his breath.

"Live ones?" Scott repeated.

"Two more characters," Wells said. "They've already made it through to the Reality Field. We almost completely missed them coming in."

"I thought you were supposed to know in advance," Scott said. He took one last large bite of his burrito and pushed his chair away from his table. He stood and walked as quickly as he could on his sore leg over to Wells.

"We were so distracted with your other characters that we missed them."

"Were you still able to open a portal?"

"Briefly," Wells said, "but it's already closed."

"What does that mean?"

"That your characters have already moved," Wells said. "It might take some time to track them down."

"How?" Scott asked. "Do we know where to start looking?"

"I was able to tell where the portal opened," Wells said. "I can teleport you there."

Wells straightened and stretched his back as he looked around Scott at the table where Liz, Curtis, and Dylan still sat. Dylan stared dreamily at Lilly.

"You've just eaten?" Wells asked.

"Yes," Scott said.

"You're supposed to wait at least two hours after eating before you teleport," Wells said. "So you might feel a little sick."

"I always feel sick when I use those things," Scott said.

"You'll feel more sick, then," Wells said. He grabbed one of Scott's hands and placed a round, silver teleporter in it. "But you've got to go."

Scott looked down at the teleporter with a groan. "Fine."

He looked over at his brother. "Want to come with me on this one, Dyl?"

Dylan stood from the table, but instead of walking to Scott, he walked toward Lilly. Scott wanted to follow Liz's example and put his head in his hands in shame.

"You know what? Maybe it's good I'm leaving," Scott said as Dylan approached Lilly. "I don't want to see this."

He looked back at Wells. "Where am I going?"

"North Carolina," Wells said. "Good luck."

"Hey, I'm Dylan," Scott overheard. "You know, I think I saw you in a dream once?"

Scott sighed and pressed the button in the middle of the teleporter. His body disintegrated painfully, like his entire body fell asleep at once. Everything went black.

And then everything turned blue and white as his body reassembled itself. His stomach heaved, and he clutched at his belly while he tried to take in his surroundings. This proved difficult because all he could see was sky, and nothing would focus.

Then, as Scott's body finished pulling itself together, he realized the horrible truth: he had materialized in the sky, high above the ground, and he was plummeting to his death.

CHAPTER TEN

S cott screamed as he fell. He struggled against the wind and brought his arms together, frantically slapping the button in the middle of the teleporter.

Nothing happened. He continued to fall.

"Help!" Scott yelled, though he knew it wouldn't do him any good. "Help me!"

Only the screaming wind answered him as it rushed past his ears. Scott tried desperately to think of movies he'd seen where people had gone skydiving. What did they usually do? Didn't they spread their arms or something?

Scott tried to lift his arms, but the wind was stronger than he was. He couldn't manage to keep his arms in one place. He couldn't keep *any* of himself in one place. He just continued to fall.

He tried pressing on the teleporter again, but he remained fully intact as he fell from the sky. Why wasn't it working? Scott screamed shrilly as he remembered: the teleporter had to charge for at least five minutes before it would work again. Looking below him, he didn't think he had that long. Why had Wells given him only one teleporter? Surely they had more.

Scott tried to twist himself around or spread his arms, but he couldn't manoeuvre his body in the wind. It seemed that all he could do was fall, until a pair of strong arms seized his waist, causing him to yelp.

Scott struggled to turn his neck to see who had grabbed him, but then someone else encircled him from the front. He stared down at the person who had hold of him. Scott couldn't properly see the person's face, as the head was partially covered by a helmet and goggles, but seeing the stranger was better than seeing the ground that Scott knew was quickly approaching.

"Who are you?" Scott yelled. "Where are we?"

If either person answered, Scott couldn't hear them over the shrieking wind. He could have sworn he saw the man beneath him smile, though, before he let Scott go and glided to the side. Scott watched him deploy his parachute and felt a strange relief in his gut: these people had a way to save his life.

At least, that's what he thought before he saw the ground.

It was too close.

One of the arms around Scott's waist released him, and then Scott felt his body being thrust upward as the person's parachute escaped from the deployment bag. The pressure of the person's arm against his stomach did nothing to help his nausea.

Scott gritted his teeth together and squeezed his eyes shut. He tried to force his body to relax as he and the person holding him shifted positions in the wind. It helped him to notice that they had slowed considerably since the parachute had deployed.

It still came as a shock when his feet hit the ground. He stumbled at the impact, tripping his saviour and bringing her down with him. The parachute tumbled on top of them, closing them in. Scott heard the man land easily next to them and run as he slowed down.

The woman released Scott. He slowly opened his eyes. He was on hands and knees on hard sand. Scott grimaced; he'd had enough of dirt when he'd been in New Mexico to retrieve Paul.

The red parachute dimmed and tinted the sunlight that streamed through the cloth above him. He looked behind him at the woman, who was releasing the parachute from her body. With a *snap* it came undone, and the woman stood, throwing the parachute off of her and Scott.

"There you are," the man said, jogging up to them. "I was afraid the parachute swallowed you."

Scott stood slowly on shaky legs. "Thank you," he said. "Thank you for coming to get me."

"You're welcome," the man said. He removed his helmet and goggles, and Scott recognized him immediately.

"Yang?" Scott asked.

The man paused and frowned at Scott. He had black hair and dark eyes. He was shorter than Scott, but he carried himself like he'd never had a doubt about himself in his life, and that made Scott feel small and insignificant next to him.

"Do I know you?" Yang asked.

Scott turned to the woman. She had removed her helmet and goggles as well, so Scott could see her long black hair and brown eyes.

"Yin?" Scott asked.

Yin gave a pointed look to Yang. "And you wanted to save him."

"Why not?" Yang asked.

"He knows who we are," Yin said. "He could be one of the people we stole the jet from."

"The jet?" Scott repeated.

"Why would someone that was chasing us choose to do it by falling from the sky?" Yang asked. "With no parachute?"

Yin frowned. "We can't be sure."

"I'm pretty sure," Yang said. "But where did you come from, kid? I didn't see a plane or jet or 'copter around you anywhere."

"I teleported here," Scott said.

"See?" Yin hissed. "He *is* with the government."

"The government?" Scott repeated.

"No he's not," Yang laughed.

"How else does he know who we are, Yang?" Yin asked. "And how else did he *teleport*? Only the government has teleporters."

"I'm not with the government," Scott said. "But I was sent here for you."

"But we only took *one jet*," Yang whined. "Surely you won't miss one little jet?"

"Or the parachutes," Yin said.

"Or the laser cannons," Yang added.

"And definitely not the computer database we copied and subsequently deleted," Yin said.

"I'm not from the government," Scott repeated. "I just need you to come with me."

"Kid, we just got out of a nasty situation back there," Yang said. "We did some pretty awesome—"

"More like horrific—" Yin interjected.

"Some pretty *awesome* things to get away," Yang said. "We deserve a break. Don't we, Yin?"

"I don't know if we *deserve* one, but we'd like one."

"Fine, whatever," Yang said. "So basically, I don't think we're going anywhere with you."

"But we need you," Scott said. "The entire world is at stake here."

"That's what the government said," Yin retorted. She removed the harnesses from her shoulders and walked over to Yang. "And... well, you don't want to know what we just did to the government."

"It depends on when you came through," Scott said. "Are you at the point where you've stolen the part of the video surveillance from Quadrant Z, or have you collected the bits from Sector K yet?"

Yin and Yang stared at him.

"Yang," Yin said, "I thought I told you not to tell anyone about Sector K."

"I didn't," Yang said.

Yin glanced at her brother skeptically. "How do you know about Sector K?" she asked Scott.

"Have you done the job yet or not?" Scott asked.

Yin and Yang looked at each other and then folded their arms across their chests at the same time, mouths pursed in silence.

Scott looked between the two of them, trying to match the situation to the timeline in his book. "If you just stole the jet, you must have been leaving Quadrant Z," he said slowly. "You're on your way to Sector K. You should be meeting a buyer close to here. But I have news: they won't be at the rendezvous."

"How do you know all of this?" Yin asked.

Scott paused. He wasn't sure how to tell them, especially while they were out here. He needed to get them back to the Castle before he disclosed that information.

"I'll tell you if you come with me," Scott said finally.

"Go with you where?" Yang asked. "And how are you going to get us anywhere, kid?"

"With this," Scott said. He lifted the teleporter in his fist and shook it, beyond grateful that he had managed to keep ahold of it while he'd accidentally skydived. He squinted as bright sunlight reflected off of the metal.

"A shiny metal disc?" Yin rolled her eyes. "Kid, we don't have time for this. We've got to go."

"The buyer isn't there," Scott said. "I'm fairly positive he did not cross over with you."

"Cross over?" Yang asked.

"Into the Reality Field," Scott said.

Yin and Yang each frowned at Scott.

"Look, I really don't want to talk about it here," Scott said. "Just let me take you to the Castle."

Yang perked up. "Did you hear that, Yin? A *castle*."

Yin glared at Yang. "You can't be serious, Yang. We're not going with some stranger just because he says he's going to a castle."

"But I've never seen a real castle," Yang whined. "The aliens destroyed all of them in the First Alien War."

Yin sighed deeply and shifted positions, which brought her slightly closer to Scott. He was actually grateful for this, as her head blocked some of the sunlight that had been blinding him.

"We have to meet Ryan," Yin said. "He's waiting for us."

"Kid here says he's not," Yang said.

Scott bristled at the word *kid* and opened his mouth to protest, but Yang cut him off.

"I trust you, kid." Yang walked, a bounce in his step, toward Scott. Scott didn't notice Yin move imperceptibly closer as well.

"We'll go with you to your castle," Yang said. "I really want to see it."

Yang put an arm around Scott's shoulder, and Scott tensed.

It probably would have hurt less if he hadn't.

Yang's arm tightened around Scott's neck, and Yin pounced on him and held his arms down.

"Who are you?" Yin demanded.

"Where do you want to take us?" Yang asked.

Scott gasped against Yang's arms.

"My name..." Scott choked, his airways blocked off by Yang's strong grip.

"You'll tell us soon enough," Yang growled.

And his arms tightened.

CHAPTER ELEVEN

Scott could feel the teleporter in his left hand, but he couldn't move his hands enough to press the button to take them back to the Castle. Even if he could, had it been five minutes? Was it recharged?

"I'm going to loosen my hold on you," Yang said. "Just enough so you can speak. Don't bother screaming for help—there's no one around for miles."

The pressure around Scott's neck lessened slightly, and Scott gratefully gulped a breath.

"Talk," Yin commanded.

"My name..." Scott choked and tried again. "My name is Scott Beck."

He tried to twist his hand against Yin's grasp, but she tightened her hold on his wrists.

"That doesn't tell us anything," Yang said. "Give us something useful."

"You're right about the government," Scott said. "There is a conspiracy."

Yin squinted at Scott. "Do you know that because you work for the government?"

"Look at me," Scott said. "Would the U.S. government give a sixteen-year-old that kind of intel?"

Scott felt Yin's grip loosen on his wrists ever so slightly.

"Whose side are you on?" Yang asked.

"I'm against the aliens, if that's what you mean," Scott said. "But really, I can tell you more in the... at my base."

"Where is your base?"

"I already told you," Scott said. "The Castle."

Yin rolled her eyes and Yang tightened his arm against Scott's throat again.

"There aren't any castles anymore," Yang said. "You think we don't remember the First Alien War?"

"Not... here..." Scott choked out. "Let me... take you..."

Yin's eyes widened momentarily.

"The disc," she said. "The disc he has. It's a teleporter. He wants to take us back to Quadrant Z."

"No..." Scott tried to correct them, but Yang tightened his grip.

Yin let go of Scott's right wrist and tried to grab the teleporter out of Scott's left hand, but Scott reached the teleporter first and pressed the button.

Scott would have sighed in relief if his body had still been intact.

The three of them rematerialized in the Field Room in the same positions they had been in in the Badlands. Yang and Yin released Scott involuntarily as they collapsed to the ground, nauseous from teleporting. Scott felt a bit sick himself, but he managed to stay upright.

"Scott!"

Dylan's voice rang through the room, and Scott's brother ran up to him, worry etched on his face.

"Scott," Dylan panted, "I didn't even realize you had left until it was too late! Are you okay?"

Scott sidestepped Yin and Yang and walked to the chair that had previously held Paul prisoner. He plopped down, exhausted.

"I'm fine," Scott said. "Just tired and a little shaken up."

"Your voice sounds strained," Dylan noted.

"That's due to a lot of screaming, and some choking."

"Choking?" Dylan repeated.

"Where are we?" Yang asked. He and Yin seemed to have recovered themselves. They both stood warily against the wall, back to back, hands up in a defensive position.

"Welcome to the Writers Castle," Shakespeare's voice said.

Scott looked behind him to see Shakespeare walking down the right theatre stairs, Wells trailing along. Scott frowned. Shakespeare always had to interfere, and Scott hated it. But then again, there was no doubt that Shakespeare was better with words than Scott. He'd let the bard handle telling Yin and Yang the truth.

"The castle story again?" Yin said. "I guess you should count yourself lucky, Yang. You've always wanted to see a castle."

"The interior doesn't look very castle-y." Yang arched an eyebrow. "Where are we? The truth, please."

Shakespeare paused at the foot of the theatre stairs and stared at the newcomers, head tilted to the side, hand under his chin. "You are Yin and Yang, correct?"

"How do you all know who we are?" Yin asked. "How long have you been spying on us?"

"We're not spies," Shakespeare said. He slowly walked forward, then sat on the ground, legs crossed in front of him, and placed his hands on his knees. "We're friends."

"Friends?" Yang repeated.

"I find that unlikely, since we were just kidnapped," Yin spat.

"Why does everyone say that?" Shakespeare asked.

"Maybe because you kidnap everyone," Wells said. He stood at the foot of the stairs, leaning against a wall, his arms crossed against his chest.

Shakespeare nodded thoughtfully. "There is that."

"How can you prove to us that you're our friends?" Yang asked.

Scott looked at Shakespeare with a grim smile. The only way Shakespeare would know the answer to that question was if he had read Scott's book, and Scott didn't see Shakespeare as someone who would have stooped low enough to read someone *else's* work.

"Your mother's name was Yuri," Shakespeare said. "Your father was named Shang. They were killed in the First Alien War when you were both three years old. You both still remember watching them die. You don't speak of it. You don't even speak your true names. You only go by your nicknames, given to you by Yuri because of your natures: Yin and Yang."

"That's not unusual knowledge," Yin said. "That doesn't convince me to trust you."

"But I know your real names," Shakespeare said.

Yin and Yang tensed as Shakespeare turned his gaze to Yang. "You are Liu Wei," he said, and he bowed his head. "And you are Wang Li," Shakespeare said to Yin, and he bowed to her.

"How do you know that?" Yang asked. "How do you know our names?"

"They're pretty common names, Yang," Yin said. "He might have guessed."

"Those would be some lucky guesses," Yang countered.

"You…" Scott interjected and then paused, trying to decide what to say. "This may be hard to understand, but I know you, from when you were in a different world."

"A different world?" Yang asked.

"Are you aliens?" Yin tensed.

"No," Scott reassured her. "Maybe the more accurate description is that you come from a different time, in a different dimension."

"I've often wondered about alternate dimensions," Yang said. "We're in an alternate dimension now?"

"Of a sort," Scott said. "I heard you from the dimension you came from. We call your dimension the Imagination Field. And in the Imagination Field, the year was 2134. We're still in the twenty-first century in this dimension."

"What dimension are we in now?" Yang asked.

"We call this… *dimension*… the Reality Field," Shakespeare said.

"So you think we're imaginary?" Yin said.

"No, not at all," Scott said.

"In a sense, yes," Shakespeare said at the same time.

Scott glared at Shakespeare. He ignored Scott and looked serenely between Yin and Yang. "You see, your story came to Scott, and he wrote the whole story down," he explained. "His words were so pure, and all of his characters and plots were so realistic, that they came to life."

"We weren't living before?" Yin asked.

"Yes, you were," Scott said. "You were alive. Just in a different place."

Shakespeare nodded. "In a way, you did live… just in the Imagination Field, which is where all stories come from."

"So according to you, we're just stories?" Yin mocked.

Shakespeare raised his eyebrows. "Just stories?" he repeated. "*Just* stories? My dear lady, do not mistake stories as mere trifles. No tale should be undervalued. Great stories… the epics, the classics, the fables of magic, and legends of heroes… these are things to be treasured by all peoples throughout time. Stories should not be treated so lightly. I mean you no disrespect by telling you that you came to be through story. You should be honoured that Scott, as an author, heard your voices and heard your story, and was able to pull you through into a different world because your story was so powerful. Powerful stories… well, those may be the strongest force in all the world, competing with the greatest forces of nature known to man, even love, and faith."

Yang smiled. "You speak eloquently. Who are you?"

"William Shakespeare."

Yang blinked. "The playwright?"

"The very same," Shakespeare said.

"You don't actually believe all this, do you?" Yin turned to Yang, her eyebrows raised.

"I don't know, Yin," Yang said. "It's… possible. If we came over to this Reality dimension, that would explain why the government didn't track us down when we stole the jet. Didn't you feel that jump while we were flying? What happened to the missiles that were chasing us? And where did the jet go after we ejected from it?"

Yin frowned in thought.

"You all are taking this better than Paul or Caspiz did," Wells commented. He still leaned against the wall.

"Paul Ether?" Yang laughed. "I like him. He's nuts."

"Caspiz?" Yin asked. "*Jane* Caspiz?"

Wells nodded.

"Where is she?"

Scott stood and put a hand on Yin's shoulder.

"She can't hand you over to the government," he reassured her. "The government from your dimension didn't cross over."

"I'm not worried about that," Yin said. She nodded to her brother. "I'm worried about him."

"Why?" Wells asked.

"Hell has no fury like a woman scorned," Scott said.

"The correct quote," Shakespeare said, "comes from the play *The Mourning Bride*, and is 'Heaven has no rage like love to hatred turned, nor hell a fury like a woman scorned.'"

Scott frowned. He hated being corrected. "So? Same thing."

"You might meet William Congreve here, Scott," Shakespeare said. "He hates it when people misquote him."

Wells nodded fervently from behind Shakespeare.

"Where is Caspiz?" Yang asked.

At that moment the door to the Field Room opened, and Caspiz stormed in, followed by an out-of-breath Paul.

"So it's true," Caspiz said. "You brought in the twins. How are you, Yang?"

Yang swallowed loudly.

"Stay away from my brother," Yin said, stepping in front of him.

Scott wisely backed away. He couldn't help but be a little pleased when Shakespeare stayed put. The bard wasn't worried, but he should have been.

Caspiz descended the theatre steps. Yang unsteadily backed away, hands in front of him defensively.

"Jane," he said slowly, "can I call you Jane?"

"No," Caspiz spat.

"Look, I'm really, *really* sorry about—"

But Caspiz wasn't listening. She sprinted toward Yang.

To Yang's eternal discredit, he turned and ran.

CHAPTER TWELVE

"Yang!" Yin yelled after him.

Yang ignored his sister and ran up the theatre stairs, away from Caspiz. Scott watched as Yin tried in vain to block the Air Force officer, but Caspiz knocked her down and chased after Yang, barely missing a step.

"Scott, you should do something," Shakespeare commanded from where he still sat on the floor.

"No way." Scott grinned. "Yang deserves it."

"You'll need your characters to get along," Shakespeare pointed out. Caspiz caught up with Yang and tackled him. "You will all need to work together in order to stop the alien army."

"I know," Scott said. "But it won't hurt Yang to have Caspiz beat him up."

"Do you hear yourself?" Shakespeare asked. "Of course it will hurt Yang."

Scott sighed. "I just want to watch this for a second, okay?"

Shakespeare frowned, stood up, and walked over to Wells. Scott watched his characters with fascination.

Yin had caught up to Caspiz and was attempting to pull her off of Yang, but Caspiz was too well trained to let that stop her. She punched Yang in the face. Yin grabbed her arm, but Caspiz grabbed her and flipped her over Yang's body and onto the ground. Caspiz punched Yang's gut and then drove her elbow into his side. Yin dove at Caspiz, but the officer easily sidestepped her, kicking Yang in the process.

But suddenly Wells approached the fray, two orbs in his hands. He clicked both of them, and green beams of light shot out from each of the spheres. One beam surrounded Caspiz, and the other swallowed Yin.

Wells lifted his hands and spread them apart. The two women were lifted up into the air away from each other, completely frozen in the light.

"Prison Orbs," Wells explained, nodding toward either hand. "They're perfect for breaking up character fights when the author chooses to do nothing."

"It was entertaining," Scott defended himself.

"Come look at Yang and tell me again how entertaining it was," Wells suggested.

Scott looked over at Dylan. He did not seem to be very proud of his little brother at the moment. His arms were crossed against his chest, and he frowned at Scott, who sighed and sauntered over to Yang.

A little voice in the back of his mind, which he quickly silenced, admitted that Wells was right.

Yang looked awful. His nose was bloody, and his neck and face were already purple with bruises. His white flight suit was rumpled and torn in a few places. He moaned from the floor, barely conscious.

"Would you like to explain to me what just happened, Scott?" Shakespeare asked. He and Dylan had walked up the theatre steps behind him.

"You've read the book," Scott said. "You know that Yang had it coming."

"That's not what I'm asking," Shakespeare said.

"Why did you let Caspiz do that to Yang?" Dylan asked.

"It's not like I could have stopped it," Scott protested. "I wouldn't stand a chance against Caspiz."

"But you didn't do *anything*." Dylan flung his hands in the air in frustration. "You stood there smiling like it was the coolest thing you'd ever seen."

"It's funny," Scott said.

"Doesn't look funny to me, Beck," Wells said. "We've got to get this kid to one of the doctors in the Castle."

"Can't Curtis, or whatever his name is, just heal him?" Scott asked.

"He's still exhausted from healing you," Wells said.

"And I don't recall a wide grin on his face when you came back with half of your leg shredded," Shakespeare said.

"Oh, please," Scott snapped. "That was different."

"H-hey," a voice said from the Field Room door. "What's going on?"

Scott looked up. Paul stood nervously at the door; it seemed that he hadn't moved since Caspiz had come barrelling in. Paul's bright eyes shifted between Caspiz and Yin, both of whom were still levitating in the air, trapped in the beams radiating from the Prison Orbs.

"Just breaking up a fight," Wells said. He handed the Prison Orbs to Shakespeare and turned to Dylan. "Will you help me take Yang to the medical wing?"

"Why not just teleport him?" Scott asked.

"Teleporting him will only make his condition worse," Wells explained. "That's why we didn't teleport Dick, remember?"

He and Dylan bent down and grabbed Yang. Dylan, who was clearly the stronger of the two, lifted Yang's shoulders while Wells held on to his legs. Paul grimaced as they carried the pilot past him. Yang's arms dangled limply in the air; he had lost consciousness.

"What happened to him?" Paul asked.

"Caspiz attacked him," Shakespeare said. He carefully placed both orbs on a table behind him, keeping the beams pointed upward so that Yin and Caspiz remained imprisoned in the air.

"Now," Shakespeare sighed. "May we converse about the impending alien attack? Without any of us trying to harm one another?"

"I'm fine with that," Paul said.

"You'd lose in a fight anyway," Scott snickered.

"What about you, Yin? Jane?" Shakespeare asked.

Neither of the women moved.

"Oh, I'm sorry," Shakespeare said. "I forgot that the Orbs don't let you move. If I let you go, you must be civil. Otherwise I'll beam you up again."

Shakespeare touched both orbs and slid two fingers down the back of each one. As he did so, the beams lowered until Caspiz and Yin touched the floor. Shakespeare gave both of them a stern look and then waved his hands once in front of the orbs. The beams disappeared, and the women were released.

Yin and Caspiz stumbled forward, but neither moved more than that, choosing instead to eye each other warily.

"Now that we're all here and able to converse *civilly*," Shakespeare said, "we should discuss the approaching alien army."

"Do Caspiz and Paul know where we are?" Scott asked. "Do they understand that they're characters from my book?"

"We discussed it," Shakespeare said.

"I still find it hard to believe," Paul said. He was closer to the group now. His arms were wrapped around his torso, and he rocked back and forth on his heels. "But I can't think of any other explanation for this. Unless, of course, you're all aliens... which also doesn't seem likely. None of you look anything like the Betans, or the other aliens I've met."

"I think we're all struggling to wrap our heads around this concept," Caspiz said. "But whether it's true or not, the aliens are coming, and we need to be ready to fight them."

Shakespeare nodded. "I concur. But can you work with Yang, Caspiz?"

"You mean that lousy, low-life, son of a—"

Yin stepped forward threateningly, and Caspiz changed tactics midsentence. "Yes," she said. "I think I've beat him up enough. For now."

"Why did you do that to him?" Paul asked.

"He's a liar and a deserter. A traitor."

Yin laughed. "You don't want to admit what *really* happened, do you?"

Caspiz's face turned red. "I think *liar*, *traitor*, and *deserter* sums it up."

"Yang had Caspiz convinced that he was in love with her so that she would share intel with him," Yin explained. "He had her fooled completely."

Caspiz stepped toward Yin, her fists tight against her sides.

"Ladies." Shakespeare lifted the Prison Orbs threateningly, and Caspiz backed down, glowering at the Orbs.

"So, aliens," Paul said. Scott smiled. Whenever Paul was uncomfortable, he changed the subject to aliens. "When are they going to be here?"

Shakespeare eyed Caspiz and Yin, and then slowly put the Prison Orbs down, keeping them pointed at the women in warning.

"Anne," Shakespeare called.

"Yes, William?" A disembodied woman's voice spoke clearly in a British accent from somewhere in the room.

"Please show us the galaxy and the Betan ships."

"Yes, William," the voice said.

"Anne?" Scott asked.

"I may be an Immortal Writer, but my wife, Anne Hathaway, was not," Shakespeare explained. "I have been alone for many years, Scott. The science-fiction authors were able to program her beautiful voice into the computer system. It is not the same, of course, but it helps me feel less alone."

Scott blinked in surprise. He hadn't realized that Shakespeare would have lost people like he had. It didn't fit with the picture he had painted of the bard in his head. Scott shifted uncomfortably.

The Field Room dimmed slowly, and then the room filled with stars and planets and constellations. Scott had to admit that it was beautiful. It was like he was standing in the most complex and realistic planetarium in the world.

"Anne, please explain the situation," Shakespeare said.

"The Earth is here," Anne's voice said. A bright green light pulsed next to Scott's head. "The Betans have been approaching from the Milky Way's centre, which is here." A similar bright green light pulsed around a large, bright star in the middle of the room, which was also the centre of the swirling arms of the galaxy.

A bright, dashed red line appeared from the centre of the galaxy and drew steadily closer to the pulsing green light near Scott.

"The red line is the path the Betans are currently following," Anne said. "In two weeks, they have travelled ten thousand light years. They only have approximately fifteen thousand light years left before they reach Earth.

At this rate, you have a little over two weeks to prepare for the oncoming attack, assuming the Betans do not accelerate or slow their pace."

"Only two weeks?" Scott gasped.

"And a few days," Shakespeare said. "Look on the bright side."

"You're not helping," Scott said.

"Are we sure they're going to attack?" Paul asked. He pulled on his bottom lip anxiously. "What if they come in peace?"

"Don't start with your hippy crap, Paul," Caspiz said. "You're only a few years younger than I am. Surely you remember the First Alien War."

"I *do*," Paul said, "but you never know if..."

"But I know," Scott interrupted. "I wrote the book you all came from, and I know they're going to attack. It would be somewhat of a miracle if they didn't."

Caspiz raised her eyebrows at Paul, as if daring him to believe in miracles. Paul looked down at his feet and said nothing.

"Anne," Shakespeare said, "please zoom in on the alien ships."

"Of course, William," Anne said.

The projection filling the room shifted and flew inward toward the end of the red line. It made Scott dizzy to watch everything move, but soon the zooming stopped and rested on three ships. They were dark grey. All three were spherical, with two arms reaching from the front of each, which Scott knew housed the command bridge and missile launchers on all of the ships. The spacecraft had dark black windows made of some sort of glass that reflected the lights of the engines and the lights from the stars. It was hard to discern much else about the alien vessels.

"Why are they blurry?" Yin asked.

"We're having trouble fully focusing on the ships because they're moving so quickly," Shakespeare explained. "That's part of the reason we can't teleport you there for a reconnaissance mission."

"Can you do that?" Caspiz asked. "You have the power to send us onto the ships?"

"Yes," Shakespeare said. "We can teleport you there... or at least, we should be able to, in theory. But Anne is having trouble locking on to them."

"Do you have to program the teleporters?" Yin asked.

Shakespeare shook his head. "Not exactly, but the teleporter has to be able to locate your desired location based on your thoughts. Or, at least, the thoughts of someone who touched it recently. That's how Scott found you, Yin. Wells had sent the location to the teleporter telepathically before handing it to Scott."

"So you have to know exactly where the ships are before you can send us up there," Yin confirmed.

Shakespeare nodded. "Not knowing the precise location could be extremely dangerous."

"I'll go," Caspiz said. "I want as much intel on the Betan ships as possible."

"Every one of you will go," Shakespeare said.

Caspiz folded her arms and leaned back on her heels. "I'd prefer it if Yang didn't come."

"He's highly intelligent, and a good fighter," Shakespeare said. "And aside from Yin, he's the best pilot you've ever seen or heard of. Correct?"

Caspiz frowned. "Yes, sir."

"Then, if you will be so kind, Colonel, you will work with Yang."

"Yes, sir."

"I want to go," Paul said. "I've always wanted to see the inside of the Betan ships."

Scott shrugged. "Sure, Paul. I know you'll pick up the details, and you'll have some creative ideas about what it all means."

"Sweet," Paul said.

Caspiz raised her eyes to the ceiling and shook her head.

"You know you'll have to go," Shakespeare said to Scott.

"What?" Scott asked. "Why?"

"You're the author," Shakespeare said. "You'll know more about those ships than any of your characters, except for Dygavery. Not that he'd help you."

"Who's Dygavery?" Caspiz asked.

"This is why we duped you, Caspiz," Yin said. "You didn't know enough to suspect us, but you knew enough to give us just what we needed."

"I don't know what you're talking about, deserter," Caspiz said.

Yin glanced at Shakespeare. "Can I plug something in to one of these computers to show Caspiz what I'm talking about?"

"Yes," Shakespeare said. He walked over to a computer. "Just—"

"I know what I'm doing, old man." Yin pushed past Shakespeare and sauntered toward a computer. She reached up and lifted a long black cord from her neck. A black USB drive was attached to it.

"You used a USB drive?" Caspiz laughed. "Those haven't been relevant in over a century."

"Which is exactly why the government didn't have any security to prevent us from hacking into their computers this way," Yin said. She plugged in the USB drive. "And clearly *this* place isn't equipped to handle biotech, so it works out."

Scott raised an eyebrow at Shakespeare.

"We'll work on it," Shakespeare said.

Yin typed on the computer for a moment. "Now, if you'll all gather around the monitor here."

"We can project it," Shakespeare said. "Anne, please project the data currently visible on monitor thirty-one."

"Yes, William," Anne said. Scott wondered if she ever said no.

The galaxy around them disappeared, and a video clip materialized in front of them, hovering about a foot in front of the Imagination Field screens.

"Is that General Davis?" Caspiz asked, indicating a man in the video feed.

"Yes," Yin said. "Why isn't the sound working on this thing?"

Shakespeare reached his arm past her and pressed a volume button on the computer keyboard.

"I thought you knew what you were doing," he said. Yin glared at him for a moment while the sound began to play.

A deep voice with a guttural accent Scott couldn't place floated across the room. The sound of it raised the hair on the back of Scott's neck at the same time as a flash of heat seared through his head.

"General Davis, have you agreed to my terms?"

"Yes, Dygavery," General Davis said. He was a short but muscly man in a black Air Force uniform. He had very little hair on the top of his head, and it glinted slightly in the fake light of the room. Colourful stars covered the left side of his chest.

"And what about your president? Your world leaders? Will they resist?"

"If they do, my men will take care of it," Davis said.

"Then swear it, General Davis," the voice instructed.

Davis knelt on the floor. The camera followed him down at an angle, and the camera's shift captured Dygavery standing in a corner of the white room. Scott grimaced at the sight of him. He was only just aware that Paul had taken a slight step backward when Dygavery had come on screen.

The alien was at least eight feet tall. He was humanoid, but his skin was grey, scaly, and scarred. His hair was long and thick, similar to dreadlocks. His eyes were strange, all black except for the irises, which were light green. He wore heavy metal armour that covered his torso, though it stopped just past his shoulders. His legs were heavily plated as well. The alien held a spear in his right hand, and several bronze plasma guns were holstered to a metal belt around his waist.

"Swear to me, General Davis," Dygavery said. He blinked, and his eyelids closed from the sides like he was a reptile.

Davis bowed his head and lifted a knife with his right hand. "Are you... are you sure you need...?"

"*Swear to me, General Davis!*" Dygavery commanded.

Davis took a deep breath and carved a symbol into his left wrist. Scott couldn't see it clearly, but he knew what it looked like: a distorted infinity symbol with a straight horizontal line drawn through the centre of it. It was the symbol of Dygavery's reign, and it meant *Conquer*.

General Davis dropped the knife and turned his wrist over so that the blood streamed onto the floor.

"I swear fealty to you, Dygavery, King of the Betans," Davis cried. "Take my blood, my image, my strength, my home, and my people."

Dygavery smiled as General Davis bled. After a moment, the general passed out and fell to the ground. Dygavery stomped up to Davis and held on to the man's wrist, his armoured fingers pushing into the wound.

"Thank you, General Davis," Dygavery said. After a moment, he released the unconscious general's wrist and lifted his now bloodied hand to his face. He licked the blood and then smeared it across his armour. The armour began to glow, and then it shifted and changed. Dygavery metamorphosed into General Davis.

"Perfect," he smiled.

Then the screen went dark.

CHAPTER THIRTEEN

Everyone stood in silence as the video disappeared and the lights flicked back on. Scott blinked rapidly against the light and stole a glance at Caspiz. Her face was pale and her shoulders were tense.

"What did I just see?" Caspiz whispered. Scott quickly looked away, pretending that he hadn't seen the tears in Caspiz's eyes.

"You just watched General Davis, one of the major leaders of the U.S. army, surrender the human race to Dygavery, the king of the Betans."

"But… why would he do something like that?" Caspiz asked.

"It's a conspiracy, man!" Paul threw his hands up in the air. "I knew the government was covering something up."

"Shut up, Paul," Caspiz growled.

"He's technically correct," Yin pointed out.

"I'm right a lot more than people think," Paul said. "Everyone's always surprised."

"Shut *up*, Paul," Caspiz repeated. "General Davis wouldn't do that! He wouldn't do something like this!"

"We don't know what this means," Yin said. "But we have solid proof that General Davis, at least, was in league with the Betans."

"No," Caspiz insisted. "He's like a father to me. He *never* would have…" She indicated the empty air where the video had played moments before. "This can't be true."

"I can interpret," Scott offered. Caspiz, Yin, Paul, and Shakespeare turned to look at him. "After the First Alien War, which most of you remember—"

Yin and Caspiz winced. Paul, on the other hand, looked starry-eyed, which Scott supposed was appropriate, in a sense.

"After the First Alien War, the government formed a shield to protect the Earth from being located by alien species so easily. The humans eventually defeated the Alitations, but the leaders of the planet in 2132 weren't sure... won't be sure?"

Scott looked inquisitively at Shakespeare. Shakespeare shrugged.

"Well, your leaders weren't sure that you could fend off an attack by another species of alien, and what would happen if the next race was stronger?"

"So there is a force field around Earth?" Paul checked.

"In your dimension, yes, there was," Scott said.

"We called it the Shield Protocol," Caspiz said. "It doesn't hide our planet, exactly, but it projects... projected... will project... an older civilization, one not quite as advanced, so that we wouldn't seem worth invading. No nuclear weapons, no advanced warfare, no space travel, not even any internet."

"I wouldn't invade that planet," Paul said.

"Exactly," Caspiz said. "The idea was that no one would think we were worth it. No one knew how the Betans found us, but we started receiving threatening messages."

"The Alitations had been slaves to the Betans centuries before," Scott said. "Even though the Alitations had won their independence, the Betans paid close attention to their activities. So when the location of the highly advanced Earth was masked, the Betans still knew where the planet was. And eventually, after looking through the Alitations' systems, they discovered how to communicate with us."

"Which is how we got the first transmission," Yin concluded.

Scott nodded.

"So what was General Davis supposedly giving away?" Caspiz asked.

"Clearance," Scott said. "Clearance to everything. Davis thought that the human race had outgrown itself, and that the best future for them lay in serving a more advanced species. He'd been serving the Alitations, too, and decided to serve the Betans. In order for Dygavery to get everything he needed, he wanted to be able to turn into Davis. The general isn't dead, but now Dygavery, using transmutation technology and Davis's blood, can walk around and obtain all of the information he needs incognito."

Caspiz folded her arms and stared at the ground. "Well, it doesn't matter," she said after a moment. She looked up at Shakespeare. "If I understand correctly, the government in this Field doesn't know about these aliens. General Davis didn't come over to this world, so Dygavery's power is useless. And Davis's betrayal means nothing in the end. It's just us. We're on our own, aren't we?"

"Yes," Shakespeare said.

"We're supposed to fight an entire alien invasion *by ourselves*?" Yin exclaimed. "Come on. There's no way."

"You don't understand the kind of power the Immortal Writers have at our disposal," Shakespeare said. "In place of an army, you can create drones. No one even has to die in this fight."

Scott's shoulders tensed. He wished he could believe that.

Yin shook her head. "How can we possibly create enough drones in time to defeat an alien attack? You already told us we only have a little more than two weeks."

"The Writers Castle can do truly phenomenal things," Shakespeare reassured them. "But you're right: haste is essential. I shall continue to work with Anne on locking in the exact location of the alien ships. That way you can teleport aboard and plant bombs to easily obliterate the Betan army before it even reaches Earth. Scott, do you know where we should place the bombs? Your book said engineering but never went into detail. Where is that, exactly?"

Scott detested the doubtful look on Shakespeare's face, but he had to tell the truth. It wouldn't help them if he lied. "I have no idea," he admitted.

"Then I'll need plans from their computer systems before we can plant the bombs," Shakespeare said. He rubbed his chin. "Isn't Dylan a computer genius?"

Scott glared. "He's not coming with us."

Shakespeare raised his eyebrows. "Why?"

Scott leaned forward. "I'm not risking his life. And I won't let you risk it either."

Shakespeare tilted his head. "If you don't let him go, everyone's lives may be at risk."

"I said he's not coming."

"Who's not going where?" Dylan asked. He and Wells stepped back into the Field Room. "Yang will be fine, by the way. He just needs to rest."

Caspiz sighed loudly and shook her head.

"Scott and I were just discussing—" Shakespeare began.

"*No,*" Scott hissed.

"What?" Wells asked.

"Why don't we let Dylan decide, Scott?" Shakespeare suggested. "I shall leave it between the two of you, as long as you give him the choice to decide for himself."

Scott frowned.

"What am I deciding?" Dylan asked.

"We need to send a reconnaissance team to the alien ships," Shakespeare said.

Scott seethed, fists clenched.

"We need a computer expert up there," Shakespeare continued.

Dylan's face brightened. "Sweet! I want to go!"

Scott felt his face heat with anger. "You're not going."

Dylan turned to face his brother. "Why?"

"Haven't you heard anything I've told you?" Scott yelled.

Dylan waved his hand dismissively. "I'll be fine, Scott. I want to go on another adventure."

"That's what Dad said, Dylan," Scott said. "And then he didn't come back."

"Scott—" Shakespeare started.

"No," Scott interrupted. "*You are not coming, Dylan.*"

Dylan straightened. "You can't keep me out of it, Scott. I'm in this with you. I want to help. And you can't stop me from going. I'm your older brother."

Scott pivoted and punched through a monitor. He barely felt the bits of glass push themselves into his fist.

"You're not going!" Scott shouted.

Dylan approached him slowly, hands raised. "Scott, buddy, remember what we talked about…"

But Scott could barely hear him over the anger pulsing in his ears. He tried to focus on his breathing, tried to slow it down, tried to focus on anything but his fear and hatred, but he was lost in it, lost in the red fury.

And then shapes started to emerge.

A red wolf ran forward, its jaws snapping—

Two pairs of large green eyes stared at him through the fog—

"Not again," Scott dimly heard Dylan say.

The volcano erupted and a large cloud of ash smothered the sunlight until everything was—

The graveyard was empty except for one crow perched atop a child's grave—

A demon smiled and lunged—

"Catch him!" Shakespeare yelled.

Everything tilted as Scott drowned in the Fever.

CHAPTER FOURTEEN

Scott drifted in and out of consciousness.

"What's happening?" a voice said. "When did he go down?"

"The Fever…"

Dylan's voice. Scott recognized that one. He tried to reach out for it, but he couldn't focus. He floated away before he could catch it.

Scott was adrift. Wherever he was, it wasn't dark. He might have felt better if it was. Instead, it was full of images, images that flashed too quickly for him to make any sense of them.

A fire lit up the night as a star—far too large to be safe—shot across the world's black sky—

The man took a deep breath and readjusted his site, then crossed himself with one hand as he exhaled and pulled the trigger—

The planet glowed red in the middle of space, the only source of light for a million miles, glowing wickedly against the stars—

The clock face was broken, the glass shattered, and the hands were frozen forever at midnight—

The woman screamed, her shrill cries echoing off the church walls and reverberating to the ears of her young son—

And then Scott would come back to silence and grey static. This was when he knew he was back in his body, but he could never force himself to open his eyes, no matter how hard he tried. He couldn't really feel his body, even though he knew it must be there. He was only aware of what was happening in his mind.

Eventually he'd fade out again. The images would come back, slowly at first, like a camera focusing, and then they'd speed past.

A tornado wrenched up trees and houses, massacring everything in its path and slaughtering the father's only son—

A fire raged on the mountainside, lighting everything in terrible hues of orange and grey—

Scott didn't know how long he suffered, trapped in his mind, watching miles of scenes pour through his mind. In different ways, every image disturbed him to some degree. But nothing unnerved him quite like the image of a dark, bearded man with a smile on his face.

His father.

In his mind, Scott stared. Slowly, his father blinked. "Scott."

If Scott had been able to control or even feel his body, he would have wept at the sound of his father's voice.

"What are you doing, son?" Kent Beck's voice was deep and rich and one of the most comforting sounds in the world to Scott. "You're at the Castle, but you're fighting the Writers. Why?"

Scott wished he could answer. He wished he could scream *because they killed you!* but he couldn't. He was trapped in his mind. He could only watch and listen.

"Scott," his father said. "You've been hiding from who you are. Some of it is my fault. I know that, and I'm sorry. But I had to, Scott. I had to save the world from all of the evils I'd created. I'd like to think I did the best thing for everyone. Can you ever forgive me, Scott? It's my fault; not Shakespeare's, not the Writers'. They didn't know. They still don't know all of it."

Scott didn't understand. Was his father still talking about how he had died? How was his father talking to him at all?

"If you're seeing this message, then your brain is activating, and I'm not around anymore. I'm sorry. Since I'm not there to guide you, you have to do what's right on your own. I've left this recording in your mind in the event that a triggering event happens... and, if you're seeing this, it has."

How had Scott's father left something in his mind? How was that possible?

"Do the right thing, Scott," Kent said. "I know it's... different, now, but... I love you. You're always my son, no matter what. Trust Shakespeare. I can't save you, but they can help you save yourself, and then you can save them. But you have to choose to."

The portrait of Kent Beck smiled at Scott one last time. "Goodbye, son."

And then the image faded. Scott wanted to cry out for his father to stop, to come back, but he couldn't open his mouth. Instead, he felt himself transition into the grey of his conscious body. He could feel his arms, heavy at his sides. His legs seemed distant and far away at first, but slowly, painfully, he started to feel them again, starting at his thighs and trickling down toward his toes. He could feel his neck, and his head. His head was so heavy. But he was in his body at last.

And finally, he slowly opened his eyes.

He stared up at an orange and pink silk tent. Sunlight streamed through the silk cloth and warmed Scott's body.

"Where am I?' Scott said. His voice sounded raw, and it hurt him to speak.

"Here, drink some water."

Scott rolled onto his left side and sat up.

"Slowly, slowly..."

Scott looked up. A balding man with round spectacles and a slight smile sat on Scott's left side, extending a cup of water to him. Scott took it and sipped. The water was cool and comforting as it trickled down his sore throat.

"Where am I?" Scott repeated.

"This is one of the hospital wings of the Castle," the man said. "A character named Healer used to reside here, but she passed on some months back. The best way her author could think to memorialize her was to create a hospital out of where she lived. It was fitting. Many injured authors and characters come here now."

Scott looked around. The large tent was full of beds, chairs, and medical equipment. He was relieved to see he wasn't connected to any of the tubes and glad that no one else was currently in the hospital aside from the man speaking with him.

"Why am I here?" Scott asked.

The man patted Scott's hand gently, and then leaned back in his brown chair. "You were under what your brother Dylan called your Writing Fever."

Scott tensed at the secret being said so openly, but then he remembered the words that his father had felt were important enough to leave in his head. He looked down, swallowed, and forced himself to relax. He took a deep breath.

"He told you about that?" Scott asked.

"He told Shakespeare and the others that brought you here," the man said. "I just happened to overhear. I was present already, praying with some other patients."

"Praying?" Scott frowned. "Who are you?"

"Clive Staples Lewis." He extended his hand, and Scott shook it.

"How can you be an Immortal Writer and still believe in prayer?" Scott asked.

"I'm not sure I understand your question," Lewis said apologetically.

"How can you be immortal and still believe in God?"

Lewis smiled. "Just because God did something I didn't expect doesn't mean He does not exist. He just created more than I ever had imagined in my previous phase of life."

Scott pondered this, taking a sip of water.

"Tell me about your Writing Fever," Lewis suggested softly.

Scott swallowed. His instinct was to turn away and close himself off, but his father's face and voice lingered in his mind. It prompted him to speak with Lewis.

"It started after my father…" Scott paused.

Lewis nodded. "After you left the Writers Castle?"

"Yes," Scott said, thankful that Lewis hadn't forced him to explain that part of his history. "After I left the Writers Castle. A cacophony of voices and a mirage of images… they overwhelm me and distract me from everything else. I can't focus or function until the Fever passes."

"Why do you call it a Writing Fever?" Lewis inquired.

"Dylan and I found that when I wrote down what I saw and heard, the images and voices went away. Writing seems to be the only treatment."

Lewis frowned. "Then why not write consistently to avoid it? I do not mean to patronize you; I simply wish to understand."

Scott hesitated. "I… I knew the potential consequences of writing. I didn't want to become…" he trailed off.

"Ah." Lewis sighed and steeped his fingers together. "You did not want to become an Immortal Writer."

Scott nodded.

Lewis leaned back and stared at the tent ceiling. "You're drowning in consequences now, Scott Beck. Why avoid writing at this point? The damage has already been done."

"Habit, I suppose." Scott shrugged.

"Writing is like praying," Lewis said softly as he looked back at Scott. "It can be difficult to begin, but once you start, you feel better."

Scott considered this. He didn't believe in prayer, but he didn't begrudge Lewis his belief. Even if he had wanted to argue, he knew he would lose a debate with one of the greatest Christian writers of all time. And in any case, Scott *did* know the power of writing. He had witnessed it first-hand, time and time again.

"How do I start?"

"Praying, or writing?" Lewis asked with a smile.

"Writing," Scott said firmly.

"You know how to write," Lewis said. "If you didn't, you wouldn't be here. You just have to get into a ritual or a habit of it. I imagine you don't enjoy writing, since you've avoided it… so I suppose for now you can think of it as medicine or therapy. I'm no doctor, Scott, but I'm prescribing you with fifteen minutes of writing a day, at minimum. I'd also recommend prayer."

Scott dismissed the latter recommendation. "I'll try to write every day." He massaged his scratchy throat. "Why is my voice so sore?"

"Though you were unconscious, you were screaming when they brought you here," Lewis said.

"How long have I been out?"

"You've been under the influence of your Fever for a few hours short of three days," Lewis said. "It could have been much worse."

Scott's eyes widened. He'd never had an attack last so long.

"If you're feeling up to it, Shakespeare was wondering if you would like an Immortal Writers initiation," Lewis said. "He and I recognize the... special circumstances surrounding your arrival. He said he would not be put out if you choose to forego the usual festivities."

Kent Beck's loving, pleading face filled Scott's mind.

"I'll... I'll try one," Scott said slowly. He didn't look up, but he could feel Lewis's surprise.

"I shall notify Shakespeare, then," Lewis said. "We'll set one up right away. For now, just rest."

"I'm afraid to close my eyes," Scott admitted. "I'm afraid to be sucked back into the Writing Fever."

Lewis nodded thoughtfully and then pulled a small notebook out of his pinstriped jacket pocket, along with a black ballpoint pen.

"Why don't you write first, then?"

Lewis offered the notebook and pen to Scott.

Scott hesitated. If he took the notebook and wrote, he'd be accepting his position as an Immortal Writer. Could he do that? Did he want to?

He didn't know.

But he did know that he wanted to please his father more than anything. And his father had cared enough to leave him a message. Scott didn't understand it, and it would take him time to process it, but he knew what he had to do.

Scott took the notebook and the pen, and, for the first time in months, he began to write.

CHAPTER FIFTEEN

"You saw Dad?" Dylan gasped as he shrugged on a suit jacket. He turned from where he examined himself in the bathroom mirror and looked at Scott.

"Just in my head," Scott said. "I don't even know if it was real, but it seemed like it was. He somehow managed to leave a message in my mind."

"And he told you to work with the Immortal Writers?"

"And that my brain was activating, or something," Scott said. "I think he was talking about me becoming an Immortal Writer. I don't know what else he could have been referring to. But how did he know I'd end up as one of them?"

Dylan turned back to the mirror and straightened his tie, avoiding Scott's reflected gaze. "I don't know. But I have to admit, I'm a little jealous. Why did Dad share all of this with you? Why didn't he leave a message in *my* head?"

Scott put his arms through the sleeves of his new suit jacket and frowned. "I wish I knew the answer to that, but I don't. I'm sorry. I guess I shouldn't have told you."

"No, it's okay." Dylan sighed and looked at himself in the mirror. "I look good, right? Lilly will like it?"

Scott groaned. "Dylan, *please* don't pursue Lilly. *Please*. She drives me crazy."

"She drives me crazy too, but for different reasons." Dylan winked at his brother in the mirror and turned around. "Besides, I thought you were going to turn a new leaf and all that, since Dad visited you in the midst of your Fever?"

"That's why I agreed to the Immortal Writers initiation, but this is different and you know it," Scott said. He flipped off the bathroom light as he and Dylan walked from the double-sinked bathroom and into their room. It was still space-themed, but the constellations had changed. They changed every night, so there was always something new to look at and new shapes to draw in the sky. Scott found it fascinating and often got so absorbed in the stars that he forgot for a while to sleep.

He and Dylan walked through the black hole that was their door and into the science fiction hall. Scott tried to rid his mind of images of Lilly as they walked toward the library.

"Just stay out of it, little brother," Dylan said. "You let me handle the ladies."

"Can't you pick another Immortal Writer?" Scott pleaded. "Or, you know, just someone else entirely? Someone *not* in the Castle?"

"Why?" Dylan asked. "Lilly is beautiful, and she's got brains. I know you keep saying she's an idiot, but she has to be smart and creative if she's an Immortal Writer."

Scott shook his head. "Not necessarily. Just because someone can write doesn't mean they can write anything of value."

"Have you read her books?" Dylan challenged.

"No," Scott admitted, "but I don't have to. I've met her, and that was plenty of insight into her head for me. The last thing I want is to let her talk at me for eighty thousand words uninterrupted." He shuddered at the thought.

"I just want to get to know her," Dylan said. "Is that too much to ask?"

Scott sighed. "Do what you want, I guess. But keep her away from me. I'm planning to make more of an effort to be pleasant around the Immortal Writers, but I have my limits."

"Deal," Dylan agreed.

Dylan and Scott entered the library. Scott still couldn't quite grasp how large the library was, and he knew that the large room around him was more than it seemed. When he'd been here two years ago with his father, he'd explored the library more fully. It tended to shift according to what you were looking for, and Scott distinctly remembered the room growing taller, as if it was trying to look more impressive, when he had just been browsing for nothing in particular one spring afternoon.

"Where's the initiation?" Dylan asked. He straightened his tie again nervously.

"In the ballroom," Scott said. He turned around and walked back into the hallway he and Dylan had just left, but he kept the ballroom in mind when he passed over the threshold. Before him, instead of the Science Fiction Wing, was a pair of golden double doors. Scott paused outside of them and took a deep breath, his hands hovering above the handles.

"Are you sure you want to go in there?" Dylan asked. "I know this whole experience has been hard for you."

Scott frowned. "Dad wanted me to work with them. All I want is to make Dad proud."

"But what about how *you* feel?" Dylan asked.

"Has Dad ever done anything that wasn't best for me?" Scott looked up at Dylan. His brother shrugged.

"I don't know, Scott."

"I'm going to try," Scott said. He squared his shoulders. "For him."

He pushed the doors open.

Immortal Writers mingled in the golden ballroom, but they quieted when Scott entered. They seemed unsure about what to do with him. Scott understood how they felt, seeing as he was unsure himself.

There was a moment of absolute stillness as everyone stared, and then an author he recognized walked up to him and extended her hand.

"Welcome to the Immortal Writers, Scott," Liz said. Scott took a deep breath and shook Liz's hand.

And with that, it seemed the spell of silence and awkwardness was broken. The writers continued chatting with each other, and the string quartet, which was situated atop a platform in the right corner of the room, continued to play. Scott didn't recognize the music, but then he'd never been very musical.

"Thank you," Scott mumbled to Liz as he exhaled in relief.

"Why does everyone seem so edgy around you?" Liz asked.

"You don't beat around the bush, do you?" Scott accused. He looked away from Liz, who was dressed in a simple blue strapless dress, and glanced around the room. Weren't there supposed to be refreshments somewhere?

"I don't mean anything by it," Liz said. She sipped some champagne from a tall, clear glass. "I can't believe they let you wear that."

Scott looked down at his tux and bow-tie and back up at Liz. "Why?"

"I had to wear fighting leather to my initiation," Liz said. "I assumed all of the writers had to wear something from their books."

Scott considered. "Maybe they're just trying to be nice to me."

Liz frowned. "Your refreshments are different, too."

"Where is the food?" Scott asked. "I'm hungry."

Liz gestured with the hand holding her champagne glass to the centre of the room. "In the middle of that throng of people," she said. "You'll have to brave the crowds if you want to eat anything."

Liz walked away toward an author leaning against the east wall. Scott thought he recognized Langston Hughes, but he wasn't certain, and he didn't care enough to go over and introduce himself.

"I'm not sure you and McKinnen are getting along very well," a woman said to him.

Scott turned toward the voice and frowned. He tried not to strangle Dylan at the sight of Lilly Foer standing so close to him. Scott could see why Dylan found her attractive. She had short brown hair, dark eyes, and a beautiful smile. She looked stunning in her lavender dress, but her personality negated any physical traits Scott could appreciate. Scott just prayed his brother would come to recognize that eventually and be done with her.

"Well, I hope *you* aren't expecting a warmer reception from me," Scott said.

"Scott, be nice," Dylan reprimanded.

Scott rolled his eyes at Dylan then took a deep breath and worked on fixing an image of his father in his mind. He could get through this initiation. He only needed to keep it together for a few hours.

"I'm getting some food," Scott mumbled. He walked in the direction Liz had indicated.

It was easy to get through the crowds. The Immortal Writers parted in front of him like he was Moses and they were the Red Sea. Scott tried not to feel hurt by this. He had pushed them away, after all, but it still bothered him. He wanted to make an effort to work with these people, but they were all keen on avoiding him, and Scott wasn't comfortable enough to try to engage anyone in conversation.

Scott meandered past L.M. Montgomery and Louisa May Alcott, who were deeply engrossed in conversation, and stopped short at the sight of a bizarre silver table in front of him. The table looked like liquid metal, and large silver blobs floated above it. It was slightly disturbing to look at, and, to Scott's dismay, there was no food.

He felt his temper rise. Was Liz messing with him? Had Shakespeare tricked him? Was he trying to humiliate Scott? He knew it shouldn't matter—they were just refreshments—but for some reason, Scott was livid.

"It's not as eldritch as you think it is," someone said to him.

A man with a long, pale face, dark eyes, and dark hair stood to his side. He wore a rather grim expression.

"The science fiction authors are trying very hard to claim you as one of their own," the man explained. "So they tried to make something special for your initiation."

"Sorry... who are you?" Scott asked.

"Howard Phillips Lovecraft." The man introduced himself with a slight nod, though he continued to stare at the table and didn't make eye contact with Scott. "I've seen my fair share of initiations. Each genre tries to make their authors feel as at-home as possible, but I do believe that, occasionally, the science fiction authors miss the mark."

Scott glanced back at the bizarre table in front of him. "What is the table meant for? What are the blobs supposed to do?"

"The spheres are there for decoration."

Scott furrowed his eyebrows.

"Who made that design choice? They're horrible."

"Indeed," Lovecraft agreed. He stared forlornly at the blobs.

Scott waited for Lovecraft to say more, but the horror author offered no further insight to the science fiction authors' attempts at decorating. He simply stared, his mouth a thin straight line.

"Is there any food?" Scott finally asked.

"Of course," Lovecraft said. "I shall demonstrate."

Lovecraft approached the table and placed his hand inside the liquid metal. The metal encompassed his palm and then released him. Lovecraft stepped back, and Scott waited.

In a matter of seconds, a plate of food floated to the top of the table from inside the metal. The plate was full of pasta. A cup of coffee appeared next to the plate. Lovecraft took the plate and the cup. He took a sip of coffee and nodded to Scott.

"Simple as that."

Scott blinked.

"But what...?"

Lovecraft sighed. "The science fiction authors have discovered a way for the metal to read what your body is craving from the imprint of your palm. I love Italian food, and since I don't drink alcohol, I drink a great deal of coffee. The table knows this and brought it forth."

Scott couldn't fathom how the science fiction authors accomplished this, but he decided to give it a try. He walked up to the table and placed his hand on the shimmering surface. His hand sank down into the table, but it wasn't painful or uncomfortable, like he had feared it would be. It was like dipping his hand into warm water.

"What villain did you have to defeat when you first became an Immortal Writer?" Scott asked Lovecraft as the metal released him. He removed his hand.

"Cthulhu," Lovecraft said dismissively.

Scott couldn't understand his bored tone. Just thinking about the Old One coming to the Reality Field sent shivers down his spine. "How did you defeat Cthulhu?"

Lovecraft blinked. "The same way he is put to rest in the story. I simply changed the star pattern to which he awakens to one that does not exist on our planet. He still lives, but the eldritch god will forever slumber in the depths of the sea."

"But what if—" Scott began.

"He slumbers," Lovecraft said sharply. He nodded to the table. "Good day."

Scott watched Lovecraft walk away, but when his stomach growled he remembered the table in front of him.

A tall milkshake waited for him next to a container of fries. Scott couldn't help the grin that slid across his face. It was perfect.

The glass that held the milkshake was cold to the touch, and little beads of moisture dripped down the side of the glass. Scott picked it up, grabbed all of his fries in the other fist, and stuck them into the milkshake. The empty fry container sank back into the table.

"Having a bit of fun?"

Scott turned to C.S. Lewis.

"This has been one of my favourite foods for as long as I can remember," Scott confessed. "I love the salty sweet combination."

Scott took a fry out of the milkshake and stuck it in his mouth before the ice cream could slide off.

"You seem in better spirits than when I saw you in the hospital," Lewis commented.

"Writing helped," Scott admitted. He considered mentioning the vision of his father, but he couldn't bring himself to speak of it. It was too sacred to him.

"Your brother also seems to be in good spirits," Lewis said. He pointed behind Scott.

Scott turned and then immediately wished he hadn't. Dylan and Lilly were lip-locked in one of the corners.

Scott groaned and turned back to his milkshake. "Why?" he muttered pitifully to his ice cream. "Why her?"

"That's what I'm wondering." Jane Austen laid her palm on the table. "That brother of yours is quite handsome, Scott."

Scott grimaced. No one ever said that *Scott* was attractive. Not that he wanted Jane Austen to think he was handsome, exactly. It would just be nice to be noticed next to his macho brother. Austen removed her hand from the table, and a brownie emerged from it. She took the dessert and left.

Many authors came to the bizarre refreshment table. Some talked to him, but only briefly. The majority of authors that bothered to speak with him offered their condolences on the Dylan and Lilly situation, including L.M. Montgomery, which Scott thought was interesting, since she was generally so kind-hearted. The Grimm brothers introduced themselves. They seemed incredibly uncomfortable. The way they stood, hunched together, made them seem like they felt out of place. Scott got the impression that they didn't interact with the other writers much, but Scott could hardly blame them. They were incredibly old. T.H. White and Leo Tolstoy came and spoke with him as well, but both of them only exchanged a few words with him, which Scott found surprising since their works suggested they were both somewhat long-winded.

Eventually, Shakespeare walked to the centre of the room and called for everyone's attention.

Scott straightened. He knew what was coming. He had been present for his father's initiation. Everyone in the room was supposed to welcome him. But would they?

"My fellow Immortal Writers," Shakespeare said to the crowd. "We have a new writer in our midst! Scott Beck's stories have crossed the threshold of the Imagination Field and entered reality. His words, his stories, and his characters are so powerful that they have sprung forth from the page and into the living, waking world.

"Scott is well on his way to defeating his villains and saving the world. He has had the unique opportunity to go and retrieve his own characters, and has shown valour and wisdom in his adventures thus far. It is now time for us to welcome him into the fold of the Immortal Writers."

Shakespeare looked at Scott and beckoned him forward with a hand. Scott took a deep breath and forced himself to walk at an even pace toward Shakespeare. It felt like the longest walk he had ever made in his life.

Eventually, he reached the bard. Scott remembered that Shakespeare had placed his hand on his father's shoulder, but Shakespeare did not try to touch Scott, and he was grateful for this. He would try to work with the Immortal Writers for his father's sake, but his bitterness and anger were not gone, and these emotions were certainly not dead. Everything was merely buried.

For now.

"Who will join me in welcoming Scott Beck into our midst?"

There was a deafening silence. Scott held his breath.

"I welcome you," Liz said. She approached him but followed Shakespeare's lead and did not touch him.

"I welcome you," Dick said. Scott was glad to see that he was already recovered from being shot, though he still looked pale.

"I welcome you," Wells said.

Many other authors approached, but not as many as Scott remembered welcoming his father. Scott noted with disappointment that although Lovecraft had spoken with him earlier, he did not welcome him.

The circle around Scott was sparse, but Shakespeare spared Scott from waiting for more authors to step forward. He raised a glass of champagne in the air.

"Do the rest of you welcome Scott as one of you, and as an Immortal Writer?" Shakespeare asked the crowd.

"We welcome him," a chorus of voices chimed together.

The circle around him began to disperse, but Wells took Scott's arm and leaned in toward Shakespeare.

"Anne's done it," Wells murmured to them.

"Done what?" Scott asked.

"Pinpointed Dygavery's army," Wells said. "We have access to the alien ships. And now that this little party is over, we need to move quickly."

CHAPTER SIXTEEN

They were gathered in the Field Room. Scott, Shakespeare, Dick, Yin, Yang, and Caspiz stood in a semicircle facing a galactic map that hovered in front of the Imagination Field screens. The map that Anne had pulled up clearly marked the alien ships, which were about twelve thousand light years away from Earth.

"They're travelling faster than I'd hoped," Shakespeare murmured as he rubbed his chin. "We're not going to have a lot of time."

"Why can't we just shoot them before they come any closer?" Yang asked. He was still a bit purple but was mostly recovered from having his ass handed to him by Caspiz. The pilot and the colonel stood far away from each other. "We don't want the mortals to know about the Betans coming anyway, right? We could avoid teleporting aboard altogether."

"Their shields won't let anything through," Scott said. Being welcomed by the authors, even though the initiation had been somewhat strained, helped him feel warmer toward the Immortal Writers. The vision of his father had changed something in him as well. He wasn't ready to save the world, not yet, but he was finally willing to do it.

"Scott's right," Caspiz said. "They have Singularity Shields. Anything that comes close to their ships is sucked into a minuscule black hole and carried to God knows where."

"That doesn't make any sense," Wells complained to himself from behind a desk. "The ships would be sucked in, too. How did this cross to the Reality Field? How?"

"Then what do we do?" Yin asked, thankfully ignoring Wells.

"Can we teleport aboard and place the bombs now and be done with it?" Paul asked.

Caspiz sighed loudly. "We can't do that, Paul."

"I know I'm not military," Paul said, "but that's what makes the most sense to me. Why teleport aboard just to walk around when we can plant the bombs immediately?"

Scott swallowed. "I don't know where to place the bombs," he admitted. "I never designed the interior of the entire ship. I just know the basic layout... three levels. The bridge is the bottom arm that extends away from the third level. The third level itself houses all of the weapons, and the first level has sleeping pods and living quarters."

"What about the second level?" Wells asked.

"I never had to worry about that before," Scott said. "So I don't know."

Wells shook his head and rolled his eyes.

"We need to send a team up there to map it out," Shakespeare said.

"As we've already discussed," Yin said, shooting a glance at Paul.

Scott took a deep breath. "Could we hack into a computer?" he asked. "I'm sorry I don't know where to place the bombs, but I know there's a computer in the sleeping quarters. It's there mainly to control the pods, but it should still have everything we need on it. Dylan may be able to hack into the system and retrieve the schematics of the ship."

Shakespeare arched an eyebrow at him but thankfully didn't comment on Scott's sudden change of heart in regard to Dylan helping the team.

"That's a good idea," Shakespeare said. "How do you propose we hack into the alien system? Do you know how it works?"

"I know it uses binary," Scott said. "So I was thinking... could you make another orb like you used on Caspiz and Yin? But this orb could be commanded by binary and hack into anything that uses that language."

Shakespeare frowned and rubbed his chin. "I presume that's possible," he mused after a moment. "I'll confer with some of the authors. Octavia Butler and Madeleine L'Engle have been itching for something to do. They'd probably jump at the opportunity to make your... Memory Orb. Assuming you have someone in your party who knows binary and can control it?"

"Dylan can do it," Scott said. He tried to sound like this idea didn't terrify him. He didn't want to lose his brother, but he knew he had to do what was necessary.

"I can come, right?" Paul spoke up. "I might be helpful."

Yin snorted. "How?"

"I know they weren't the Betans, but when I was thirteen, I was abducted by aliens."

"Here we go," Caspiz muttered.

"So I might be familiar with some things," Paul continued, ignoring Caspiz. "I'll have perspective none of you have."

"You were *not* abducted by aliens, Paul," Caspiz said. "Give it up."

Paul furrowed his brow and opened his mouth, but Scott spoke first.

"Actually, he was," Scott said. "He learned a lot about the different alien species. In the book you end up listening to his theories, Caspiz, because they tend to be correct."

Caspiz gaped at Scott. "That's ridiculous," she sputtered. "This guy's a nut job."

"He's incredibly helpful in the book," Scott said.

Yang laughed as Caspiz stared between Paul and Scott.

"This job isn't for civilians," Caspiz finally said.

"He should go," Shakespeare countered. "Your team now consists of the Immortal Characters and the Immortal Writers... and Dylan."

"Where *is* Dylan?" Paul asked.

"With Lilly Foer," Scott grumbled. "I eventually stopped arguing with him and came here by myself."

Dick patted Scott's shoulder. "My condolences, Scott."

"We'll need supplies," Caspiz said, "so that we can survive on the ship."

"The science fiction authors can make anything at a nearly impossible pace," Shakespeare said. "What do you need?"

"I need weapons," Caspiz said. "I'd like particle guns and gravity guns. You can look at my particle gun as an example, if that would help. Assuming that magician didn't hurt it when she so stupidly threw it away from me."

"We can make the guns," Dick said. "Do you need anything else?"

"Suits," Caspiz said. "The ones I'm thinking of are blue and have headsets in the helmets that will allow us to communicate..."

"I know just the ones," Shakespeare said. "Scott described them in the book."

Caspiz nodded. "Speaking of Scott, if the civilians have to come, I want to train them first. Nothing major—I know we need to hurry—but some basic shooting, how to infiltrate, how to clear a room... things like that."

"You can use the Imagination Room," Shakespeare suggested. "Scott can imagine the parts of the ship he knows. That way you won't be teleporting onto the real ship blindly."

"What's the Imagination Room?" Paul asked.

Shakespeare smiled.

Scott, Caspiz, Paul, Yin, Yang, Dylan, and Lilly stood outside of the Imagination Room. It hadn't been hard to talk Dylan into coming, but it was on the condition that Lilly could come as well. This annoyed Scott, but Dylan was an essential part of the plan, so he had acquiesced. Mary Shelley stood in front of the Imagination Room and gestured toward its silver doors.

"This is the pride and joy of the science fiction authors," Shelley said. Her long, dark hair swept up in a bun behind her head, and it bounced as she moved her arms. "Gene Roddenberry was instrumental in developing it. He's usually the one to introduce it to the authors, but he's not at the Castle at the moment."

Paul walked up and stroked one of the silver double doors. "What does it do?"

Scott smirked. Paul's look of wonder reminded him of when Scott had first seen the Imagination Room with his father. He could clearly see himself two years previously, standing before the doors with his dad while Roddenberry welcomed them.

"The Imagination Room is virtual reality at its finest," Shelley said. "Each of you will need to touch the handles. Prepare yourselves for a bit of an electric shock; it's just the room reading you and preparing you to enter."

"Like being probed?" Paul asked.

Caspiz squinted at Paul in disgust. "What is up with you and being probed?"

Paul shrugged.

"No, it is not like being probed," Shelley said. "The electric shock injects microchips in your system to help the room read your body movements. That way you can interact with what's inside."

"What's going to be inside?" Yang asked.

"Whatever is in Scott's head," Shelley said.

"Not to interfere," Caspiz interrupted, "but maybe it should be whatever is in my head. I know how to run the training exercises we need to do."

"But I know some of the layout of the alien ships," Scott said.

"That won't be helpful if the exercises aren't set up well enough to teach the civilians how to clear a room," Caspiz said.

Shelley twirled a piece of loose hair anxiously. "True. We'll let the Imagination Room read both of you. You can have control at first, Character, but after, Scott can show you what he knows of the Betan ship. I'll program the Imagination Room to read both of your minds. It will know when it needs to."

Caspiz nodded. "What do I need to do?"

"You just need to walk in first. An orb will surround your head so it can accustom itself to your brainwaves. Then it will reflect what you're picturing."

"How large is the room?" Caspiz asked.

"As big as you need it to be," Shelley said. "It'll grow and shrink according to what you think and see."

"Can we go in now?" Paul asked. He sounded like a little boy at a candy shop.

"Caspiz first, and then Scott," Shelley said. "All of you follow him."

Caspiz squared her shoulders and walked up to the double doors. She grasped the handles, and then her body froze for a moment as electricity coursed through her. After a moment, the doors swung open, and Caspiz stepped through into the dark room beyond. The doors shut themselves just enough that the handles were close enough together to grab them both, and Scott stepped forward.

He touched the handles, and the familiar electric shock entered his body. He felt himself tense, but then the electricity released him. Scott stepped back as the doors swung outward. He walked into the dark room and watched the orb snap apart from Caspiz's head. The blue orb flew over to Scott and surrounded his skull. A horizontal line of blue light scanned him, and then the orb cracked open and flew away. By the time it had released him, everyone was inside the Imagination Room. The doors swung shut.

"It sure is dark in here," Lilly said. Her voice was high-pitched, and it grated against Scott's ears.

"One of the primary goals of a reconnaissance mission is not to get caught," Caspiz said. "That means *keeping quiet.*"

Scott heard Lilly click her tongue in disdain. For a moment he was grateful it was too dark for him to be able to see. He would have been too tempted to slap her.

Slowly, the Imagination Room grew lighter, until it finally looked like the seven of them stood in front of a moonlit brick maze. Scott looked up. He knew the sky wasn't real, but it was exquisite. He didn't recognize all of the constellations, though, and it took him a moment to remember that what he was seeing was from Caspiz's sky and not his own. Scott's attention snapped back to the ground as a table piled high with guns materialized next to Caspiz.

"I've asked the Writers to make two different types of weapons for us," Caspiz said. She picked up a long silver-and-blue weapon from the table and held it up for them to see, one hand firmly gripping the handle and the other holding the long, wide barrel.

"This is a gravity gun," Caspiz explained. "It doesn't shoot any bullets or other materials; instead, it shoots out force. If I were to shoot one of you, the area of your body I hit, and up to six inches in any direction from the point of contact, would react the same way it would if your body fell from a great height."

Lilly shrieked. Dylan put a comforting arm around her shoulders as Scott rolled his eyes.

"If you shoot someone in the leg with this gun, that leg will be gone in less than a second," Caspiz continued. "If you shoot them in the chest... well, it's not pretty."

She set down the gravity gun and picked up a smaller weapon. Scott thought it looked more like a highly advanced pistol than the almost shotgun-looking gravity gun.

"This is a particle gun." Caspiz held it away from her in one hand. It was dark grey, with white accents lining the length of the weapon. The gun sloped steadily upward from the handle to the barrel. "Some people believe that it's a kinder way to kill someone. This gun does have bullets, which contain a liquid that dissolves the target into particles. This does not separate atoms; it will not cause a nuclear detonation. But it does separate molecules, so if I were to shoot you in the arm, a chunk of it would disintegrate and disappear. The liquid can spread up to a foot in any direction."

"Would we, like, breathe in bits of people that disintegrated?" Paul asked, his hand raised. "I mean, are particles of them still in the air? Does that hurt our lungs?"

Caspiz blinked. "I..." she frowned. "Well, there have been no problems with my lungs yet, and I use this gun all the time. So I'm assuming you'll be alright."

"Okay, but will I be breathing in particles of dead people?" Paul asked. "I really feel like this is an important thing for me to know."

Caspiz shook her head and gestured toward the table of weapons. "Each of you come choose a weapon," she commanded. "Don't worry; they won't be live until I imagine they are. I normally wouldn't teach this way, but these guns can't cause any damage, since they're just from my imagination. They're not loaded. This gives you the unique opportunity to become familiar with the guns without possibly killing everyone."

"Wait, we actually have to use guns?" Lilly asked.

"This is a military operation," Caspiz said slowly.

"You're in a sci-fi world now," Scott said. "Feel free to leave at any time, if you feel uncomfortable."

Lilly raised her chin. "I'm perfectly comfortable, thank you." She stomped to the gun table and looked at the particle guns and gravity guns in dismay. "Don't you have anything more dainty?" she asked.

Scott could hear Yin's knuckles crack as she clenched her fist beside him.

"More dainty?" Caspiz repeated. "You can't be serious."

"I refuse to be seen carrying a weapon like this," Lilly sniffed.

"You could just not carry a gun, and we can all let you die," Scott suggested hopefully.

Dylan punched him on the shoulder.

"I can protect myself, I just prefer a different weapon," Lilly insisted.

"What qualifies as *dainty*?" Caspiz asked.

"Something… old fashioned and romantic," Lilly said.

Caspiz arched an eyebrow and blinked. A small .22 pistol appeared on the table.

"How's that?" Caspiz asked.

Lilly touched the silver handgun but didn't pick it up. "It's not very pretty, is it?" she sighed.

"Do you want flowers on it?" Yin asked, exasperated. "It's not an accessory, it's a weapon. And not a very good weapon for what we'll be doing. It's mostly used for shooting rabbits."

"Oh no, not poor bunny rabbits!" Lilly whined.

Scott turned and glared at Dylan. He shrugged sheepishly.

"Just take the damn gun, civilian," Caspiz barked.

Lilly picked up the gun gingerly between her thumb and forefinger and held it far away from her chest.

"That's not how you hold it," Caspiz growled.

"Even I know that," Paul said.

Lilly adjusted her grip.

"Whoa, whoa!" Caspiz yelled. She stomped forward and twisted the gun away from Lilly.

"Don't put your finger on the trigger until you're ready to shoot," Caspiz reprimanded. "Do you want to shoot yourself or someone in your squad?"

Lilly sighed. "Well, how would I know what to do? I'm not a barbarian. I don't handle guns all day."

Scott saw Caspiz's knuckles turn white as her grip tightened on the gun she'd wrenched away from the romance author.

"I don't think I would be very responsible if I let you handle a weapon. Even though this isn't live yet, this is foolish," Caspiz said. "I don't think it would be very wise of me to let you come on this reconnaissance mission."

"Yeah, why are you here again?" Paul asked.

"She's with me," Dylan spoke up. "I'm not going unless she's allowed to come."

"You'll be putting her life at risk, as well as all of ours," Caspiz reprimanded.

"It's alright, sweetheart," Lilly said. She walked up to Dylan and patted his cheek. Scott grimaced. "I don't have to come. You just be safe and come back to me."

Lilly turned away from Dylan and glanced around. "How do I get out of here?"

Caspiz blinked and a doorway appeared in front of Lilly.

"Oh, thank you," Lilly said. She walked through the doorway, and it disappeared.

Scott raised an eyebrow and looked at Caspiz. "Did you really send her out of the Imagination Room?"

Caspiz stared at Scott. "Of course I did," she said flatly. "I certainly wouldn't have sent her anywhere that she'd have to run away from terrifying 'poor bunny rabbits,' now would I?"

Dylan opened his mouth to complain, but Scott nudged him with his elbow. "She'll be fine," he muttered. "Let's focus."

"Scott's right," Paul said. "I want to learn how to shoot aliens!"

"I know Yin and Yang can handle a gun," Caspiz said. "What about you, civilians?"

"I know how to shoot, more or less," Paul said. "I've read a lot of books and blogs about it."

"That's not the same thing as actually *shooting* the gun," Yin pointed out.

"But I know the basics," Paul insisted.

"Dad took me shooting when I was a kid," Dylan said. "I haven't shot for a few years, but I think I can handle it."

Scott frowned at Dylan. "Dad never took me shooting."

"Well, Dad never brought me to the Immortal Writers Castle," Dylan said as he intently studied the moonlit maze.

Scott grimaced. That probably hurt Dylan quite a bit, though he'd never come right out and say it. He wished he knew the reason his father had never included Dylan, but his dad had never offered explanation.

"I've never shot a gun before," Scott admitted.

Caspiz frowned. "Well, you'll be with all of us, so hopefully you won't have to do much shooting... but we should be prepared just in case."

Caspiz turned, and a strange-looking replica of a Betan appeared about twenty-five yards away. The alien looked similar to Dygavery. It was tall and had long, thick, dreadlock-looking hair. Its skin was orangeish instead of grey, though, and it looked slightly translucent.

"What is that made out of?" Scott asked.

"Ballistics gelatin," Caspiz said. "It replicates flesh. I'll shoot it for you so you can see what will happen when you shoot a real Betan."

"Why not just imagine up a Betan?" Paul asked. "Why make it out of ballistics gel?"

"Because you can see inside of the gel to watch what's happening," Caspiz said. "I'll slow it down so you can see things clearly."

She picked up a small particle gun and held it away from her, both hands around the weapon. She aimed longer than she should have needed to. Scott peered at her face. It was drawn and slightly red. Scott felt like he could understand. Davis had betrayed the world, betrayed Caspiz herself, for this Betan. She probably wanted nothing more than to shoot the alien king.

Caspiz took a deep breath and fired.

The shot didn't make a sound, but Scott watched carefully as the bullet that contained the dissolving liquid entered the Betan replica. Caspiz used her imagination to slow down the bullet, so Scott was able to see what happened when it entered the ballistics gel.

The bullet shot through the gel easily enough, and inside, Scott saw it tear itself apart as dark green liquid spilled out of it. The liquid greedily devoured the interior of the Betan, and the gel dissolved and disappeared. A gaping hole was left in the replica's chest.

"That doesn't look like a kinder way to die," Dylan said. "He dissolved slowly."

"I slowed down the effects so you could see what happened," Caspiz said. "It's much faster in real time. Come grab a gun, everyone. Make sure the barrel is pointing toward the ground. *Do not* point your weapon at anyone."

Scott walked forward and picked up a gravity gun by the pistol grip. He was surprised at how heavy the gun was. He hoped he would be able to hold it up long enough that he wouldn't embarrass himself.

"How quickly can the Immortal Writers make guns for us to take on the reconnaissance mission?" Yang asked as he picked up a particle gun.

Scott shrugged. "From what I remember from when Dad… from when I was at the Writers Castle last time, they can make things pretty quickly. I'm sure they've improved their processes even more in the last two years."

"Can they make us walkie-talkies or something?" Paul asked excitedly. "So we can communicate?"

"Radios like that are outdated, even for us," Dylan said. He picked up a particle gun identical to Yang's.

"They're making us full-body suits, remember?" Yin said as she grabbed a gravity gun. "There'll be a way for us to communicate in the helmets."

"They should look something like this," Caspiz said.

She was suddenly covered in a fitted dark-blue body suit. A belt with magazines surrounded her waist. She wore combat boots over the suit. A dark blue and black helmet covered her head.

Yin nodded. "Yes," she said. "The new suits the military created. Exactly."

Scott jumped as his head was encompassed by a helmet identical to the one Caspiz wore. He looked down at himself. He was now dressed in the body suit, too. He tapped his chest with his gloved hand. The material was surprisingly hard and was less like spandex than Scott had imagined upon seeing it at first.

"Can everyone hear me?" Scott jumped again as he heard Caspiz's voice in his helmet.

"Loud and clear, boss," Paul said.

"Everyone stand in a line next to me. Leave about five feet between each of you."

They lined up. Six targets appeared before them. These were not made of ballistics gel but looked real. They also looked human, instead of Betan.

"Who's that supposed to be?" Paul asked. "It's not me, is it?"

"It's not you," Caspiz said. "Blowing up the ballistics gel was satisfying, so I wanted to try killing this scumbag six times in here."

"Who is he?" Yang asked. He sounded nervous.

"His name's Justin," Caspiz said. "An ex from years ago. God, I hate him. I can't wait to blow him up."

She lifted her gun—she had grabbed a gravity gun this time—and pointed the barrel at the Justin down her line of sight.

"Keep your finger off the trigger until you're ready to shoot," Caspiz said. "And remember, don't point your gun at anything you're not willing to destroy. Hence me pointing it at Justin."

Scott smirked and lifted his gravity gun.

"Press the stock of your gun against your shoulder," Dylan instructed. "Otherwise it'll kick back and hurt you."

Scott pressed the gun against his right shoulder.

"Press the bolt catch down," Yang said.

"The what?" Scott asked.

"The little lever on the left side of the gun," Dylan said.

Scott flipped the lever then held the gun tightly around the pistol grip.

"Now you're ready," Yang said. Scott saw Dylan nodding on his other side.

"Just look through your sight now," Yang said.

Scott put his cheek against the stock of the gun, closed his left eye, and looked through the sight. He could see a red dot on the left arm of Caspiz's ex.

"Turn your safety off," Dylan whispered. Scott didn't know why Dylan bothered to whisper; everyone could hear inside their helmets.

"Where's the safety?" Scott asked. He felt himself grow hot with embarrassment.

"Left side, above the trigger," Dylan said.

Scott flipped the safety off and looked through the sight again. He could more clearly see Justin now. He was tall and thin. He had a ferret-looking face with dark brown eyes. Scott wasn't sure if his eyes looked dead because he was from Caspiz's imagination, or because he was a horrible person.

It didn't matter either way. He was going to shoot him regardless.

"Everyone aim and get ready to shoot this bastard," Caspiz said.

"What did he do to you again?" Paul asked.

"Let's just say he's a manipulative, selfish, horrendous excuse for a human being," Caspiz said.

"He sounds pretty bad," Yang said.

"You're not much better," Caspiz pointed out.

"I'm glad it's not me out there," Yang said.

"Don't tempt me," Caspiz said. "Everyone aim for his chest. Fire on my mark."

Scott peered at Justin's dead brown eyes for a moment before he focused on his chest.

"Fire."

Yin, Yang, and Dylan hit Justin in the chest. Dylan and Yang's targets' chests disintegrated. If the target had been a real person, no vital organs would have been left, and Justin would have died. However, he would have died cleanly.

Yin's target, on the other hand, exploded in a bloody mess, spewing gore around the room. Paul missed his target completely and exploded a shadowed wall behind him, but Scott managed to graze Justin's arm. The arm exploded and bits of flesh hit Scott's helmet, even from twenty-five yards away.

The force from Caspiz's gun hit Justin... somewhere else. He exploded while Caspiz laughed.

"I like this room," Caspiz said. "I might come back in here for target practice more often."

"Maybe I made a mistake by having you dupe her to get information," Yin murmured to her brother. Yang shifted uncomfortably.

"Scott, Paul, try to hit Justin again," Caspiz commanded.

Scott lifted his gravity gun to his chest. It was heavy in his grip. His arm shook a bit, and he fired faster than he should have because he was embarrassed of his weakness. The bullet hit Justin's left leg, and it exploded as well. Paul, on the other hand, managed to hit Justin's head.

"I was totally aiming for his head," Paul said. "His chest is way too easy a target, you know?"

Scott rolled his eyes and fired again, this time hitting Justin in the chest. He exploded messily. Scott wrinkled his nose in disgust.

"Now that all of the targets are destroyed, can you clean this up?" Scott requested.

"Why?" Caspiz asked. "This is the best I've ever seen Justin look."

"Caspiz," Yin said. "Even I'm having a hard time stomaching this."

"Let's go back to the ballistics gel," Yang suggested.

Caspiz sighed. "Fine."

The blood and gore disappeared. Scott exhaled in relief.

"Well, none of you are *awful* at shooting," Caspiz said. "But we'll run through this a few more times after the reconnaissance drill. Mostly, though, we're going to hope that Paul and Scott don't have to shoot anything."

Scott frowned. "I can learn quickly."

"I'm sure you can, civilian," Caspiz said, "but we don't have that kind of time if we're going to board the enemy ship soon. The most important thing I can teach you now is how to be as discreet as possible. If we do our job right, none of the Betans will hear or see us, and we'll be in and out quickly without ever having to use our guns.

"We're going to walk single file," Caspiz continued. "Stay about arm's-length apart from the person in front of you. I'll take point. Yang, take right; Yin, you be the rear. Dylan, you're easily the best shooter out of the civilians, so I want you to take left."

"What does that mean?" Dylan asked.

"While we're walking, I'll be looking right, and only right, watching for Betans," Yang explained. "Caspiz will be looking ahead, and Yin will be walking backward looking behind us. You need to be looking for enemies on our left. If you see any, shoot immediately."

"Will we see any in the Imagination Room?" Dylan asked.

Caspiz looked at Scott. "Why don't you imagine up the area of the ship we'll be in, and I'll place enemies randomly in our way," she suggested.

Scott nodded.

"When we round corners and cross corridors, wait for me to clear it first," Caspiz said. "I'll beckon each of you forward, one at a time. Don't wait and look around; just trust me. We have to work together to keep each other safe."

"What are Scott and I going to do, since we don't have a position or whatever?" Paul asked.

"Just stay low and follow me," Caspiz said. "And all of you stay quiet. Silence is key. I don't want to hear a lot of chatter while we're running this exercise, and especially not when we're really on the ship. Understood?"

"Don't the suits block sound from escaping?" Dylan asked.

"They make it easier for us to communicate, yes," Yin said, "but we want to make as little noise as possible. If the Betans hear us talking to each other at all, we're screwed."

"They do have excellent hearing," Scott said, "but they'll all be asleep. It really shouldn't be too difficult to get to the computer in the sleeping quarters. I doubt we'll run into trouble."

"If they have excellent hearing, won't they wake up?" Yin asked.

"They have to sleep in salt water to regain their strength, so they sleep in pods," Scott explained. "Still... I think Caspiz is right. We want to be as quiet as possible."

"But what if we have a question?" Paul asked. "What if we get lost? What if...?"

"Silence is imperative, Paul," Yin interrupted. "And you'll be with us. You'll be fine. The real question is, are you capable of shutting up?"

Paul sniffed and lifted his head in defiance.

"When we approach a room, Yin, Yang, and I will clear it to make sure it's safe," Caspiz said. "Wait to follow us until after we've told you the room is clear."

Everyone in the group nodded.

"Alright, Scott. It's your turn to take over," Caspiz said. "Let's go."

CHAPTER SEVENTEEN

The scene around them changed as Scott's thoughts took control of the Imagination Room. Within seconds, they stood in a large blue room littered with rows upon rows of green and yellow boxes, which were mostly submerged into the floor, making them easy to see over.

"What's in the boxes?" Paul asked.

"The Betans," Scott said. "The water in the pods is why they always smell like brine."

"What did I just say about silence being imperative?" Caspiz snapped.

Scott pursed his lips together as Caspiz stepped in front of him.

"Yin, Yang, Dylan, fall into position," Caspiz commanded. Yin trotted to the back of the line, and Yang ran to the left of Scott. Dylan walked more hesitantly to the right of Paul.

"Watch and follow me," Caspiz said.

She hefted her gun against her shoulder and crept forward. She was quick but quiet. Scott and Paul followed her with Yin trailing behind, keeping watch behind the group. Dylan and Yang walked along either side of Paul and Scott, keeping guard to the left and right. Yang watched with confidence, but Dylan stumbled occasionally, and Scott could hear his nervous breathing through the speaker in his helmet.

Caspiz manoeuvred expertly around the pods, never pausing as she stalked through the room. As they reached the end of it, she moved to the side, and they lined up against the left wall.

"We're going to clear the next room," Caspiz whispered. "Wait for all three of us to say it's clear. Understood?"

They nodded.

"Yin, Yang, you're with me."

Yang walked forward and placed a hand on Caspiz's shoulder. Yin took her place behind Yang, holding on to his shoulder as well. Caspiz glanced at Scott and pointed to the door.

"These doors aren't like human doors," she said. "How do I open them?"

Scott pointed to a keypad on the right hand side of the door. "You have to enter the code," he whispered.

"Do you know the code?" Caspiz asked. She sounded somewhat impatient.

Scott nodded. "It's—"

"No," Caspiz interrupted. "We'll have you do it. Follow me."

The six of them crept over to the right side of the door, each of them maintaining their positions.

"Enter the code," Caspiz commanded.

Scott turned to the keypad. The keys were covered in the moon cycle Betan numbers, and for a moment he panicked. He didn't know how to interpret their language... but it didn't matter with their numbers. Numbers were universal... or at least, that's what Scott had heard. Had anyone really tested that theory?

Praying that he remembered the Betan numbers correctly, Scott pushed at the keypad, entering in *21345793*.

The door slid open. Caspiz, Yang, and Yin ran inside in quick succession, Caspiz in the centre, Yin taking left, and Yang going right. Scott, Paul, and Dylan watched as the three military officers swept the room.

"Clear," Caspiz whispered into the headset.

"Clear," Yin said.

"Clear," Yang repeated.

Caspiz lifted a hand and beckoned the rest of the group forward. Dylan, Paul, and Scott entered the room slowly. Scott looked around, his heart hammering and his breathing shallow. He wasn't sure why he was nervous. They weren't really on the spaceship. He had complete control over their surroundings. Still, something about the exercise raised his adrenaline and made him sweat.

"Fall back into position," Caspiz said.

Everyone drew together into the same pattern that they had been in before, with Caspiz in the lead and Yin behind the group. They walked through the large sleeping quarters, manoeuvring around sleeping pods, and then entered another room after Scott opened the door. Not much had changed from before, and Scott felt his heart rate slow and his breathing become more even as he became used to the routine of the exercise.

Caspiz stopped the group in the middle of the next room. "This is what it will be like when we clear rooms," she said. "It's pretty straightforward. But do any of you know what to do if we come across a Betan that's awake?"

Yang raised his hand. Caspiz glared at him.

"Not you, Yang," she said. "A civilian."

Yang lowered his hand, and Scott could see his lower lip sticking out under the glass on his helmet.

Paul spoke up. "We shoot them, don't we?"

Caspiz nodded. "We shoot them. I know our goal is to be quiet and remain undetected, but hopefully the authors will be able to create guns that will remain almost completely silent, like these are. Also, we can't count on any of the Betans *not* being an enemy. We must shoot on sight. Don't try to determine if the creature is a threat or not. All Betans are threats.

"Hopefully Yin, Yang, Dylan, or I will spot the Betans first, since we're on the lookout for hostiles," Caspiz said. "I hope we can shoot the Betans and keep moving. But if we're somehow surrounded, I want everyone to get low and shoot anything that moves, as long as it's not us. Does everyone understand?"

They all nodded.

"I'm going to start imagining Betans coming at us from random places," Caspiz said. "We'll keep clearing rooms as we've been doing, but it will be different now. Is everyone ready?"

Scott nodded hesitantly. His heartbeat sped up again as he gripped his gun tightly. He wished it wasn't quite so heavy. More accurately, he wished he were stronger.

They walked forward through the room. Scott entered the same code in the door, and Caspiz, Yin, and Yang ran through the opening.

Scott tensed as he heard the bodies fall. He craned his neck to see past Paul and the door, but it was no use. He could only see the strange green lights that emanated from the alien sleeping pods. They reflected eerily off Paul and Dylan's helmets.

"Clear," Yin, Yang, and Caspiz said after a moment.

Scott, Dylan, and Paul walked into the room one at a time. Scott grimaced at the Betan bodies on the floor. He wasn't sure why it bothered him. He had just seen different versions of that Justin fellow blown to bits, and it hadn't really fazed him, whereas seeing the dead Betans made his stomach turn. He couldn't make himself look away from their green blood spilled all over the chrome floor.

Scott was so focused on the Betans that he forgot what they were doing. He ran into Dylan, who was standing in front of him. Scott looked up, confused.

"Watch where you're going, Scott," Caspiz said. "If you only focus on the dead, you'll soon be one of them. Pay attention."

Scott raised his shoulders, frustrated with the reprimand. "I just wanted to see what they looked like up close," he said.

"Why?" Yang asked.

"Yeah," Paul said. "I was close to some aliens once, and let me tell you, man, it's not worth it."

"It's different for me," Scott said. He stood up straight. "I'm their creator."

"Their *creator*?" Yin scoffed.

Yang chuckled. "What were you thinking? Those things are *gross*."

Scott glanced back down at the dead Betan closest to his left foot. Green blood covered his combat boots.

"Only because they're bleeding," Scott said. He looked closer at the slightly scaly grey skin and long, dark dreadlocks. "I don't think they look so bad."

"They're pretty disgusting, dude," Paul said. "The other aliens I met weren't quite this gross. Did you make anything, you know… not repulsive?"

"He made you, Paul," Dylan pointed out.

"That doesn't help his argument," Yang countered.

"And you," Dylan continued.

"Oh," Yang said. "Right."

Scott continued to stare down at the Betan, his stomach turning uncomfortably. He felt strangely hot.

"I'm their creator," he repeated.

He felt like he was missing something important. He felt like he should know something specific about this creature, but he couldn't think of what it might be. Whatever he was trying to remember was just out of reach. Scott was constantly ashamed of how little he knew. Usually he tried to hide from his ignorance. But something bothered him about seeing the dead Betan on the floor. It made his head ache.

And then Yin's voice cut across his thoughts through the headset. "Contact rear," she said as she fired her gravity gun.

Scott looked up. The Betan's head ruptured as the gravity force hit it. Scott swallowed down the acid in his throat.

"I told you they're disgusting," Paul said.

"That Betan was able to get way too close to our unit before anyone noticed," Caspiz said. "This may only be an exercise to you, but if you can't do it correctly here, then you don't stand a chance when we teleport to the actual ship."

"They'll all be asleep," Scott insisted. "We won't have anything to worry about."

"Are you sure about that, *Creator*?" Caspiz snapped. "Can you guarantee it? Are you really willing to bet your life on it?"

Scott took a deep breath and shook his head.

"That's what I thought," Caspiz nodded. "Now let's keep moving."

They continued the exercise for hours. Scott wasn't certain how long they stayed in the Imagination Room clearing the sleeping quarters and shooting imaginary Betans, but his arms grew steadily weaker. The gun shook in his hands. He wished he had time to grow stronger before they had to teleport to the Betan ship. Just when Scott thought his arms might actually fall off, they rounded a corner.

"Contact right!" Dylan yelled.

A woman screamed.

"Don't shoot!" she yelled. "Please, please don't shoot!"

Scott peered around Paul and Dylan in confusion then sighed in disappointment as Dylan lowered his gun.

"Aw, come on, Dyl," Scott said. "Why didn't you shoot her?"

"I'm so glad I found you!" Lilly said. She ran forward and wrapped her arms around Dylan's neck. Scott wrinkled his nose.

"I've been lost in the Imagination Room for hours," Lilly continued. "I don't know what happened. I thought I'd left, but then killer bunny rabbits were chasing me—Beatrix Potter would be *furious* at such a depiction! And then everything changed and I somehow ended up in here. Maybe you can help me find a way out."

"We've been training for hours now," Dylan said as he patted Lilly's back. He glanced up at Caspiz. "Can we be done?"

Caspiz lifted her head and stared at the ceiling. Scott distinctly heard her sigh in frustration.

"Fine," Caspiz said. "We'll be done... for now."

Scott shook his head, and the Betan ship surrounding them disappeared like his head was an Etch A Sketch. They were left standing in a blank white room. Caspiz blinked, and their guns and space suits disappeared. Scott was back in his regular clothes—blue jeans, white Chucks, and a black shirt with a blue phone box on it.

Scott took the lead and headed toward the door of the Imagination Room. Caspiz fell into step behind him, and the others trailed behind.

"How long should it take the authors to finish the guns and suits?" Caspiz asked.

Scott shrugged. "I don't know. Not long, though. Nothing ever takes them long to build."

"I want to meet back here tomorrow and go over everything again while we wait."

Scott nodded absently.

"Is that okay with you, Creator?" Caspiz asked.

Scott stopped and looked at her, his brow furrowed. He regarded her carefully, but her eyes were serious. She didn't appear to be making fun of him. He felt his shoulders relax.

"Of course," Scott said.

"Then prepare for more work tomorrow," Caspiz told everyone. "You're not nearly prepared enough, and I don't want all of your blood on my hands when we teleport to the Betan ship."

CHAPTER EIGHTEEN

"Come on, Scott! Focus!" Caspiz stomped up to him and knocked the gun out of his hands.

Scott pivoted to face Caspiz, his face inches away from hers.

"Give me a break!" Scott yelled. "What are you expecting here? A miracle? I've never shot a gun before yesterday."

Caspiz jabbed a finger into his chest. "That's not the problem, and you know it," she said. "I can forgive you for being a poor marksman, but you're hesitating."

Scott pushed her finger away. "Of course I'm hesitating," he said. "I don't know what I'm doing!"

"Maybe everyone should just calm down a minute," Dylan suggested. He, Yin, Yang, and Paul stood off to the side of the Imagination Room. They were in the moonlit maze from Caspiz's mind again. Yin and Yang lounged against some brick ruins, but Dylan's body was tense. Paul chewed nervously on his lip.

"Yeah," Paul said, "I mean, he's not going to become like you overnight, you know. Give him some time. And maybe we shouldn't be throwing guns around—just saying."

Caspiz rounded on Paul. "Don't start with me, you crazy alien enthusiast. And we're in the Imagination Room; that gun wasn't going to go off. I know how to handle firearms, unlike some of you."

Scott pointed to Paul. "Why aren't you mad at him? He's just as bad of a shot as I am!"

Caspiz shook her head violently. "It's not the same thing. You're *hesitating*!"

"Maybe I'm just not used to killing people like you are," Scott said. "Maybe it just doesn't come quite as naturally to me as it does to you, *Colonel*."

Caspiz turned and glared at Scott. They held each other's gaze for a moment, and then Caspiz turned to the rest of the group. "Leave," she commanded quietly.

No one moved.

"*Now*," Caspiz growled.

Yin, Yang, Paul, and Dylan jumped forward. Scott moved to leave as well, but Caspiz reached behind her and grabbed his shirt, holding him in place while she watched the rest of the group march toward the door of the Imagination Room.

"Not you," she said. "We need to talk."

"Ugh." Scott yanked himself free of Caspiz's grip but stayed put as Yin, Yang, and Paul left. Dylan gave Scott one last worried glance as he walked out of the Imagination Room, closing the door behind him.

There was a moment of silence. Scott stared out at the moonlit ruins Caspiz had imagined for training. It had been a long day. They'd woken up early that morning to run through clearing rooms again, and had spent hours upon hours shooting at replicas of Betans. Or in Scott and Paul's case, *trying* to shoot at Betans. Something had pushed Caspiz over the edge, and now here they were, staring stonily into the silence.

"I want to make a couple of things very clear," Caspiz said after a moment. "The first one is that killing people doesn't come easily for me. I get no joy out of it."

"You seemed to enjoy shooting Justin yesterday," Scott reminded her.

"Look at where we are!" Caspiz threw her arms up and gestured at the Imagination Room. "He wasn't really hurt. That did *no* damage. It was simply entertaining."

"Killing people is entertaining to you, then," Scott said as he folded his arms across his chest.

Caspiz lowered her arms and stared at Scott with hard eyes. "He wasn't really here, Scott Beck. He doesn't even exist in this reality. And don't pretend that other people's pain doesn't interest, if not entertain, you. You were all too happy to let me hurt Yang."

Caspiz walked over to him and stood directly in front of Scott. He stared at the ground, tapping his foot, but Caspiz wouldn't have it.

"Look at me," Caspiz said.

Scott rolled his eyes and looked up at her.

"I do not enjoy killing people," Caspiz said. "That's not the reason I'm in the military. Do not ever make that assumption."

"But you do it so easily," Scott argued.

"No, I don't," Caspiz said. "It's been years since I've had to take a life, and it still haunts me, Scott."

"That's not true," Scott said. "Maybe it haunts you, maybe not, but I know exactly when you've crossed over into the Reality Field. I know where you are in your timeline. You killed three Betans that were hiding on Earth a week ago."

Caspiz gave a short laugh. "Betans?" she repeated. "Betans aren't people, Scott."

"They're living, breathing, thinking creatures," Scott said.

"But they're not *people*," Caspiz said. "They're not human. There's nothing human about them. They're all murderers. All they want is to conquer and destroy. And yes, there have been some people like that, but we've always classified those people as monsters. That's all the Betans are. Monsters."

"But it's so easy for you!" Scott shouted. "I can't just kill them as easily as you can."

"Look at them, Scott!" Caspiz commanded.

The moonlit maze disappeared as the Imagination Room changed. Caspiz and Scott stood in an enclosed white room that had one dark window. The room was brightly lit, and Scott squinted his eyes against the harshness of the light.

"Do you know where we are?" Caspiz asked.

Scott glanced at Caspiz and shook his head slowly.

"I guess that shouldn't surprise me," Caspiz said. "You don't know everything about the Betan ships, so you wouldn't know everything about the military bases."

Scott watched her as she walked closer to the window and stopped inches away from it.

"Look inside," Caspiz commanded.

Scott walked forward and stood beside Caspiz. He gave her one last look and glanced inside the window.

Three Betans stood inside at three points of a triangle, which was outlined on the ground with grey bed sheets that were tied together. Five beds were against the far side of the room, which Scott could easily see because the room was minuscule.

"These are the other Betans I didn't find in time to kill, like I did those other three you just mentioned," Caspiz said. "We took these creatures prisoner. I think it was foolish; they should have been killed on the spot. But there are people out there, people like you, who think we should study them, that maybe there's a peaceable answer."

The Betans clasped hands.

"What are they doing?" Scott asked.

Caspiz gritted her teeth. "Watch."

Scott continued gazing through the glass. The Betans' arms tensed, and then the aliens began to shriek and writhe. Their hands were moving, but Scott couldn't quite tell what was happening.

"What are they doing?" Scott asked, glancing at the colonel.

"Watch," Caspiz said again.

A particularly loud howl brought Scott's attention back to the Betans, and he gasped at what he saw. One of the Betans had ripped off the hand of the other alien it had a hold of. The mutilated Betan gnashed at its brother, and the alien on its other side ripped off its other hand.

"What are they doing?" Scott cried out. He stumbled backward a step and looked at Caspiz with wide eyes.

"They're seeing who's strongest," Caspiz said. "Watch."

Scott looked back in the window but couldn't watch for long. There was too much blood and too much screaming. His head burned, and he backed away.

"Change the scenery," Scott choked. "Please."

The Betan screams were cut off, and once again Scott and Caspiz stood in a moonlit maze. Caspiz still faced away from him, where the Betans had been moments before.

"There were five in there originally," Caspiz said. "But every day, they joined hands, and the alien that lost the tug-of-war was slaughtered as a sacrifice to some awful deity who they thought would save them."

"Why did you show me that?" Scott asked.

"Because I want you to understand something," Caspiz said. She turned to face him. "The Betans are not human. They're not 'people.' If you can't get that through your thick skull, and if you can't pull that trigger when we're up on the ship, and if you're not willing to kill every last one of them, then you don't belong on that mission. I don't care *what* Shakespeare says. I will not have your back, because you don't have mine if you have any remorse when you explode those things to bits."

Scott stared at her, the image of the Betans fresh in his mind. He could understand what she was saying. Even though it made him sick to think about, he knew she was right. The Betans were monsters, and he shouldn't hesitate. He just hoped he had the strength to do what she was asking.

"I'm sorry," he mumbled as he looked down at the ground. "I... I don't know why it's so hard for me."

Caspiz took a deep breath. "I want to know why you did it."

Scott looked up. "Did what?"

"Why did you create them?"

Scott opened his mouth to respond, but no words came out. He wasn't sure what to say.

"How could you make monsters like that, Scott? What's inside your mind that you could think something that awful, that disgusting, that... *inhuman*... into existence?"

Scott shook his head slowly. "I don't know," he said softly.

Caspiz stalked up to him and held his gaze for what felt to Scott like several minutes. He resisted the urge to back away. "Can you kill them, Creator?"

Scott stared at her. He knew why she was asking. This was about more than just protecting her world. Her dead family cried for justice, and she was the only one left to deliver it. Scott knew that Caspiz would not let him stand in the way of her doing that.

And he didn't want to be in the way. Caspiz was right. He had written them—he knew that what he had just seen did not begin to cover the horrible things they could do, and had done.

"I'm on your side, Jane," Scott said. Caspiz stiffened at him using her first name but continued to stare him down. "I'll do what I need to do. I... I'm sorry."

Caspiz nodded and stepped back from him. The room around them swirled until it disappeared and they were left in an empty white space.

"Let's get ready to go," Caspiz said. "They should have locked on to the Betan ships by now. And if they have, then we need to start moving. I just pray that you're telling me the truth and that you really are ready. Because I'm warning you... if you're not, I may not be the one to pull the trigger, but I won't stop the Betans from killing you."

CHAPTER NINETEEN

"Are you sure they all have to come?" Caspiz asked again.

Shakespeare folded his arms across his chest and leaned back against a desk in the Field Room, where the group stood together, holding their guns and wearing their suits, which the sci-fi writers had made perfectly in practically no time at all.

"You're all stronger together," Shakespeare insisted. "You have to bring Scott because he's the writer. You need Dylan because he is the one who will hack into the system with the Memory Orb."

"And Paul?" Caspiz asked. "Do you really have a good reason for me to bring Paul?"

"Hey!" Paul complained. "I'm a valuable member of this team!"

Caspiz tilted her head and gave Shakespeare a skeptical look, an eyebrow raised.

"He was the hero in Scott's book," Shakespeare said. "He's a vital part of this story, too."

"*Paul* was the hero?" Caspiz repeated. Scott flinched as she started shouting. "*Paul?* Are you kidding me?"

Paul grinned broadly. "Aw, yes!" He pumped his fist.

Caspiz turned her glare to Scott. He raised both of his hands in surrender.

"I'm sorry," Scott said. "You were really important too, if it makes you feel any better. You were all important."

"You still are important," Shakespeare said. "That's why you're all going."

Caspiz opened her mouth to argue yet again but was interrupted by the Field Room door sliding open.

An older woman with short, dark hair walked into the room, followed by a black woman with greying hair. The black woman held a small silver orb in her hand.

"Who are you?" Caspiz asked.

"I'm Octavia Butler," the black woman said. She pointed to the other woman. "This is Madeleine L'Engle. We're science fiction authors."

"We have something for you," L'Engle said. The two women walked up to the group, and Butler handed Dylan the orb.

"Here's the Memory Orb you requested," L'Engle said. "It can get into anything that knows binary and store all of its information."

Dylan lifted it up and peered at it. "It's not very heavy."

Butler frowned. "Does it need to be?"

Dylan paused. "No, I just…" He trailed off, unsure of himself.

"How, exactly, does it take the information from the computer?" Scott spoke up.

"When you reach the alien computer, hold the orb up against it and command it in binary to start downloading," Butler said. "One of you does know binary, correct?"

Scott saw Dylan roll his eyes. "Of course I know binary."

"It shouldn't take terribly long to download the information, but it depends on what's stored on the computer," L'Engle said. "You'll know when it's done because it will flash blue and float back down into your hands."

Anne's voice interrupted L'Engle. "Scan complete," the computer said. "Life forms detected."

"We knew there would be life forms," Scott said. "We're just hoping they're all asleep."

"There was no movement detected," Anne said.

"Thank you, Anne," Shakespeare said. He turned to face the group. "You'd better get your helmets on and go before that changes."

Scott grabbed his helmet and pulled it over his head. It hissed as it sealed to his suit.

"I'm really impressed at how quickly you were able to make the suits and the guns," Caspiz said as she put her helmet on.

"We have more power at our disposal than you could possibly dream of," Shakespeare said.

"Speaking of your guns," Wells cut in, "why are we sending you into space with explosive weapons? What happens if one of you hits the side of the ship with a gravity gun, and it blows a hole into it? You'll be dead in seconds."

Scott shook his head. "There are shields on the interior of the ship too," he said through his helmet, loud enough for Wells to hear.

Wells shook his head. "You know that nothing you write makes sense, right?"

Scott glared at him.

"Don't forget to grab the drone we teleported there to check for you," Wells sighed, handing Scott two teleporters. "After you have the information you need, teleport back here immediately. You don't want to be there longer than you have to be."

"Two teleporters?" Scott asked as he took them from Wells.

"One to get there," Wells said, "and one to get back, just in case you can't wait five minutes for the first teleporter to charge. We'd give each of you a teleporter, but we don't have enough. Plus, if one of you were to drop or lose a teleporter, it could be disastrous. We don't want to give the Betans that kind of access to Earth."

Scott nodded and zipped a teleporter into a pocket in his space suit. He clutched the other teleporter in his left hand.

"You should know," Shakespeare said, "that we plan on having Curtis here after this mission, and after any other, just in case anyone needs medical assistance. I don't want a repeat of... the past."

Scott raised his chin and nodded slightly. "Thank you."

"Are you all ready to go?" Wells asked.

They all started to nod, but Caspiz intervened. "One minute," she said. She turned and looked at all of them. "We've been through the drills of how this is going to work, but I want to remind you that this is different.

You'll be facing real Betans up in the ship. Hopefully they'll all be asleep like Scott says, but we might still run into trouble. Remember to stay close together, stay low, only shoot at the Betans and not your comrades," she glared purposefully at Paul, who blushed, "and *stay quiet.*"

Scott and everyone around him nodded.

"Let's get into position, then," Caspiz said. She walked to the front of the group. Yin took the tail, Yang went left, and Dylan moved to the right. Paul and Scott stayed in the middle.

"Everyone grab Scott," Caspiz commanded.

Scott tensed as hands touched his shoulders and back.

"Good luck, Scott," Shakespeare said.

Scott took a deep breath, and they teleported onto the Betan ship.

Scott gasped as they materialized. It was warmer than he had expected… far too hot for his comfort. For some reason, he hadn't thought about the Betans being cold-blooded and requiring so much heat, since they were tall. He hadn't thought to have the science fiction authors make the suits cooler.

Scott breathed a little easier as everyone let go of him and gripped their guns with both hands. He put the teleporter in his suit pocket and zipped it up, then secured his grip on his gravity gun. He hoped that the science fiction authors really had made the guns as silent as possible. He didn't want to be attacked on the ship because their weapons made too much noise and drew attention to them. He had the teleporters, so he could get out, but he couldn't guarantee he could get to everyone else in time for all of them to escape uninjured.

Scott looked around the room. It was exactly as he had pictured it in his books and existed precisely as he had created it in the Imagination Room. The walls and ceiling were blue. Sleeping pods littered the room, but they were mostly submerged in the floor. This comforted Scott, because he wasn't worried that Betans might be lurking behind the pods… though it did little to ease his fears to know that Betans were, undoubtedly, inside of them. He just hoped they'd stay asleep.

Scott shuffled his feet slightly, and he heard his right boot clatter against something on the floor. He tensed and felt everyone's eyes shift to him. He looked down and saw the scanner, which looked like a miniature black jet, that they had teleported in before they'd transported themselves aboard. They had decided they only wanted to send in a scanner that would secure one room before the team teleported onboard. If Betans were awake and wandering around and happened to notice a flying scanner, it could have caused problems. If the Betans had grabbed hold of it and the scanner had teleported back to the Castle, the Betans could have come with it. It was safer to have the team collect it themselves.

Scott bent down and picked up the drone. He placed it in his pocket, straightened as he zipped it up, and gripped his weapon tighter. Still, everyone stared at him.

Scott glanced at Caspiz and shrugged. He wasn't sure what they were waiting for, and he had no desire to dawdle.

Even through the helmet, Scott could see Caspiz's glare. She pointed behind Scott and in front of him, then raised both hands. Embarrassed, Scott understood. She was waiting for him to indicate which way they should go.

Scott swallowed. He honestly wasn't certain which direction to choose, but he pointed ahead of him. Caspiz nodded, turned, and walked forward. The group followed, one by one. They stayed in the formation they had practiced over the last two days in the Imagination Room. Scott supposed it helped that everything looked so familiar. He didn't feel like he was in any real danger. He knew he should have been more afraid, but he feared less for their safety and more that they wouldn't eventually run into a computer, and that this would all be for nothing.

They paused outside of a door, and Scott quickly punched in the access code. It sounded like the door gasped as it slid open. Caspiz, Yin, and Yang ran inside.

"Clear," Caspiz whispered over the headset.

"Clear," Yin repeated.

"Clear," Yang whispered.

Dylan crept inside, followed by Scott, and then Paul. Nothing moved in the room except for the reconnaissance team as they manoeuvred past the sleeping pods in single file. They reached another door, and Scott entered the code. The door opened, and the three military officers swept the room beyond.

Scott took the opportunity to peer inside one of the sleeping pods. The greenish water glowed slightly, lighting up the sleeping Betan. Seaweed crept around the alien, folding in from the sides and covering the creature like a blanket. The seaweed waved slightly in the water, undulating up and down with the Betan's underwater breath.

The alien itself looked peaceful in the water. Seeing the Betan asleep, Scott found it hard to believe that they were such a violent people… but he'd written about them; he'd created them, and he knew how terrible they could be. He'd just seen it first-hand a few hours earlier in the Imagination Room. He shuddered at the memory.

Scott could see the individual scales on the Betan. Each one was small and grey. Peering at the scales, he could see the salt from the water seeping into the cracks and mending all of the flaws in the Betan's armour. It took six hours to replenish the Betan skin and mind. Scott just hoped they had enough time left in that cycle to reach the computer, grab everything they needed, and teleport back to the Field Room before any of the Betans woke up.

Dylan nudged Scott's shoulder. He looked up, startled. Dylan nodded toward the next room and motioned Scott forward. Scott glanced once more at the sleeping alien and then jogged into the next room.

Caspiz, Yin, Yang, and Paul stood around a tall pedestal in the centre of the room. Caspiz stared at him, a warning look in her eyes. Scott nodded to her. He could do this. He was on her side.

Scott reached them and looked at the pedestal. A dark black screen shone from the top of it. Tiny buttons covered with the squareish Betan alphabet surrounded the screen in groups of diamond patterns. Scott hoped that the Memory Orb really could hack into the network and gather the information they needed.

Dylan joined them, and Scott nodded to the screen. He heard his brother take a deep breath through the headset as he approached the computer. Caspiz pointed to the group and drew her hand in a circle around the podium. Scott and Paul hesitated for a moment, but Yin and Yang took their arms and guided them in a circle around the podium, facing outward.

Scott turned and looked at Dylan. He had taken the Memory Orb from his pocket and held it in front of him. He looked at it, his mouth twisted, and took another deep breath.

Dylan began to murmur in a low voice. "Zero, one, zero, zero, zero, one, one, one, zero, one, one, zero…"

Scott eventually lost track of the zeros and ones, but he felt like it took Dylan five minutes to finish giving his command.

Dylan exhaled loudly when he was done, and the Memory Orb levitated in the air. It made a soft beeping noise. Scott saw Caspiz tense at the sound, but she made no other movement. The Memory Orb continued its soft beeping, and eventually the screen on the pedestal lit up. Slowly, numbers and images rose from the screen and flew into the Memory Orb. Blue light slowly filled the orb from the bottom, like a glass being filled with water, as more and more information poured into it.

"I hope it's doing what I wanted it to," Dylan muttered quietly. "What if I got a number wrong?"

"You only had to remember ones and zeroes," Paul murmured.

"Be quiet," Caspiz whispered.

Paul stood at attention, and Dylan continued to watch the Memory Orb anxiously as more and more data poured into it from the screen below. Scott looked at his brother's worried face and felt a surge of pride at Dylan's intelligence.

But then multiple low hisses split the silence in the room. Low gurgling sounds followed. Scott stopped breathing, panicked.

The gurgling continued as the sleeping pods rose up from the floor, stopping only when they were four feet higher than they had been before.

The glass above the pods swung open. The gurgling stopped as the water drained down into the ship and out of the pods. And then there was silence.

None of them had had a chance to move. They could only stare, terrified, as over twenty Betans crawled out of their sleeping pods, scaly legs first, until all of them, standing over eight feet tall, towered above them.

CHAPTER TWENTY

The Betans and the humans stared at each other for a brief moment, each group unsure of what to do. Scott could hear his loud, panicked breathing in his helmet, echoed by the fear of his comrades' breaths via the headset. There was no other sound, save for the soft beeping of the Memory Orb behind the humans.

That is until Caspiz fired.

Somehow it was worse that Scott couldn't hear Caspiz's gun. He hadn't expected it to make a difference, but it did. He didn't hear a blast, just the sickening sound of flesh and blood and gore rupturing around the room as the force from the colonel's gravity gun tore an alien to shreds.

The Betans howled in anger and bloodlust. Their screaming made Scott's stomach twist violently. He tried to cover his ears, but he immediately felt stupid as his hands slapped against his helmet. The helmet did nothing to impede the horrible sounds of the screeching aliens around him.

Scott reached again for his gun, but his stomach plummeted when he realized he had dropped the weapon when he'd reached to cover his ears. At first he hadn't noticed, because he couldn't hear it clatter to the ground over the sound of the screaming.

He cursed himself as he dropped to the ground and grabbed frantically for his gravity gun. A Betan crouched down with him and snagged the weapon out of reach. Scott's blood chilled as the weapon scraped against the ground and into the Betan's hands.

Scott stared at the Betan for a moment in terror. He was defenseless, on his hands and knees before an invading alien race, his own weapon held against him. The Betan grinned and growled. Its teeth were pointy, and its dark eyes glinted in the eerie glowing lights from the pods.

"We need to get out of here!" Yang yelled over the headset.

"The Memory Orb doesn't have everything yet," Dylan said.

"That doesn't matter if we're all dead," Yin shouted.

Scott backed away from the Betan, his hands behind him on the floor as he attempted to scramble away. He ran into the podium behind him, and a sharp edge dug painfully into his shoulder. The Betan crawled forward, still clutching Scott's gun.

"Everyone gather around Dylan," Caspiz commanded.

"There are more Betans coming in!" Paul shouted.

Scott looked past the Betan chasing him and realized that Paul was right. The howling Betans had called more into the room, but the aliens streaming in were armed.

"They have guns!" Scott yelled.

Caspiz swore as the Betans began to fire. One shot narrowly missed Yang, and a plasma dart pierced a sleeping pod behind him.

"Take cover behind the pods," Caspiz said. "We need the information on that computer."

Scott leapt forward, trying to pass the Betan, but it reached out and grabbed his arms. It was surprisingly strong, and Scott yelped as he felt his arms instantly bruise in the alien's grasp.

Scott looked into the Betan's black and green eyes and saw it sneer. Scott said only one word.

"Please."

The Betan paused and peered at Scott. Slowly, its expression changed. Its eyes became wide instead of narrowed, and its snarl disappeared and was replaced by a gaping mouth. The Betan looked like it was in shock.

And then its head exploded.

Scott's visor was covered with green blood and bits of Betan flesh. He gasped as the grip on his arms loosened and the Betan fell forward on top of him. The alien was heavy.

"Take cover, Scott!" Caspiz commanded.

Scott managed to shove the Betan off him and grabbed his gun. He shot blindly toward the amassing alien horde. He didn't have time to worry about remorse now.

Scott turned around and found Dylan crouching next to the podium, taking turns firing his particle gun at Betans and looking up at the Memory Orb. Scott could hear Dylan muttering a prayer under his breath.

"Prayers aren't going to help you," Scott said. He scurried over to his brother, ducking as a plasma dart flew above his head.

"Let it go for once," Dylan said. "If you can be immortal, then there can be a god."

Scott knocked Dylan flat to the ground as a plasma beam hit the podium beside them. Dylan raised his head and fired his gun.

"I think praying might be working," Dylan panted.

"How close are we to having all of the data we need?" Caspiz shouted. She crouched to Scott's left, partially hidden behind a sleeping pod.

Scott let Dylan up and continued aiming and firing at Betans. Dylan looked up at the Orb.

"I think we're almost done," Dylan said. "We probably only have about twenty percent left."

"What does that mean in *time?*" Yang shouted. He and Yin shot at the Betans from opposite ends of an abandoned pod. "More Betans are piling in. They would have killed us all by now if they'd had a clear shot."

"Ironically, it might be lucky there are so many aliens in here," Paul commented. He cowered next to the twins, covering his head.

"Not if we're all trampled," Yin said.

"How much longer, Dylan?" Caspiz's voice cut through the group's frantic jabber and the noise of exploding bodies and cracking sleeping pods.

"No longer than a minute," Dylan said. "Hopefully."

"Everyone make your way toward Dylan and Scott," Caspiz said. "By the time we get there, whether the Orb is done or not, we're teleporting out. Move!"

Scott got up on his knees and shot into the throng of Betans as his teammates army-crawled toward him and Dylan. They moved one at a time. Paul crawled in first as Yin, Yang, and Caspiz covered for him. He seemed to move slowly, and Scott grew frustrated with his progress. He released his pent-up panic on the aliens.

Scott was lucky there were so many Betans. If there hadn't been, it would have been even more obvious that he was a horrible shot and that he wasn't hitting his target. Yes, he was killing aliens, but never the ones he meant to hit. Still, enough Betan bodies ruptured and spewed gore that he didn't feel ashamed about his aim.

That didn't stop his shame from all of the death he caused, even though he remembered what Caspiz had shown him. He knew he had to defend himself and his unit.

Paul finally reached him, and then Yin crawled forward. Dylan, Scott, and Paul knelt back-to-back in a triangle, shooting outward as the pilot crawled toward them. Within moments she had joined the group, and Yang crawled forward.

Scott noticed a Betan aiming for the squirming pilot. Scott swerved his gun and fired at the alien. He missed, but his shot hit the pod in front of the Betan. The exploding glass and stone obscured the alien's vision enough that his shot missed Yang... mostly.

"Damn it!" Yang shouted. Scott heard him breathing through his teeth.

"Keep going," Yin encouraged. "You're almost here. We can get back to the Castle, and that magician will fix you up."

Yang inched forward as the rest of them continued to shoot.

"It's done!" Dylan shouted. He raised his hands in the air. "Zero, one, zero, zero, zero, one, one, zero, zero, one, one, zero..."

"What the hell were you thinking making him command the Orb in binary?" Paul asked as Yang reached the group. Caspiz didn't bother to crawl; she open fired toward the aliens and sprinted for them. "There must have been an easier way."

"The Betans will have shot us all by the time he's done telling it to do whatever he's telling it to do," Yin said.

"Let him focus!" Scott said as he fired at another Betan and completely missed.

The Orb blinked and descended toward Dylan's hands.

"Everyone grab on to Scott!" Caspiz shouted as she reached them.

They all grabbed Scott's arms, back, and even legs. Scott's eyes widened as he realized he didn't have the teleporter in his hands.

"Oh shit," he muttered. He dropped his gravity gun and fumbled with his pockets.

"Hurry up!" Yin commanded.

"I'm trying!" Scott said.

"I've got it!" Dylan said. "I've got the Orb!"

Scott finally managed to unzip his pocket with shaking hands.

"Hurry, Scott!"

Scott grabbed his gun and the teleporter and pressed the black button in its centre, just as he heard a plasma dart pass dangerously close to his head. He felt his elbow hit Paul in the back, felt Paul shift, and then they were gone.

CHAPTER TWENTY-ONE

They rematerialized in the Field Room. Dylan and Scott were the only ones that managed to remain on their knees. Paul, Yin, Yang, and even Caspiz collapsed.

Shakespeare ran up to them. "What happened?" he asked. "Is everyone alright?"

"Help... me," Paul moaned.

Yin crawled over to Paul and lifted his hand from his side.

She swore.

"He's been shot," Yin said as she pressed on the wound.

Paul passed out.

Scott released Dylan, and after glancing at his brother to make sure he didn't see any blood on him, turned to Paul.

"How bad is it?" Scott asked. He was afraid to know the answer, especially since he could see blood wetting Paul's suit.

Yin pursed her lips and lifted her hand from Paul's side. There was a large hole there, gurgling blood. It looked like someone had taken a bite out of Paul, except that the shot was too clean. Blood seeped out of the wound and pooled around him on the Field Room floor.

Scott's mouth hung open in shock. He had been kneeling right next to Paul. How had this happened? Scott should have been protecting him. Instead, he remembered hitting him with his elbow. Had Scott put him in the line of fire?

Curtis leapt forward and crouched next to Paul, opposite where Yin was trying to stop the bleeding with her hands. Scott was incredibly grateful that Shakespeare had thought to have the Body Magician waiting for their return just in case something like this happened.

"You've got to let go of the wound," Curtis said. "My magic will be more effective if I touch the injury directly."

Yin nodded and lifted her hands. Paul's blood gushed for a moment, but Curtis was quick to put his hands on Paul's side and start working.

Scott stood up and backed away from where Paul bled. He couldn't handle being so close to Paul, especially if this was his fault. Shakespeare took his place and knelt next to Yin in Paul's blood. Yang sat beside his sister, holding on to his leg, but he didn't speak up or mention his injury. Dylan hesitantly crawled over to Paul, careful to avoid the blood. His fist was tight around the Memory Orb.

"I was too slow," Dylan whispered. "If I had been faster hacking into the system, we could have gotten out before Paul was hurt."

Scott couldn't say anything. His mind couldn't process what was happening. He could only stare at his fallen protagonist.

"Don't blame yourself," Caspiz said. She stood up and helped Dylan to his feet. They walked over to Scott and stood beside him. Dylan couldn't stop staring at Paul, and Caspiz's face was drawn as she unsealed her helmet and laid it on a desk to her side. "This is war. This kind of thing happens all the time. It isn't pleasant, but it's a fact of warfare. Blaming yourself will only get in the way of you doing your job."

Scott still stared blankly at the scene before him, not bothering to remove his helmet, despite the gore that obstructed his view.

It all looked so familiar. His father had already been dead by the time they'd materialized, his blood clotted and still, but other people had been bleeding like this. Scott could see the scene so clearly, and he remembered well how desperate he had been for *anyone* from that mission to survive.

"Scott!" Dylan jostled his shoulder.

Scott shook his head violently. His brother's voice and touch had reclaimed him. Dylan had taken off his helmet. His hair was dishevelled and his eyes were full of tears.

"Are you okay, civilian?" Caspiz asked. "Are you in shock? Do you require medical attention?"

Scott took a deep breath and looked up at Caspiz. "No," he said. He paused as he took off his helmet and placed it next to Caspiz's. "I'm alright. Let's just focus on Paul."

Caspiz looked at him for a moment then said, "You did a good job up there."

Scott didn't bother to answer. He just looked back at Paul; the evidence would suggest Scott had failed miserably.

Scott couldn't tell if Curtis was helping Paul or not. Nothing seemed to change; the blood still ran from underneath Curtis's fingers. Curtis's face grew more drawn, and his breathing grew haggard while Paul's shallow breathing slowed. Then, for several terrible minutes, everything was still.

Finally, Curtis rocked back on his heels and removed his hands from Paul's side.

"I did my best," Curtis said quietly.

There was a terrible moment of silence.

"*What?*" Scott gasped.

Curtis looked up at Scott and raised his bloody hands in a placatory gesture. "I did my best," he repeated. "I'm sorry, Scott."

Scott felt cold wash over him. The wave started in his neck and flooded his chest as all of his body heat fled from him in shock.

This couldn't be happening. This could *not* happen all over again. His father had promised that things would be different, that the writers were good...

But it wasn't the Writers' fault that this had happened, was it?

It was his.

He had shoved Paul at that last second. *Scott* had put him in the line of fire. Not Wells, not Dick... and not Shakespeare.

"Wells, Curtis, can you take him to our morgue?" Shakespeare asked. His voice was soft and seemed almost reverent.

Curtis nodded and stood slowly. His hands shook, but Scott watched him and Wells carefully pick up Paul's body and carry him out of the Field Room.

No one spoke for several minutes. They all just stared at the pool of Paul's blood. Scott was too numb to do anything but look at the mess on the floor. He couldn't even cry.

"Is anyone else hurt?" Shakespeare asked quietly.

"My leg was hit," Yang said, "but it's more of a scratch than anything serious. I'll be fine."

"Yin," Shakespeare said, "please help your brother to the hospital wing. They'll take care of him. Do you know where to go?"

Yin nodded and helped Yang stand. They removed their helmets and dropped them on the floor. Yang swung an arm around his twin sister's shoulders and together they left the room.

"Scott, I..." Shakespeare paused and clasped his hands behind his back. He took a deep, shaky breath. "I'm so sorry."

Scott swallowed against the lump in his throat. He blinked slowly, trying to find any emotion in his chest besides the awful cold and numb of panic and grief.

"Was the mission successful?" Shakespeare asked carefully.

Everyone looked at Dylan. He raised his fist, which still tightly clutched the Memory Orb.

Shakespeare nodded.

"Let's see what you've found, shall we?"

"Can't we wait?" Scott choked out. "Paul... Paul just *died*. His blood is still staining the Field Room floor."

"We need to keep moving, soldier," Caspiz said softly from beside him. "Time is of the essence. The Betans will not wait to attack simply because we grieve."

Shakespeare shook his head slowly. "I'm sorry, but Caspiz is right. The authors have to know what kind of weapons they need to create to protect the Earth, and we need to figure out how you're going to save the world."

Scott looked over at Dylan. He still looked scared—eyes wide, nostrils flaring, creases on his brow. Scott was sure his own face reflected his brother's.

"Let's see what was on the computer," Scott mumbled as Dylan's wide eyes met his own.

Dylan released his grip on the orb and lifted his open palm up toward the high ceiling of the Field Room. The Memory Orb lifted off his hand and floated up about three feet. Dylan lowered his hand to his side, and the orb stopped its descent and hovered in the air above their heads.

"Zero, one, zero, one, zero, zero, one, one…" Dylan began. Scott furrowed his eyebrows. He vaguely wondered how Dylan remembered all of those numbers in their proper sequence.

They all waited for a moment in silence after Dylan had finished speaking.

"Why isn't it doing anything?" Caspiz asked after a minute.

"Anne, please turn off the lights," Shakespeare called out.

"Yes, William," Anne said in a soft voice. Even the computer system seemed hesitant to speak.

The lights dimmed, but they were not left in darkness. Instead, they were surrounded by strange, square-like symbols and dots projected from the Memory Orb.

"What is that?" Caspiz asked.

"It's what the orb took from the computer," Dylan said. "The symbols don't have anything to do with computers, though. I don't recognize them."

"I do," Scott said. "They're the alien language."

"Can you read it?" Shakespeare asked.

Scott bit his lip and shifted his feet uncomfortably. "I never went so far as to create a language," he admitted. "But I can turn each symbol into a letter from our alphabet. I just don't know how they all fit together."

"Tolkien may be able to help with that," Shakespeare mused. "I'll see if he can spare some time to work on this. In the meantime, it would be helpful if you could give us the information you do have."

"That'll be great for later," Caspiz said. "But we can't understand anything on the Memory Orb right now. What if this Tolkien guy never translates the language? Was the entire mission useless? Was Paul… was his death pointless?"

"Maybe not," Dylan said. "This is just some of what was on the computer. There might be more. Hold on."

Dylan listed off so many zeros and ones that Scott couldn't keep track. The light blue images that surrounded them in the room seemed to scroll up until they disappeared, and then they were replaced by a large diagram.

"This is the ship, I think," Dylan said.

Shakespeare walked up to the 3D blue outline of the ship and placed a hand on either side. He pulled his hands apart from each other, and the ship expanded so that everyone could see it clearly.

"You're right; it is the ship," Shakespeare said. "We can see what Scott already knew with the bridge, the torpedo arm, and the three living levels."

Scott walked around the diagram, carefully avoiding Paul's blood. He tried not to think about the red pool just off to the side of them, but it was hard not to smell it.

"Can we see inside?" Scott asked as he tried to focus. "I already know what it looks like from the outside. We have to find engineering."

Shakespeare touched the top of the ship and pulled up. The top of the ship came off.

"How are you doing that?" Scott asked. "I admit that I don't know everything about my creations like I should, but I do know that this is not how Betan technology works. So how is their ship design doing whatever you want it to?"

"The Memory Orb converts all files into this format," Shakespeare said. "I don't know how L'Engle and Butler made it work, but I think it's genius."

Shakespeare took off the sides of the ship as well, tossing them away, and looked inside the spacecraft.

"We were just on the top floor," Caspiz said. "We've seen plenty of that, I think, and it wasn't very helpful."

Shakespeare nodded and stripped away the sleeping quarters. It rose high into the air, out of Shakespeare's way.

Caspiz stepped forward with interest. "You said you didn't know what was on the second level, correct?" she asked Scott.

"It wasn't necessary for the story, so no. I never got around to thinking about it."

Everyone stepped closer to the glowing blue diagram. Inside the ship was a maze of hallways and rooms. Caspiz touched a larger room and expanded it with her hands the same way Shakespeare had enlarged the ship. The room grew, and they could more easily see details.

"This looks like a training barracks," she said. "I suppose that's good to know, but it won't help us figure out where to place the bombs."

Caspiz shrank the room back down to size by touching either side of it and compressing her hands.

"What else is here?" Dylan asked.

They investigated the second level but found nothing of major interest. It mostly consisted of storage rooms with extra repair parts for the ship. There was an infirmary on the second level as well.

"The engineering section must be on the third floor," Scott said.

He lifted the second level off the ship and pushed it into the air, where it narrowly avoided hitting the top level that Shakespeare had removed earlier.

The third level was different than he had expected. Instead of just housing weapons, there was also one enormous tunnel that spanned the middle of the entire floor.

"What's that?" Caspiz asked, pointing.

Scott enlarged the tunnel and took the top off it. As the tube broke apart, he could see inside the walls. Tiny wires crisscrossed each other in the tunnel walls. This was what they were looking for.

"All of engineering is in a Jefferies tunnel?" Dylan asked.

"What's a Jefferies tunnel?" Caspiz asked.

"Jefferies Tubes are from a popular TV show," Dylan said. "They're built for engineering and utilities… but they're not usually *the* engineering. And they're certainly not that large."

"Gene Roddenberry will be pleased to hear that you know all of this, Dylan," Shakespeare said.

"There weren't any Jefferies tubes in my book," Scott said. "I think they're stupid."

"Clearly the Reality Field doesn't agree with you," Shakespeare said. "It needed to make the ships work, so it had to add an engineering section to the ship. The Reality Field must have figured this would be best, and the most natural way of integrating something necessary. At least it looks like it might be larger than a typical Jefferies Tube. You should be able to stand and have plenty of room to manoeuvre."

"But where do we put the bombs?" Scott asked. "I don't care how it got to be there; we're going to destroy it anyway. I just want to know how we're going to blow it up and live through it."

Caspiz pointed to either end of the tunnel. "These two ends of the tunnel should be enough," she said. "Both explosions would get either side of the ship. We could place them, teleport out, and activate the bombs."

'That doesn't sound too bad," Scott said. "At least we don't have to go into a bunch of different rooms. It's all in the same place."

Caspiz shot Scott an annoyed glance. "Do you know how large this tunnel is? It spans the entire ship. If we run along this tunnel, we can cross the entire thing in five minutes. If we *run*. And we'll have no cover for those five minutes, because there are no corners to hide behind. We'll be out in the open the entire time."

Scott swallowed.

"Hold on," Shakespeare muttered. He separated his hands and enlarged the image of the tunnel. "Look at that."

Scott peered closely at the tunnel. As Shakespeare enlarged the tunnel, Scott could see that a thin green wall encased the interior of the tube. "A force field."

"Can't we teleport past the force field?" Caspiz asked. "Why does that even matter?"

Shakespeare expanded the image again. "Look closely. The force field zigzags across the tunnel like a laser all through the tube. And knowing the Betans, those shields aren't friendly."

Caspiz swore. "Then how do we place the bombs?"

"There's one spot in the middle of the tunnel that isn't protected." Scott pointed to the space. "Could we teleport here, disable the force field, and then run to opposite sides of the tunnels and place the bombs?"

"How do we know we can disable the force field from there?" Caspiz asked. "That seems like a rather large risk to take."

"Jules Verne has made it a point of analyzing spaceships," Shakespeare said. "I'll have him look more closely at these plans and see if that might work, Scott. I'll speak with him right away. At least now we know where the bombs go, and that's invaluable."

Scott shook his head. He could see this ending badly for everyone, like it just had for Paul... and like it had for his father. He squeezed his eyes shut and tried to focus on the task at hand instead of the past.

"Go back," Dylan said. "Let's look at their weapons."

Shakespeare reached into the image of the ship and zoomed away from the engineering tunnel, then zoomed up to the images of the weapons, which littered the outside of the engineering tube.

"They don't look too massive," Shakespeare said. "Are they nuclear? Will they implode planets? What do these weapons do?"

Scott shook his head. "They're just missiles. They'll puncture holes in the Earth. If all of the missiles on all three ships were fired at the Earth and hit, there wouldn't be much planet left."

"There wouldn't be a planet left at all," Dylan frowned.

"How do we stop the missiles from hitting the Earth while we're placing the bombs?" Caspiz asked.

Shakespeare sighed. "Hopefully, Scott will be ready to go on the ships and place the bombs before the ships get much closer to the Earth. I'm hoping that the ships stay out of range."

"Look at how close they are to us already," Dylan said. "Can we really hope for that?"

"Why can't we go place the bombs now?" Caspiz asked. "We know where to go. Let's move."

Shakespeare shook his head. "Scott has to be the one to destroy the alien ships, and especially to defeat Dygavery. It was acceptable for him to passively go on this mission, but to defeat the Betans, he must take on a more active role. Do you think he could do it at this point? Not you, and not Yin, and not Yang, but Scott? Do you think he's ready?"

"Of course he isn't." Caspiz laughed. Scott clenched a fist. "But why does he have to be the one to do it? I don't understand."

"When stories first leave the Imagination Field, they're not fully integrated into the Reality Field. It takes time for this to happen. While Reality is adjusting, there is little that can be done to those characters by anything outside of their original world, because they don't quite fit in yet. So that is why you all must be working on this, and the real world leaders and militia cannot know what is happening. Their efforts would have no effect. You are alone."

"But then I could do it," Caspiz said. "I'm part of the story. I still don't understand why Scott is necessary."

Scott felt his face heat with anger. He didn't appreciate being talked about like this, like he wasn't there and like he didn't matter.

"Scott is essential," Shakespeare said. "He's the creator. For this sensitive period of time, he can still mold things, adjust the story, and change what happens. He has the most power out of everyone. While you can help him, and while you can cause damage with him by your side, you cannot do it alone. His creations are protected during this sensitive time, *unless* he is actively involved in what is happening. And you can't end a story without him leading the attack. The protections still in place from the Imagination Field will not let you."

"But Paul was shot, and Scott didn't do that," Yin said.

"But Scott was there, and he was invested in the story," Shakespeare said. "He is the creator of the Betans. He is the only one that can end them."

Caspiz folded her arms and stared at the blue ship in front of her. "This makes no sense," she growled.

"But truth is truth, whether you understand it and agree with it or not," Shakespeare said.

"Then we should prepare a way to defend the Earth in case Scott isn't ready in time," Caspiz said. "We can't rely on such a large variable."

"I agree," Shakespeare sighed. "We need a backup plan."

Everyone was silent for a moment, thinking. Scott brooded. It frustrated him that Caspiz saw him as expendable. For once, Scott was thankful for Shakespeare, because at least the old bard stood up for him.

"What kind of shields did you say the aliens have?" Dylan said.

Scott looked at his brother. "Why does that matter?" he asked. His voice sounded dead.

"They're black holes, right?" Dylan said. "Black hole shields?"

"Singularity shields," Scott corrected.

"Same thing." Dylan rolled his eyes. "Okay, so why don't we make singularity bombs?"

"To destroy the ships?" Shakespeare asked. "We couldn't make a black hole big enough to pull the ships in without it also swallowing the Earth. That seems a bit counterproductive."

"No," Dylan said. "The singularity bombs can make small black holes to take away the missiles. And then the black holes can disappear."

"That's impossible," Caspiz said.

"Not if we use teleportation technology," Scott said slowly.

"It might work," Shakespeare mused. "Caspiz and Scott can teleport aboard the ships and place the bombs. Yin and Yang can be in a sort of command ship, similar to the one in your book, Scott. They can control some drones, which will fire the singularity bombs and protect the Earth. If we have to wait until the ships are in range, we'll probably need to stage an attack on the ships as well, so they don't suspect that anything is going on inside of the ships themselves. We need to keep them distracted so Scott and Caspiz have a chance."

"Just fire on them," Caspiz said. "We know that whatever we throw at them won't get past the ships' singularity shields, but they don't know we know that. They'll just think Yin and Yang are trying to destroy them. They won't suspect a diversion. Scott and I will be safe to do what we need to do in the ships."

Shakespeare nodded slowly. "I think this plan could very well work. I'll talk to the science fiction authors, and we'll see what they can create. But for now, go rest. Take time to grieve."

Everyone except for Scott glanced toward the pool of blood on the ground. Scott just stared at the image of the Betan ship in front of him, his face blank. It took him a moment to notice that Shakespeare had turned back to look at him. He reluctantly raised his gaze to the bard's.

Shakespeare's brow was drawn, and his eyes looked sad. "You have to be ready for what's coming, and you don't have a lot of time."

"I know," Scott said.

Shakespeare took a deep breath. "You'll need to get back to work tomorrow. I know that doesn't give you much time to recover, or to grieve..."

"I'll be fine," Scott said.

He turned away from the bard so that he wouldn't see that was a lie.

CHAPTER TWENTY-TWO

"Hey, Creator," someone whispered in Scott's ear. "Want to see something cool?"

Scott bolted up in bed, gasping for breath as terror seized him. He wasn't used to being woken up so suddenly. His and Dylan's room was dark except for the stars that shimmered from the ceiling. Scott glanced over to Dylan's bed. It was empty, but Scott could see a silhouette of a man next to his bed in the darkness.

"What's happening?" Scott shouted.

"Shhh," the voice whispered. Scott squinted at the man and slowly started to make out the strong chin, black hair, and dark eyes that belonged to Yang. "You'll want to see this. Come on."

"You're out of the hospital," Scott noted as his heart slowed down to a more reasonable pace. "Is your leg okay?"

"I'm fine," Yang said. "Now come on! I have something that might cheer you up."

"Where are we going?" Scott whispered back, hesitant. He wasn't sure he wanted to get out of bed and follow the young pilot in the middle of the night. His mind was still full of the horrifying images of Paul, drenched in his own blood and dying on the Field Room floor. Scott seriously doubted Yang could do anything to cheer him up right now.

"The authors are already hard at work, and some of the drones are ready. And guess what else is already built?"

Scott couldn't help but smirk at the excitement in Yang's voice. "What?"

"The command ship where we'll be controlling the drones!" Yang said. "Do you want to come fly it with me?"

"Why don't you fly it with Yin?"

"Yin's waiting for us," Yang said. "She thought you might want to see, too, since this is all coming from inside of *your* head."

Scott twisted his mouth. It probably wouldn't hurt to distract himself from Paul's death, and he doubted he'd get back to sleep any time soon, anyway. It had been awful enough trying to fall asleep earlier amidst the tears.

"Where's Dylan?" Scott glanced at his brother's bed again.

"I don't know," Yang said. "Last I saw, he and Lilly were together. She seemed... uh... very relieved to see him after the mission."

Scott wrinkled his nose. "I'd rather come with you than dwell on that mental picture," he said. He swung his legs out from under the covers and stepped onto the hardwood floor.

"Do you need me to let you get dressed or anything?" Yang asked.

"No," Scott said. He hadn't bothered to change out of his clothes before collapsing onto his bed earlier that night.

Scott and Yang walked to the black hole door. Scott opened the door slowly, squinting his eyes and blinking rapidly as he tried to adjust to the sudden light of the hallway.

"Why is it so bright out here?" Scott complained. He shut the door behind Yang, and the two walked down the hall toward the library, Scott trying to suppress his yawns as they strolled. Why didn't the sci-fi authors dim the lights at night? Didn't anyone sleep around here? "The Castle's electricity bill must be insane."

"They probably make their own energy," Yang suggested. "The Immortal Writers want to stay off of the grid, right? Doesn't make sense to use an electric company, especially with everything they can do. I can't believe how fast they made the command ship and the drones."

"Where are they storing all of that stuff?" Scott managed to say past a yawn.

"Shakespeare said it's in the hangar," Yang said as they entered the library.

Scott frowned as they turned back to the hallway they'd exited. "I didn't know the Castle had a hangar."

"So even you don't know everything, then," Yang chuckled. "Big surprise."

Scott frowned but couldn't muster enough energy to be angry with Yang for his snide comment. He was still too tired, and too numb.

They walked into the hallway again, but it was no longer the Science Fiction Wing of the Castle. Scott had actually never seen this hallway before, and that surprised him. He hadn't bothered to do much exploring this time around, but when he'd been at the Castle two years earlier, he had explored thoroughly. He'd seen the Thriller Wing, the Fantasy Wing, and even the dungeon in the basement. But he'd not seen anything like this.

They were in a dimly lit, wide cement hallway. Large lamps hung low from the tall ceilings, and yellow and black stripes lined the bottom and top of the walls on either side. A gentle humming reverberated through the hall. It grew steadily louder as Scott and Yang walked.

"What is that noise?" Scott asked.

Yang shrugged. "It's how the Immortal Writers make things so quickly," he said. "You'll see."

They had only made a few twists and turns before the cement hallway ended and they arrived at a large metal platform that offered a great vantage point of the most enormous aircraft hangar Scott had ever seen. Neat lines of various aircraft covered the expansive open space in front of him. The ceiling was higher than even the Castle library's. At the end of the hangar, which seemed ridiculously far away, the hangar opened up into the night sky. Scott could see mounds of white sand shimmering in the empty space beyond.

"Sand?" Scott asked. "I thought we were in the Adirondacks."

"Shakespeare said that this part of the Castle is located in some obscure place in Egypt," Yang explained. "But look behind you."

Scott turned around. Next to the threshold of the hallway was a large glass room, big enough to rival the size of the hangar. Millions of tiny multicoloured lasers crisscrossed each other inside. The orange, green, pink, and blue streams of light seemed to be building several small black aircraft, like a three-dimensional printer, but far more advanced, and infinitely faster.

"That's where the sound in the hall came from." Yang said over the fizzing and humming of the lasers inside of the glass room.

"I see you finally got the all-wise creator out of bed," Yin said as she jogged up to Scott and Yang. Her dark hair was tied back in a ponytail, and she wore grey sweats. Scott envied how comfortable she looked. He was still in wrinkly jeans.

Scott gestured out to the hangar full of flying machines.

"It's only been, what, twelve hours? They made all of *this* in half of a day?"

"Not all of it is ours." Yin pointed toward the opening of the hangar, which let in the cool night air. "Only everything over there."

Scott peered past the Auroras, Voyagers, jet-powered wing suits, F22 Raptors, and other aircraft, to what looked like a small army of black jets, identical to what was being made behind the young pilots and their Creator. The jets were grouped together in four rows next to a larger aircraft.

"Those are the drones they've managed to produce so far," Yang said. "Aren't they awesome?"

"How many are there?" Scott asked.

"Right now we have around two hundred," Yin said. "Since each drone can cover about thirty miles, we'll need over eight hundred of these suckers if we want to defend the Earth."

Scott frowned. "There's no way Shakespeare has the manpower to fly all of those."

"They're *drones*, Creator," Yin said. "No one's going to be in them."

"They fly themselves," Yang said. "Or rather, a computer flies them. And we'll be controlling the computer... from that."

Yang pointed to the large spacecraft. Or at least Scott assumed that's what he was pointing to. It was so far away he couldn't be certain.

"Want to go see it?" Yang asked in excitement.

Scott surprised himself by grinning at the twins' enthusiasm. "Absolutely."

They walked across the grated platform and down the metal stairs into the hangar. Scott felt very small next to the large jets, airplanes, helicopters, and spaceships stored in the enormous room. He wasn't even eye-level with most of the machines. He was left staring up at the underbelly of most of the planes.

Yin and Yang seemed to get a kick out of the various ships. Some, they said, were old-fashioned and vintage, though to Scott they looked new; others were unlike anything they'd seen before. They were particularly keen on a white ship that looked a little like a shoe with the words *Heart of Gold* branded on the side.

After a while they reached the large, sleek black spaceship Yin had indicated. It was slender and pointed in the front but more squarish in the back to make room for its engines. Standing right up against it, Scott felt insignificant. The spaceship was huge.

"Isn't she beautiful?" Yang asked. He reached up and touched the shiny black hull of the ship.

Scott gazed up at the machine. "It's enormous."

"Yes," Yin said as she folded her arms. "It's a little overkill, in my opinion. It's not like we're going into deep space. We don't need so much room."

"We're not going into space *yet*," Yang said. "But give it time."

Yang walked around one of the engines in the back, gliding his hand across the ship as he walked. Scott and Yin walked behind him. Yin stopped to look at the engines; they opened up in silver spheres in the back, where fire would blast out and propel the ship along. Scott walked a bit farther away from the ship so that he could stare at the whole of it in awe.

They stopped in the middle of the left side of the ship. Scott could only just see a faint outline of a black door. Yang reached up and placed his hand on the top of it. The ship unlocked with a rush of air, and then the door opened and a ramp slowly descended toward the concrete floor. Scott, Yin, and Yang backed up quickly to get out of the way.

The ramp hit the floor with a *clang*. Small blue lights lit the sides of it. Yang and Yin stepped onto the ramp and started onto the ship. Scott followed more hesitantly.

The inside of the ship was black, with small pinpoints of light that looked like stars glistening from the ceilings and walls of the spacecraft. Scott was aware that he was standing in a massive space, but he couldn't see around him clearly. What he could make out, though—the different hallways, the various screens—fit perfectly with what had been in his head.

"It's kind of gloomy in here," Yang said.

"It's just like I pictured it," Scott said. "The command ship wasn't meant for controlling drones in my book, but you guys still piloted it. It seems like the Immortal Writers replicated it exactly."

"So you know where the command deck is, then?" Yang asked.

"Or are you not going to be much help on *this* spaceship as well?" Yin said.

Scott cringed. "Look, I acknowledge that it's my mistake I didn't know where everything is on the Betan ship. But I know my way around here easily enough. Come on."

He walked down the hallway in front of Yin and Yang until they reached an intersection. He took a left, then a right, and another left. His eyes steadily adjusted to the dim lighting as he went along. He never got lost, even though all of the hallways looked the same. Scott had seen this ship so clearly in his writing... or, more accurately, in his Fever.

He had been forcing himself to take C.S. Lewis's advice and write multiple times a day. He felt the delusional effects of the Fever lessen each time he sat down to write, which relieved him. He'd always felt like he was on a ledge with the Fever; he had never felt safe from it, but instead always seemed to fall off into the oblivion of his imagination. He was grateful that writing had started to ease his Fever, letting him step back from that ledge, before he and his characters had gone to the reconnaissance mission on the Betan ship. Scott shuddered to think what would have happened if he had lost control of his mind while they were in space.

What further harm could his writing do now that he was an Immortal Writer, anyway?

Scott paused outside of another door. "If this is like it is in my book, one of you will need to touch the door to get in," he said. "In my book, only certain handprints could open it. Both of you were authorized to enter in *Invasion*, and I'm not sure the Immortal Writers would have thought to put my handprint in or not."

Yin stepped forward and placed her palm against the door. It glowed dark blue for a moment, and then dissolved.

"Come on," Scott said.

He, Yin, and Yang stepped into the command room. The door reappeared behind them. Scott turned in a circle as he took in the command deck. It was much better lit than the rest of the ship. The star-like lights were brighter and cast the deck in what Scott thought looked like a predawn glow. The room was perfectly round, and its walls, ceiling, and even the floor were made of large, dark screens. The screens, Scott knew, provided those on the bridge with a 360-degree view of the surroundings of the ship. Other than that, the room was rather empty. There were no seats, no computers, no desks… nothing but a massive amount of empty space.

"Are you sure we control the drones from this room?" Yin asked.

"Yeah, no offense, buddy," Yang said, "but it's kind of bare."

Scott smirked at his two pilots and turned back to the cavernous room. He raised his voice to the computer. "Activate full bridge."

Blue lights appeared in the air and created podiums and desks and computers. All of the new furniture looked like it was made from lasers. The various new machines were scattered all over the room. Scott smiled over at Yin and Yang, who looked ethereal in the bright blue light. Their eyes were wide as they looked around the newly equipped bridge.

"Cool, right?" Scott asked.

"We can't possibly manage all of the computers by ourselves," Yin said as she gestured at all of the machines.

"There's a two-pilot system if you want to take it out of autopilot," Scott said.

"You can show us that in a minute," Yang said. "I want to see if I can figure some things out, first." He stepped deeper into the command room and looked around, peering at the laser computer screens as he passed them.

He finally stopped in front of a screen in the centre of the room. "This looks right," he mused.

Yang pushed a few buttons, and Scott felt the ship ascend. He held out both hands in an attempt to steady himself. There was nothing to hold on to.

"Let's see what space looks like in this baby, shall we?" Yang asked.

Scott swallowed as Yang pushed a few more buttons, and then his stomach dropped as they zoomed forward.

"Show live screen," Scott commanded.

The screens on the walls lit up to show them a full view of what surrounded the ship. Immediately, Scott wished he couldn't see. They were just exiting the hangar, and he could see how close the ceiling was to the top of the ship.

"We're going to crash!" Scott yelled. His breathing was so panicked that he was starting to feel tingling in his extremities.

"Calm down, Scott," Yin said. She patted his back. "We'll be fine." She paused. "The ship does have simulated gravity, right?"

"Yes," Scott moaned.

"Then yes, we'll be fine."

He squeezed his eyes shut and focused on staying upright while the ship catapulted forward.

"You're missing a great view here, Creator!" Yang whooped as the ship continued to ascend. Scott opened one eye and saw that the ship was surrounded by wisps of clouds. He thought it was beautiful for a moment, but then the view was replaced by angry streaks of red flame as the ship passed through the atmosphere. Scott squeezed his eyes shut again and hummed to himself in an attempt to ease his anxiety.

But then, impossibly soon, the ship slowed and stopped as it entered space. Scott held his breath as the engines shut off.

Yang whistled. "Look at that view."

Scott slowly opened his eyes and gasped.

They were in space, and it was the most beautiful sight Scott had ever beheld. The stars were clearer than they were even in his simulated room at the Castle. They sparkled and glinted—and there were so many. He had never realized how full the sky was until this moment. And the moon was so close, so full, and so brilliantly lit and beautiful that Scott felt ashamed that he had ever thought it was a lesser light. He turned so that he could see all around the ship in the screens. The sun was glaringly bright, and he turned away quickly, shielding his eyes. Looking at the floor was disorienting, as well; his stomach plummeted as he expected to fall.

He looked up, and his jaw dropped as he saw the Earth, with its beautiful white clouds against the blue oceans and large landmasses. The view of the Earth was more beautiful even than the stars and the moon and the blinding sun. At first he was in awe, but then he felt a stab of heat at the base of his skull. His stomach lurched with longing. His heart pounded, and his hands shook as his breathing accelerated.

For a brief moment an image from the Fever flashed in his mind, and he saw his father's face.

Your brain is activating! Scott heard his father's voice briefly, hollowly, and then it faded.

Scott gasped as he came back to his senses. His breathing was normal again, and his hands had stopped shaking as suddenly as they had started. But he could still feel the heat in his head.

"Yeah, it's beautiful, isn't it?" Yang sighed.

Scott shook his head, trying to clear it. Yin and Yang hadn't noticed him dipping into the Fever. They were too focused on the view. Scott looked apprehensively back at the Earth, but his body didn't react to it this time, and he remained firmly in his own mind.

What had happened? He'd been writing every day with no sign of the Fever. What about the view of the Earth triggered him?

Scott focused on taking deep breaths as he stared at his planet. He imagined a trickling sensation cooling the heat in his head and stared at the water on Earth to help his mind imagine the calm and cool that he craved.

"As much as I'd love to stare at the stars all night," Yin said, "I want to know how to fly this thing. *Off* of autopilot."

Scott took one deep breath, cleared his throat, and turned around, facing the front of the ship and avoiding the sight of the planet behind them. He focused instead on the moon and stars ahead of him.

"Dual pilot mode," Scott commanded loudly.

The laser computers and podiums surrounding the trio disappeared and were replaced by two bright blue cocoons, made solely out of crisscrossed lasers. One cocoon was on either half of the command deck and did little to fill the large room.

"One of you sit there," Scott said, pointing to the seat on the right, "and the other one sit on the left."

Yin and Yang walked over to the laser cocoons.

"The light will hold us up?" Yin asked doubtfully.

"Yes," Scott said. "Get in."

Yin sat awkwardly in her cocoon, grimacing like she expected to fall through the chair and the command room floor to be left to the mercies of space, but Yang jumped in and leaned back in his seat.

"This is surprisingly comfortable," he said. "But how do I fly the ship from here?"

Scott smiled. "Just wait."

He cleared his throat and spoke again to the computer. "Activate controls."

Two joysticks appeared on either side of Yang, along with a miniature display of the command ship in front of him. He reached out and grabbed the joysticks. "Finally, something I recognize. And look at how cute the little command ship is!"

Yin reached out to touch the keyboard that had appeared above her lap. There were no images in front of her.

"What's the point of this?" she asked doubtfully.

"In the book, you used that system to control different satellites, probes, and other machines you'd send out into space," Scott explained. "I imagine you'll use it to protect the Earth in this situation."

"This controls the drones?" Yin checked.

Scott nodded. "I assume so. The drones weren't in my books, but it makes sense you'd control them from that side. And you can switch who controls what if you'd like to."

"No way," Yang said. He rubbed his hands together. "I'm flying this baby first."

Yin sighed. "Fine." She reclined in her cocoon and folded her arms. "I'll figure out the system with the drones. Maybe I can signal some from the Castle hangar."

Scott shrugged. He didn't know if that was possible. "Activate manual flight," he said.

He felt the engines hum to life. Yang chuckled with glee and thrust the joysticks forward. The ship jumped ahead, and Scott lost his balance. He tumbled forward, bruising his knees as he tried to catch himself. He slid forward as they lurched to a halt.

"Whoa, sorry!" Yang said as he let up on the joysticks. "This is very responsive, isn't it?"

Scott simply moaned in response.

Yin began typing on her laser keyboard. Words appeared in the air in front of her, and she smirked. Scott and Yang watched in fascination as drones appeared above and around them on the screens and as digital replicas of the drones appeared in the space in front of Yin.

The twin pilots played with their respective systems and then switched. Scott watched in silence. Yin's face was serious and focused while she worked, her mouth in a straight line, her brow furrowed; Yang, on the other hand, seemed to be having the time of his life. He repeatedly stuck his tongue out of the side of his mouth when he concentrated, and a grin was perpetually glued to his face. Scott knew he should have been more excited to watch his characters in action, but he wasn't. He sank lower and lower into himself as he watched his pilots. Part of his anxiety was that he had nothing to do. He had taught his characters how to activate the flight systems, but that's all he seemed good for. He desperately wanted to be more useful than that. He couldn't distract himself from the ugly fact of Paul's death while he sat and stared, and it didn't help that he was still troubled over his odd reaction to seeing the planet. Why had the Fever come back? And what had his father mean: that his brain was activating? He was missing something.

"Scott?" Yang asked loudly.

Scott jumped, finally coming back to himself. He blinked. Yang was waving a hand at him from his cocoon. "What?"

"Quit zoning out," Yang said. "I'm not going to let you fly this thing if you're going to be distracted."

Scott perked up, a grin lighting his face. "I can try to fly it?"

Yang nodded. "This is the product of your imagination, after all."

Scott jumped up from where he had been sitting on the command deck floor and walked over to Yang's cocoon. Yang clambered out of the laser chair and allowed Scott to slide in. It felt like he was suspended in nothing but air.

"You're right," Scott said. "This is surprisingly comfortable."

"Do you know how to do this?" Yang asked.

Scott took a deep breath. "I wrote it," he said. "I can do it."

"But you've never flown anything before, right?"

Scott narrowed his eyes. "I can do it," he said.

Scott ignored his characters as they exchanged a skeptical glance. Yang frowned and opened his mouth to say more, but Scott ignored him and put his hands on the black and red joysticks.

"I can do it," he repeated.

But within a few minutes, everything had gone horribly wrong.

CHAPTER TWENTY-THREE

Alarms blared from the ship's sound system, but even they couldn't match the remarkable decibel level of Yin's shouting.

"Pull back on the joysticks!" she screamed.

Scott tried, but the controls wouldn't budge. He wasn't quite sure how that was possible. He had no idea what he had done wrong.

"They're stuck!" he yelled back.

Yang yanked Scott out of the cocoon, and Scott crashed to the floor. Yang repositioned himself in the cocoon and grabbed the joysticks.

"Hurry, Yang!" Yin shouted.

"I've got it!"

Scott shut his eyes and turned away from the front screens as they grazed the surface of a satellite. He could feel the momentum of the spacecraft shift. The stars reflected in the screens before and under them, then twirled as the ship rotated and spun. Eventually, they finally stopped moving.

The alarms stopped. All Scott could hear was Yang panting from behind him. Scott was tempted to look up and check on his characters, but he could only stare at the stars below him in shame.

"That was way too close," Yang murmured after a moment.

"Why did you let him fly the damn ship?" Yin shouted at her brother.

"I didn't think he'd nearly make us crash into a satellite, Yin!"

Scott clenched his jaw, grimacing at the feel of his teeth grinding together.

"You just gave him the joysticks with no instruction and didn't expect anything bad to happen?"

"We're in space," Yang yelled. "I didn't think he'd be able to hit anything!"

"I'm still here!" Scott shouted. He was relieved that his voice hadn't cracked or wavered when he spoke.

The twin pilots quieted, glaring at opposite corners of the command deck. The three of them sat in silence, the pilots in their cocoons while Scott still sat uncomfortably on the floor.

"I think we should go back now," Yin growled. She hit a few buttons on her system, and the drones flew away. Yin and Yang stood up from their cocoons.

"How do we turn on autopilot to get back to the Castle?" Yang asked.

Scott took a deep breath, trying to calm his anger and hide his embarrassment. "Activate auto pilot," he commanded. The blue cocoons and controls disappeared. "Take us back to base."

The ship zoomed back toward Earth. Scott closed his eyes and focused on the feeling of his clenched fists as they flew back to the Castle. He only relaxed and opened his eyes when he felt the ship land and heard the engines shut off.

Yin stalked out ahead of Yang and Scott, not even waiting for Scott to scramble off of the deck floor.

"You actually didn't do that bad," Yang tried to console as they exited the ship. "It's my fault for not giving you any instructions. And we're fine, right? So no harm done?"

Scott glared at the ground. "I'm going back to bed," he said. "I have to get beaten up by Caspiz later today, so I should probably try to catch some sleep."

He walked slowly out of the hangar, anger boiling inside of him.

Scott sat alone in the Imagination Room, his legs crossed beneath him. He had a pen in his right hand and a pad of paper on his lap. He wrote furiously in an attempt to avoid another attack of the Fever, no matter how brief.

The Imagination Room reflected his thoughts as he wrote. He could see everything clearly and vividly. As he jumped from one scene to another, the room shifted and changed. First it was space, and then a lava planet, which turned into a forest with dark red trees and misted sunlight.

Scott supposed that to anyone else the ever-changing scenery would have been distracting. But not to Scott. This was what it was like to be in the Fever. When he was under its influence, he was completely overpowered by the visions of large buildings and ships, the smell of pine trees and the taste of cool mountain air, the texture of sand graining against his fingers, the cacophony of voices... so many voices.

The Imagination Room was probably Scott's favourite part of the Castle. He felt in control here, because the room didn't overpower him like his mind did, and he could change what he saw. When he was in the clutches of the Fever, he didn't have a choice. The stories just appeared, unbidden and unwanted.

It was a mystery to Scott, and to Shakespeare, why the Writing Fever tortured him. Shakespeare conjectured that Scott had some sort of strange connection to the Imagination Field and that the stories and worlds and characters just spoke to him clearer and louder than they did to anyone else. At least that was what C.S. Lewis had told him when he first picked up a pen and started writing again a few days ago.

But Scott wanted to know *why* he was connected to the Imagination Field. Lewis had offered no answers to that.

Scott closed his eyes and worked on focusing his mind on one scene: a grove of trees with tall men around a pool of dark water. The men chanted in a language he couldn't quite decipher, but even without knowing what they meant, the words chilled him every time he heard them. Scott had been seeing this particular scene for years, and he was keen on figuring out what it meant.

"Scott," someone said.

Scott furrowed his brow and tried harder to focus.

"Scott, I need to teach you how to throw a punch."

Scott opened his eyes and looked up.

Caspiz stood in front of him, her arms crossed against her chest. She wore a plaid shirt and black jeans, which surprised him; he was accustomed to seeing her in uniform or the spacesuit the Writers had created.

Scott was annoyed at Caspiz's presence but pleased to see that he had focused enough on a scene to make it stand still. They were in the grove of trees he had pictured, and the pool of water shimmered in the moonlight in the centre of the ring of aspens. None of the men were present, however, and there was no chanting.

"Why do I need to learn how to punch someone?" Scott asked. "Not that I mind. There are a few people I'd love to punch in the throat."

Caspiz arched an eyebrow at his comment. "You and I will be going on the Betan ships to place the bombs," she explained. "I'm hoping that we'll be able to get in and out quickly now that we know where we're going, and I especially hope that you won't have to fight or shoot any of the Betans. But it's best to be prepared."

Scott stood, imagining the pen and paper out of existence. He commanded his subconscious to hold the scene around them in place, and then focused more fully on Caspiz. He breathed a sigh of relief when their surroundings didn't waver. At least he could do *something*, even if he couldn't fly the command ship.

"What do you want me to do?" Scott asked.

Caspiz smiled and took a few steps closer to him. She let her arms hang by her sides. "Hit me," she said.

Scott smirked. "I'd love to," he said snidely, "but I feel like that would be a bad idea."

"I'm not at all concerned that you'll do any damage," Caspiz said. She pointed to his thin, lanky arms. "Do you even have any muscle?"

Scott didn't need more motivation. He'd always been quick to anger, ever since his father died. It was not one of his finer traits.

He swung at Caspiz and hit her in the gut. To his deep dismay, she didn't double over, stumble back, or even exhale sharply. She just blinked at him with what looked like boredom.

"This is worse than I thought," Caspiz said. Her voice was normal and didn't sound breathless or pained at all. Scott had done absolutely no damage; it was like he had poked her instead of punched her.

"Well, I'm sorry," Scott said. He folded his arms. "I haven't had twenty years of military training."

"Neither have I," Caspiz said. "They didn't pick me up and teach me how to sucker punch someone when I was an infant. I've had fifteen years of training, though; they started us young. We've been a little paranoid since the First Alien War."

"Whatever," Scott said. "I don't have *fifteen* years of military training."

"I can tell," Caspiz said.

Scott rolled his eyes. "Are you gonna teach me anything, or are you just going to mock me?"

"You did one thing right," Caspiz said. "You actually hit me. I didn't have to do too much to goad you into it. At least I know you're willing to hit someone, and after the reconnaissance mission, I think I can trust you to do what you need to do with a Betan. I just need to teach you how to do it."

Scott just stared at the colonel, waiting. He tapped his foot impatiently.

"The first thing you need to know is that you don't just punch with your fist," Caspiz said. "You have to put all of your body weight into it. I have arm muscle, but even if I punched with only my arm, it wouldn't do much good. You especially don't stand a chance."

Scott frowned. He was not in the mood to be mocked.

Caspiz bent her knees slightly and leaned back. "Try punching like this," she said.

She swung her arm, and Scott noticed that all of her body moved forward with her fist as it flew into the air beside Scott. Her movement was controlled and strong. Her arm didn't waver an inch from where she directed it.

"Now you try it," Caspiz said as she stood up straight. "But don't just hit air. Hit me."

Scott pursed his lips and mimicked Caspiz's example. He squatted down, his right arm raised, then leapt forward and swung at Caspiz. He hit her in the gut, and this time, she stumbled back a step.

"That's a little better, I guess," Caspiz said.

Scott frowned. She still didn't sound out of breath or in pain.

"How are you not doubled over right now?" Scott demanded. "What do I have to do to injure you?"

Caspiz chuckled. "You have to practice, and you have to be a lot stronger," she said. "Now let's try that again. This time, follow through with your movements."

Scott tried, but again he did no damage. He didn't feel like Caspiz was much help. She wasn't a very good teacher. She didn't encourage him at all. Instead, she infuriated him, and his anger didn't make him stronger; it just made him lose control, and without any control, he couldn't focus his strength. Not that Caspiz would say he had any to begin with.

They must have worked for hours. Scott grew weary. His arms and legs shook, and sweat beaded on his face. But he wasn't about to give up. He was still furious about failing in the command ship, and it enraged him that he was failing here as well. And worst of all, he had failed Paul. He didn't want to disappoint anyone else, including himself.

"That's enough for now," Caspiz said after a while. "You're off to a decent start, I suppose. After a few weeks, you'll be somewhat competent. Maybe."

"We don't have a few weeks," Scott growled. He dropped his fists and pivoted away from Caspiz to hide his face, which was hot with shame. The scene around him began to fade, and he could clearly see the door to the room. He stomped toward it as best he could on shaking legs. The grove of trees around them disappeared and was replaced by an empty white room.

"Being angry at me isn't going to make you better," Caspiz said, easily keeping pace with him.

"I don't care," Scott said. He threw open the door to the Imagination Room and marched into the richly decorated Castle without bothering to check that Caspiz had followed him.

Not that he had time to look if he wanted to. Yang ran up to them, out of breath.

"You've got to come see this," he panted. His hair was dishevelled and stuck up wildly with sweat.

"No," Scott snapped. "I'm tired of this. I don't want to crash more spaceships or get my ass handed to me anymore. I'm leaving."

"No, Scott," Yang said. He tried to catch his breath, but Scott didn't pause to give him time to speak again. He shoved past the young pilot.

"We found something in the files from the alien ship," Yang managed to gasp.

"I don't care," Scott said. He continued to walk away and was in the dining hall before Yang and Caspiz had caught up with him.

"You will," Yang said.

"I doubt it."

"*Scott!*" Dylan ran up to him from the library, panicked.

Scott paused. If Dylan was panicking, then something was definitely wrong.

"Fine," Scott growled. "What is it?"

"I don't know how they have it, or why, but they have a picture," Dylan said.

Scott shook his head in frustration. "A picture of what?"

"The Betans have a picture of *you*."

CHAPTER TWENTY-FOUR

Scott stood in the Field Room, staring at a picture of his face floating in the air, projected by the Memory Orb.

"How did they get this?" Shakespeare asked. "Is there anything, *anything*, you've written that would explain it?"

Scott shook his head slowly. "I was never in my book."

"What do they want with my brother?" Dylan asked.

"He's probably a target," Yin said. "Look at the evidence."

"All we know is that they have a picture of him," Yang countered. "We don't know why. What's-his-face hasn't been able to decipher the language yet."

"I've been working on it!" Tolkien said from a computer toward the front of the room. "I'm not used to all of your science fiction technology, and it's not like I have a Rosetta Stone to guide me here. This language is nothing like anything I've seen on Earth, and it doesn't help that I can't *hear* it."

"Let's focus on the matter at hand," Caspiz interjected. "I agree with Yin. They're probably targeting you, Scott."

"But *why*?" Scott asked. "How do they even know I exist?"

Wells, who was leaning against a wall, spoke up. "None of the 'logic' in your book makes sense; why does *this* have to make sense?"

Scott curled a fist. He would have gone and punched Wells if he thought it would do any good, but Caspiz had thoroughly proved to him over the last few hours that it wouldn't.

"You're not helping, Wells," Dick reprimanded from beside Tolkien.

"We don't have any answers for you, Scott," Shakespeare said. "And we probably won't until Tolkien cracks the Betan language."

"Then what do we do?" Dylan asked. "We're not sending him to the ships to place the bombs now, right? Not when they know who he is."

Shakespeare hesitated. "I'm sorry, but Scott has to be involved. It's the only way we can defeat the Betans."

Dylan rubbed his forehead in frustration as he growled at the floor.

"They won't be able to see you through the helmet," Yang said hopefully. "That should help, right?"

"It's too dangerous," Dylan yelled.

Scott couldn't help but agree. They were probably walking into some sort of trap; what other explanation was there? He would end up like his father.

Dead.

"Does anyone else have a suggestion of how we could defeat the Betans?" Shakespeare asked. "A way that would be safe for Scott, perhaps?"

No one said anything. Scot couldn't think of any sort of solution; he just stared at the picture of his face hovering in the air. None of this made sense, and even if it did, he was useless anyway. He was no good to anyone, and he didn't want to work with these people in the first place. He struggled to remember the vision of his father telling him to work with the Immortal Writers.

"Paul would have had an idea," Dylan said. "He may not have known a lot about military tactics, or about shooting guns, but he knew a lot about aliens."

"I know everything he knew," Scott muttered as guilt stabbed through him. "And he's dead, anyway. He's no use to us now."

Scott hated how harsh the words sounded as he spoke them, but he didn't know how to soften that truth. He wasn't sure he could.

Caspiz cleared her throat. "Then what can *you* tell us? Do you have any ideas?"

Scott's mouth twisted as he thought. He stared at his face in the air, frowning as it rotated in front of him. "The Betans are religious," he said. "That's what drives their conquests. Maybe they think that, because I wrote about them, I'm a threat to their god?"

Shakespeare ran a hand through his receding hair. "That would make sense," he said. "Something is definitely going on with their religion. At least we think so, based on some footage we found. Maybe you'll be able to make more sense of this than I can."

Shakespeare turned and faced the projection of Scott's face. "Anne," he commanded, "please show us the footage Wells found of Dygavery."

A projection of Dygavery replaced Scott's face. The Betan king's pointy teeth glinted as he stood before them. Scott almost felt like Dygavery was in the room with them, the image was so realistic. He resisted the urge to take a step back.

Dygavery choked and gurgled. It caught Scott off-guard at first, but then he realized that the Betan king was speaking. Shame spread through him, and he shifted uncomfortably. He wished he could understand what Dygavery was saying.

"We almost skipped over this footage," Shakespeare said over Dygavery's loud, gravelly voice, "before we saw this."

Scott's eyes widened as Betan forms surrounded him. All of them were on the ground, kneeling on one knee. Their torsos were upright, and their right fist covered their chests as they watched Dygavery in awe. The kneeling Betan projections covered the entire room, and Scott felt like he was part of the crowd.

Dygavery dipped his hands in a red bowl, and when he raised them again, they dripped green—the color of Betan blood.

The Betans cried out and thumped their chests. Scott had to cover his ears to protect them from the horrible noise. Not only was it unpleasant, but it had triggered the familiar, uncomfortable heat of the Fever.

"Enough!" Shakespeare shouted over the uproar.

The images faded away, and only the Writers and Characters—and Dylan—were left in the room.

"We figured it looked like some sort of religious ritual," Shakespeare said. "Can you interpret this?"

Scott nodded slowly as he lowered his hands from his ears. "Dygavery has more than claimed himself as king; he's set himself up as some sort of deity. I'm... honestly not sure how it happened."

Wells sighed loudly from a corner.

"And if Dygavery is the god now, and the Betans think that your picture is a threat to your religion..." Dylan trailed off.

"Then they're definitely targeting me," Scott muttered.

There was a brief moment of heavy silence before Caspiz grunted. "But how did they *get* your picture?"

Scott shook his head. "I truly have no idea. But if I'm right, and they think I'm a threat to their religion..." He trailed off, unwilling to go on.

"Well, now Scott's definitely not going," Dylan said. "They'll kill him instantly."

"He has to go," Shakespeare said. "I've already told you that. I wish it weren't true, but it is."

"I think our best bet is to give him time," Caspiz said. "He's dismal at fighting now, but if you give him a couple of weeks, he'll be more competent and might stand a chance."

"But we wanted to attack the ships before they came too close to Earth," Yin reminded them.

"He'll be completely defenseless if we rush him," Caspiz said.

Scott pursed his lips. They were right. He was going to be utterly useless in this fight. And if he couldn't defeat the Betans, the world would be blasted to bits. He hated it, but he had to try. He couldn't let all of the people of Earth die just because he was too afraid to act. But how was he going to keep Dylan and Yang and the other characters safe? How was he going to survive? He only had one strength, which was writing. He wasn't sure how helpful that would be.

"Let me try something," Scott said after a moment. "Give me the night to work on it. We can meet again tomorrow."

"Time is of the essence, Scott," Shakespeare reminded him.

"I'm aware of that, Shakespeare," Scott said. He tried to keep his voice level and calm. "But I think I may have come up with something that will help."

Scott lay on his bed and stared at the laptop in front of him. This was the one time he needed the vividness of the Fever, and of course it wasn't there. The cursor on the screen mocked him.

Focus, Scott.

Scott closed his eyes and let his mind go blank. He saw no images and heard no voices. He only heard his heartbeat and the breath in his throat as he tried to focus.

The darkness in his mind was smothering. He didn't understand why he couldn't see. He had never experienced any sort of writer's block before; on the contrary, there had always been too many voices and too many stories.

Granted, Scott had never tried to write about himself before.

He waited in the darkness and focused on what he knew about himself. He was tall and black and lanky, with black hair and dark eyes. He always wore graphic t-shirts. He never wore matching socks.

Scott focused on these details individually until he began to see them. First his socks, then up and up until he could see his entire person in his mind.

He stared with his inner eye, focusing as the image shifted and changed. Scott looked the same, but he had more muscle; he no longer looked wimpy. He encouraged the image of himself to continue to morph and evolve.

Scott opened his eyes and began to type. His fingers flew across the keyboard, but he barely noticed. He was only dimly aware of his surroundings. Instead, he was completely absorbed by the scene in his mind.

He watched the vision as he manipulated it, changing him into a fighter and an excellent marksman. He allowed himself to feel power, and he wrote it all down. He wrote of impossible things, things that he never would have dreamed he would really be able to do.

But he wrote it.

Your brain is activating, he heard his father say.

He ignored the warning and wrote on.

CHAPTER TWENTY-FIVE

S cott had gathered Shakespeare, Caspiz, Yin, Yang, and Dylan in the Imagination Room. Wells had insisted on coming along, probably keen on scoffing at Scott's ideas. They stood in the same grove of trees that Scott had imagined yesterday, except that instead of being shadowed in waning moonlight, streams of light ran through the trees and motes of dust floated above shooting targets, which looked like advanced archery marks, randomly placed in the grove.

"Why are we here, Scott?" Shakespeare asked. His eyes were shadowed with exhaustion, and he wearily rubbed the bridge of his nose.

"I'm ready," Scott said. "I can go on the Betan ships, and no one has to worry."

Shakespeare sighed and lowered his hand. Dylan frowned, and Caspiz laughed.

"I fought with you yesterday, and I've seen you shoot," Caspiz said. "Trust me, you're not ready."

Scott grinned and imagined a silver gravity gun into existence. He picked it up from the ground and aimed it at one of the targets. He looked at the target for less than a second before he fired. He was the only one who wasn't shocked when he hit the target dead centre and it exploded.

There was a moment of silence.

"You couldn't hit anything you aimed at a couple of days ago," Yin commented.

"No offense," Yang said peaceably.

"I can hit anything now," Scott said. "Watch this."

He turned away from the group and again raised his gun toward the targets in the grove as they started to move. Two swung back and forth, one flew high into the air, part of it disappearing in the blinding sunlight, and one grew legs and started to run away in a zigzag pattern.

Scott fired three times. The target in the air exploded into bits, and pieces of shredded metal fluttered down toward the group; the target running away was grated apart; and he hit both of the swinging targets as they swung toward each other and intersected.

The obliterated targets and the gravity gun disappeared. Scott took a deep breath and turned to face the writers and characters.

Yin, Yang, Caspiz, and Dylan were shocked. Scott could see it on their faces. They had seen him try to shoot a gun before, and he was now years ahead of where he was days before. All of their eyes were wide. Yang's mouth was even hanging comically open.

Shakespeare's eyes were squinted shut, and his mouth was pursed together, but Scott couldn't interpret his thoughts. Wells, on the other hand, looked thoroughly disturbed. Scott opened his mouth to demand that someone say something, like congratulate him for his sudden and impressive progress, but without warning, Caspiz ran forward, head lowered, and tried to pummel him.

Scott pivoted and avoided the blow, then jabbed at Caspiz. She dodged the punch, but Scott was prepared with his other hand. He grabbed her arm, twisted it, and pulled it behind her back. His grin disappeared as he heard Caspiz's arm *snap* sickeningly. He released her quickly and stepped back. He hadn't meant to use so much force. He had meant to stop.

Caspiz swore.

"I… I'm sorry," Scott stuttered. Why hadn't he stopped?

Caspiz grunted. "It's just dislocated. Yin?"

Yin jogged forward and grabbed Caspiz's arm. With a *pop*, Caspiz's shoulder jumped back into place. Caspiz was not one to show pain, but Scott heard a low moan of discomfort, and there was a slight sheen of sweat glimmering on her brow.

"Stop," Shakespeare commanded. "I think we get the point, Scott."

"I can do it now," Scott said, excited despite the turning in his stomach from hurting Caspiz. "I can save Earth. We can go today. I'm ready."

"You look different," Shakespeare said. He slowly walked forward and circled Scott. "You've made yourself stronger."

Scott nodded.

"And you've made yourself into an excellent fighter and master marksman," Shakespeare continued.

"Yes," Scott said. "I've fixed the problem. I can fight the Betans now."

Shakespeare stopped circling Scott and looked him in the eyes. "What did you write?" he asked quietly.

Scott blinked, surprised that Shakespeare had come to that conclusion so quickly. "I wrote about myself and changed what I needed to. It all came true. Just like with the characters and the spaceships that are heading for Earth *right now.*"

Shakespeare glanced at Wells, who shook his head.

"You don't make any sense," Wells grumbled.

"What's wrong?" Scott asked. His voice was louder than he had intended it to be. "I've solved a problem. I've written my way out of it. Isn't that part of what you tell your group of Writers? That they can do anything with writing?"

"They can write themselves…. capabilities," Shakespeare said. "For example, a few months ago Liz McKinnen wrote that she had Elemental magic… but she could not make herself proficient in this new skill. She had to learn that through trial and error."

"So?" Scott asked.

"You've changed fundamental aspects of your character," Shakespeare said. "You've given yourself abilities, which is normal, but you've somehow made yourself exceptional at those abilities. You've bypassed the necessary character growth that is an essential part of a writer's work coming to life. I don't understand how you've done what you've done."

"None of what you write makes any sense," Wells said. "How does anything you come up with cross into the Reality Field when so little of it is logical? How did you write yourself into an adept enough fighter that you could incapacitate someone with fifteen years of military training in less than ten seconds? *You don't make any sense.*"

Scott gritted his teeth in frustration. "I don't understand why you're so upset! I made myself better! I fixed the problem! It doesn't matter why the Betans know about me now, and whatever they want is irrelevant. They can't defeat me now."

"I just don't understand how you've done it, and because of that, I don't know what the repercussions might be," Shakespeare said. "Before we send you up to the ships, I need to know that nothing else is going to happen. I need to know that you're stable."

Scott flung his hands in the air in frustration. "What do you mean that I'm stable?"

Shakespeare nodded to Caspiz, who still rubbed her shoulder.

"I don't know what the side effects might be of what you've done," Shakespeare said. "I've never seen it before."

Scott peered at Shakespeare and took a step forward. "Are you scared of me, old man?"

Shakespeare looked at him coolly. "Hardly, Scott. But I'm trying to protect you. I have no desire for history to repeat itself."

Shakespeare's words hit Scott like a fist to the gut. His anger withered away into fear and apprehension.

"How long do we have to wait?" Scott asked quietly.

"As long as we can," Shakespeare said.

CHAPTER TWENTY-SIX

S cott lay in bed and stared at the ceiling, his arms crossed tightly over his chest. Dylan had not yet come to their room; Scott assumed he was with Lilly. Again. It was just one more thing that made him angry.

He'd been trying so hard to work with the Immortal Writers, desperate to please the memory of his father after he'd seen him in the Fever. He'd tried to be more upbeat and less angry, less accusatory. But it hadn't done any good. Paul was dead, and Scott was right back where he started, except that now he was prepared to take on the Betans.

That was what angered Scott the most. Why was Shakespeare upset with him for doing exactly what needed to be done to defeat the aliens? Scott didn't care about character development for himself, nor did he give a damn about the laws of Immortal Writers. Why should he have to worry about them in the first place? He was prepared. He could win. That's what should have mattered, yet Shakespeare treated him like he was a little boy playing with fire. And then there was Wells, who constantly belittled Scott's writing, logic, and story.

Scott wasn't sure he could take it anymore. He didn't know if he could handle the heat in the back of his skull, the turning in his gut, the constant fury. He clenched his fists and watched a shooting star rocket across the sky.

"If only wishing on you would help," he mumbled to the fake star as it shot out of view.

Scott sighed and gazed at the stars. It was amazing how realistic the sky seemed here in his room. He could see the constellations so clearly. There was Sagittarius, Cassiopeia, Orion, Ursa Major…

He squinted as the constellations shifted, dimmed, and then swirled away. He felt helplessly dizzy, it was suddenly hard to breathe, and then he was sucked into the black abyss of space.

No! Scott tried to yell, but his voice wouldn't work. He could only scream in his mind. *Not the Fever!*

But just like before, he had no control. Scott was unaware of his real surroundings but was alert enough to know that he was seeing things that weren't real. He couldn't feel his body lying on the bed any more, even though he knew that must be where he really was. He had no sense of his body at all, or of reality.

An unbearably bright light exploded in the darkness. Scott turned away from the light, and blinking rapidly, he saw the dark, black expanse of space, lit by the light behind and beneath him. He dared to look down and saw that he stood on a monstrous, burning red star.

His heart hammered wildly in his chest as he waited for his eyes to burn and boil, or for him to asphyxiate in the depths of space, but he didn't. Eventually, his eyes adjusted to the light, and the star even enhanced his vision so that when he stared out into the darkness of the universe, he could see as far as the star's light was visible. That meant that he saw *everything.*

He saw planets and people and aliens. He saw death and disease and war. He saw religions that worshiped false gods, liars, and corrupt governments, all of which toppled and fell. And for once, he didn't feel overwhelmed by everything his eyes and mind beheld. He took a deep breath and revelled in his visions.

"Turn it off, Scott!" someone yelled from behind him.

Scott blinked, startled back into his own eyes. He turned slightly and saw his father standing on the star with him. Scott's stomach heaved, and he felt himself return a little more to his body.

"Turn it off!" his father repeated.

"Turn what off?" Scott asked. His voice sounded unnaturally loud.

"I told you before that your mind is activating," Kent Beck said. "But you can't let it control you."

"I'm angry with them, Father," Scott said. He took a step forward. "I'm furious. Why should I work with them?"

"They can help you," Kent said. "Trust me."

The star beneath him flared. An arm of flame shot out from the star and into space. Kent stumbled on the sun and started to sink.

"Trust me!" he shouted as his legs were enveloped by flame.

"Dad, wait!" Scott reached out a hand, but his father was almost completely swallowed by the red star.

"Fight it, Scott! Fight it!"

The star engulfed Kent, and Scott screamed as the ravenous flames began to lick at his own flesh.

Scott!

He heard his name in the distance, but it was barely audible over his own screams as the star tasted him again and again.

Scott!

Scott extended a hand and reached up as the star pulled him down further and further—

"Scott!"

Scott's eyes snapped open, and he found himself lying on his bed, Dylan hovering over him, blocking out the starry ceiling. Dylan's eyes were wide, and there were tears streaming down his cheeks.

"Scott!" Dylan repeated.

Scott could barely hear him. Why?

"He's awake," a woman's voice said. Scott tried to see past Dylan, but he couldn't move his neck or head.

What was that noise in the background?

"He's still burning," a low voice said. Scott shifted his gaze away from Dylan and recognized Curtis, the magic healer, standing next to his brother, closer to Scott's head.

Curtis looked down at him with bright blue eyes. "You're damaging your voice faster than I can repair it, and you're so out of air that I honestly don't know how you're alive."

Scott didn't understand.

"Try to stop screaming, Scott," Curtis said. "Tell me what's happening."

Scott realized that the horrible noise in the room was his own screeching. He took a deep breath and the screaming ceased, but that was when he started sobbing as he felt horrible pain sear through his body.

"What's happening?" Scott yelled.

"Shhh," Curtis said. "I don't know. Your body feels like it should be on fire, but it's not. You have no physical burns that I can see."

"It hurts," Scott cried.

"I know," Curtis said. "But I can't identify what's wrong."

"Scott, what happened?" Dylan asked. "I found you here thirty minutes ago, and you were burning up. About ten minutes ago the screaming started. What's wrong?"

Scott couldn't think past the pain. He shook his head, trying to clear it. "The Fever."

Dylan frowned. "It's never done this to you before."

"I don't understand what's happening," Curtis said.

"I might have a solution," the woman said, "but I'd need your permission, Scott."

"Who are you?" Scott cried. "I can't see you."

A figure came into view, and Dylan moved his head so that Scott could see.

"McKinnen," Scott said.

Liz nodded. "I have Spirit Magic. With it I can enter your mind and try to identify the problem. But I don't want to force myself into your mind without your permission."

Scott was about to refuse when pain shuddered through him again, a shock of heat that started at his head and reverberated through his body until it got caught in his toes and then rebounded back up.

"You've got to let Liz in there," Curtis said. "Please. We can't help you if you don't trust us. I'm barely keeping you under control, but things are slipping through my magic and I'm running out of strength."

Scott nodded. He closed his eyes as Liz took a deep breath. He felt her consciousness push into his mind but was surprised when he didn't feel threatened by it. Liz's mind felt friendly and cautious but curious. He let her delve, and his mind was calmer while she was present. He breathed deeper as she investigated, feeling peace for the first time since Shakespeare had knocked on Dylan's door.

But then she left, and the shock wave of pain coursed through him again.

"I'm so sorry, Scott," Liz said quietly.

Scott looked at her, sweat and tears blurring his eyes. She looked incredibly sad. "I didn't realize about your father... what had happened..."

Scott swallowed and changed the subject. "What's wrong with me?"

Liz took a deep breath. "I've never seen anything like it before," she said. "There's some sort of block in your mind."

"A block?" Dylan asked.

"It's like a wall," Liz tried to explain. "I don't know what's behind it... maybe it's your mind's way of protecting you from whatever this problem is, but whatever's behind this barricade is escaping. The dam is leaking."

"So I need to fix the wall?" Curtis asked.

"I assume so," Liz said.

Curtis closed his eyes and took a deep breath, but before Scott felt any change in his body, Curtis opened his eyes and growled. "I can't find it!"

"Let me guide you to it," Liz said. "Use our bond to work through my magic."

Liz reached around Dylan, who wouldn't leave his brother's side, and put her hands on Scott's head too, and Scott felt soothing warmth fill his mind as Curtis and Liz's magic entered. Soon his body started to cool. It was slow going at first. It felt like they poured water over his head, and the cool liquid slowly trickled down his neck and torso. The cool sensation spread through him, and he started to relax as the burning was smothered by Curtis's magic.

Scott slowly opened his eyes as Liz and Curtis stumbled away from him. They both looked exhausted. Scott barely noticed the worried glance they gave each other. He just lay gasping on the bed, trying to wrap his mind around what had just happened.

"Are you okay?" Dylan asked. His voice was more strained than Scott had ever heard it. Now that the burning was gone, he could feel Dylan clutching his hand tightly. His brow was furrowed and his eyes were full of tears. Scott felt a surge of love for his brother.

"I think so," Scott whispered.

He sat up slowly. He didn't feel any pain or heat, but he shook uncontrollably from sheer exhaustion.

"Get him a blanket," Curtis said. "He's probably in shock."

Dylan nodded and scrambled to his bed to grab a blanket for Scott.

"Scott, I don't know how long that wall will hold," Liz said slowly, "and I still don't know what's behind it. I wish I knew, but I couldn't see past it at all. Whatever is behind there is completely blocked off again."

"Did you see anything through the… the crack, or whatever it was?" Scott asked. His voice trembled.

Liz shook her head uncertainly. "Not really. I didn't understand anything. Nothing made sense."

"How do we keep the wall up?" Dylan asked as he wrapped a blanket around his brother.

Liz shrugged. "I really don't know. This is something I'm very unfamiliar with. Healer… someone I knew once might have been able to tell you, but she's not here anymore."

Scott frowned. "I was able to write some changes to myself. Maybe I could make the wall sturdier in my mind? At least until the Betans are defeated? Then maybe we can see what's back there and solve it permanently."

Dylan nodded slowly. "Let's try that."

"Here." Curtis walked over to Scott's desk and grabbed a pen and notebook. He handed them to Scott with surprising gentleness. Scott took them with shaky hands. He took a deep breath and stared at the spiral-bound notebook.

"We'll be close if you need us," Liz said after a moment of silence. "I think for now, though, we'd better let you write and rest."

Liz and Curtis quietly left the room while Scott opened his notebook. Dylan watched him with an anxious expression, probably looking for any additional sign of sickness for which he might need to call back the magicians. Scott flipped through the pages until he found a blank sheet and started to write. He'd been writing for only a minute or two when a frantic knock at the door interrupted his scribbling.

"Get up, Scott," Dick's voice called through the door. "Wells and Shakespeare need you."

Scott looked up at the black hole on his door, and he was surprised to find that he wasn't angry at the interruption. Instead, he was just confused. How odd. Maybe Curtis had healed the anger inside of him somehow, too.

"What's going on?" Dylan asked as he stood up from his bed.

"Something's wrong," Dick said. "Please, open the door."

Dylan glanced at Scott. Scott nodded and set his pen down, closing his notebook as Dylan walked to the door and opened it.

"Something's wrong with the..." Dick trailed off as he saw Scott sitting on his bed, wrapped in a blanket and shaking.

"Are you alright?" Dick asked.

Dylan hesitated.

"You can tell him," Scott said. His voice was still hoarse from screaming.

"Tell me what?" Dick asked. He looked between Dylan and Scott, his eyebrows knitted in concern.

"Scott had another Fever attack," Dylan said, his voice low. "It was worse than anything I've ever seen before. I don't know how long he was under, but he was burning up and unconscious and screaming..."

"Do I need to go get that magical healer?" Dick asked. "I can never remember his name..."

"Curtis and Liz were already here," Dylan said. "They brought him out of it. Curtis seemed pretty low on magic by the end. I'm not sure there's much more he can do."

"There's nothing else he needs to do," Scott said. "I feel better."

"You look terrible," Dick observed. "You're covered in sweat, you're shaking... are you sure you're alright?"

Scott raised a hand to wave Dick's concerns away, but his fingers trembled and ruined the façade. He lowered his arm with a sigh.

"It's better than it was," he defended himself. "It was twice that bad a couple of minutes ago."

Dick pursed his lips and gave Scott a pitying look. "I'm sorry, Scott, but… do you think you can come to the Field Room?"

"He's just been terribly sick," Dylan said. "I don't think it's a good idea for him to go anywhere right now."

"I'm feeling better," Scott insisted. He shivered as he untangled the blanket from around his shoulders. "I can go."

"Scott…" Dylan began.

"What if you pushed him in his office chair?" Dick suggested, noting how Scott shook now that the blanket didn't hide him.

"I can walk," Scott protested.

"With how much you're shaking?" Dylan asked. "I wouldn't risk it. You're not going."

"Is pushing Scott in the chair a good compromise?" Dick asked.

Dylan looked between his brother and Dick, brow furrowed. He nodded. "Fine."

Dylan grabbed Scott's office chair and wheeled it over to his brother. Scott looked up at Dylan, his eyebrows raised.

"Do I really have to do this?" Scott asked. "I honestly think I'll be fine walking."

Dylan frowned at him and pointed to the chair. Scott sighed and wrapped the blanket around himself again as he stood. He was surprised by how weak his legs were and was glad that he could quickly sit down in the chair. He stared at the ground, trying to avoid Dylan's gaze. He didn't want to admit that he was too weak to walk.

"Why do I need to go to the Field Room?" Scott asked Dick as Dylan pushed him out of the room. "What's happened?"

"Something's wrong with the Imagination Field," Dick said. "I've never seen it act like this before. Wells and Shakespeare are as bewildered as I am. We brought in Bradbury and Clarke, but they had no idea what was going on either. Then the attack calmed down, so they went to one of the labs to run some tests on the Fields."

"Why do you think I can help?" Scott asked. "If you guys can't figure it out, I certainly won't know what's going on."

"Actually, you've already answered one of the questions," Dick said as he rubbed the side of his stubbly cheek.

"What do you mean?" Dylan asked.

"You'll see." Dick opened the Field Room door and stepped inside. Dylan leaned close to Scott as they entered the room. "You owe me," he said.

"For what?" Scott whispered hoarsely.

"Do you have any idea how tempting it's been to spin you around in your swivel chair?" Dylan asked softly. "I am exercising so much self-control right now."

"That's because you have some saved up since you have none when you're with Lilly," Scott muttered.

Dylan snorted as he continued to push him.

"What's wrong with you?" Wells asked Scott. He was in front of the bottom row of computers, all of which were flashing brightly. His dark hair was dishevelled, and it looked like he'd been pulling on his mustache.

"He had the worst Writing Fever attack I've ever seen," Dylan said. "Without Curtis and Liz's help, I'm not sure he would have come out of it."

"What happened, Scott?" Shakespeare asked. He looked exhausted, and dark bags shadowed his eyes.

Scott explained his attack, leaving out the parts with his father. He didn't want to let the writers know what had caused the screaming to start or that he was still so traumatized by his dad's death. It felt like a weakness. Plus, he didn't want to say anything about his brain activating, because he didn't know what that meant, and he wasn't sure he should give the writers that information.

"How are you feeling now?" Shakespeare asked after Scott finished explaining. "Is the Fever gone?"

"I'm feeling much better," Scott said as he leaned forward in his chair. "Just tired and shaky, and a little cold. I feel stronger every minute, though. It's pretty convenient that Curtis has that healing magic."

"Curtis's Body Magic was highly useful when Liz had to face her villain as well," Shakespeare said.

"When did you find Scott in the Fever, Dylan?" Wells asked.

Dylan looked at the watch on his wrist. "About forty-five minutes ago?"

Wells turned back to the computer and hit a few keys on the keyboard.

"Look," Wells said. He pointed to the large screens at the front of the room as an image transferred onto them. It showed the blue web of the Imagination Field, but it was more active than Scott had ever seen it. It fluctuated like it was the ocean in the midst of a ferocious storm.

"'I have seen tempests, when the scolding winds have riv'd the knotty oaks; and I have seen the ambitious ocean swell, and rage, and foam, to be exalted with the threat'ning clouds: but never till to-night, never till now, did I go through a tempest dropping fire. Either there is a civil strife in heaven; or else the world, too saucy with the gods, incenses them to send destruction," Shakespeare said.

Wells rolled his eyes from where he stood next to the computers. "*Julius Caesar*," he said. His voice was flat and bored, and he just stared at the Imagination Field, not bothering to look at anyone else.

"Dammit, Wells! You beat me to it," Dick murmured. He kicked at the ground as Shakespeare smiled.

"What?" Dylan asked.

Shakespeare chuckled.

"Shakespeare always quotes himself," Dick explained. "He changes his favourite author based on who knows what he's talking about most frequently. Wells has been in the lead for the last two weeks."

Dylan shook his head, squinting in confusion. "*What?*" he repeated.

Shakespeare sighed. "I've never seen the Imagination Field behave in this manner," he translated. "The quote felt appropriate."

"*Anyway*," Wells said pointedly, "the Imagination Field was acting up, as you can see. It lasted about an hour. What you're seeing here happened around forty-five minutes ago, or around the time Dylan first found Scott in the Fever."

Dylan frowned. "Did it peak about thirty minutes after that?"

"Yes, actually," Wells said. He pulled something else up on the computer, and the enormous monitors in front showed a different view of the Imagination Field, except that it looked nothing like it usually did and more like a child had scribbled all over the screen. The concise webbing of the Imagination Field was unrecognizable, and the peaks didn't even look like waves. It was a complete mess.

"At first we thought the computer was glitching," Dick said. "That made more sense than the possibility that something was actually wrong with the Imagination Field. But we checked everything, and the computer was fine. It was the Field."

"What happened at 1:45?" Wells asked, pointing to the messy screens. "Why did you ask about this time specifically, Dylan?"

"That's when Scott started screaming," Dylan said.

Wells nodded slowly then pulled up another time period on the computer, which was reflected on the screens. The group watched for about ten minutes as the Imagination Field stormed violently. After a few minutes, it slowly began to calm down. Waves and webs became recognizable bit by bit amidst the scribbling. Then, all at once, the Field returned to normal.

"I'm assuming that Scott woke up after the peak," Wells said. "And then this is when the dragon warrior was finally able to heal whatever was going on?"

Dylan nodded.

"What does it mean?" Scott asked. "What do I have to do with the Imagination Field?"

Shakespeare lifted himself up on a table and sat on its edge, looking at Scott thoughtfully. "That is the question of the hour, isn't it, Scott?"

"But you'll be able to figure it out, right?" Dylan asked.

Shakespeare opened his mouth to speak but was cut off by Anne's voice.

"Proximity alert," the computer system said urgently.

Wells frowned as the room's lights turned red, giving everyone's faces an eerie glow. "Proximity to what?"

The computer clarified. "The Betans are less than an hour away from being within firing range of the Earth."

CHAPTER TWENTY-SEVEN

"Thank you, Anne," Shakespeare said. He sounded scared, something Scott was unused to hearing from the bard.

"How did that happens?" Wells asked. "We should have had at least another week!"

"Scott," Shakespeare said, ignoring Wells, "are you strong enough to go to the ships?"

Scott stared at Shakespeare in shock. "I don't know," he said honestly.

Shakespeare nodded. "We no longer have time to exercise caution," he said. "I shouldn't be advising this, but I need you to do what you did before to make yourself proficient with hand-to-hand combat and firearms. You must write to make yourself stronger immediately. We cannot wait for nature to do the work for you."

Scott nodded hesitantly. "I can do that."

"Only write what you need to feel ready," Shakespeare said. "We'll deal with the consequences later, if any come."

"What do I need to do?" Dylan asked.

Before Shakespeare could speak, Scott intervened. "I don't want him up there," he said.

"Scott..." Dylan began.

"No, listen," Scott said urgently, leaning forward in the chair, "I let you come last time, but we weren't going to be around all of those weapons, and I had planned for us to go where the aliens were sleeping. You were in enough danger before, but you were essential to that mission, so I allowed you to come. I'm the only one that absolutely has to go up there now, and I'm not willing to risk you."

"Scott, I'll be fine," Dylan insisted.

"Please, Dylan," Scott pleaded. "Stay here."

"I'm part of this now too," Dylan said. "I want to help."

"If I may," Wells interjected, "we could actually use Dylan here."

"How?" Shakespeare asked.

"He can help with the computers," Dick explained. "Maybe he can finish the language translator program and help Tolkien, or help us control the drones from here. It will be helpful to have an extra pair of hands."

Shakespeare turned to Scott. "Would that be acceptable?"

Scott nodded. "I just want him out of harm's way."

"I don't foresee anything happening to him here," Shakespeare said.

"Unless you fail and the Earth explodes," Wells reminded him.

Shakespeare shook his head at Wells and then turned to Dick. "Go wake Yin and Yang and tell them to board the Command Ship. When they're ready, we'll send the drones with them to protect the Earth while we prepare Scott and Caspiz to teleport into the Betan ships and place the bombs."

Dick nodded and ran out of the Field Room.

Scott stood from his chair. He still felt weak, but he wasn't shaking as much, and he wasn't nearly as cold. He turned toward the door to walk back to his room and write, but Shakespeare stopped him.

"Can you write here?" Shakespeare asked. "As soon as you're done, we need you suiting up and gathering gear so that you can teleport."

Scott hesitated. He hated people watching him while he wrote, and he didn't like the idea of Wells being in the same room, looking over his shoulder. He judged Scott's writing harshly enough as it was. At the same time, however, Scott could respect their time constraints.

"Where can I go?" he asked.

"Anywhere you'd like," Shakespeare said. "I carry a scroll and a quill with me everywhere. As long as you're not opposed to writing with a quill, you may use this equipment. Otherwise, we can let you use one of the computers."

"I'll try the quill," Scott said. He walked slowly to the end of one of the tables, away from the computers that occupied most of the space. Shakespeare followed him and handed him a roll of parchment and a red quill.

"The quill automatically fills up with ink and cleans itself," Shakespeare said. "I enchanted it, so you shouldn't have any splatters on the paper or ink on your hands."

Scott took the quill. "So you're saying it's a pen?"

Shakespeare frowned, pivoted, and walked away. "Start writing, Scott."

"Where are you going?" Scott asked.

"I'm going to collect Caspiz," Shakespeare said over his shoulder. "Even with your new skills, you'll need all the help you can get."

"Follow me, Dylan," Wells said. "I'll have you take a look at Tolkien's translation software."

Dylan and Wells jogged to the bottom of the Field Room, and Shakespeare sprinted away to wake Caspiz. Scott turned to the scroll and unrolled it, then picked up the quill. He felt a little foolish using such an old writing method, but it didn't stop the words from coming.

I can feel the weakness in my body, he wrote. *I was sick. I felt the burning, and the shocks of pain, but they're gone now. They were healed by magic and replaced by exhaustion, trembling, and weakness.*

But now I feel the weakness dissolve. It lifts into the air and disappears, lost in the cosmos. My muscles grow strong. I no longer feel weak. I feel rejuvenated. My body is fully recovered, and it is ready for a fight.

Scott barely noticed the rush of heat that coursed through him, and he didn't acknowledge the flame of anger that escaped from the wall in his head.

My body courses with adrenaline, and I am prepared to meet the Betans, and to fight them, and to win. My mind focuses on the fight ahead.

With a flash of Fever, Scott saw the blockage in his mind. He was sure he only imagined it now because of what Liz had said earlier. He saw a large hole opening in the wall. Fire danced behind it, but he didn't know what it meant. He couldn't see the paper in front of him; only the wall was visible, but he forced his hand to move.

I am safe in my own mind, Scott wrote.

He heard an angry roar trumpet from behind the wall and saw the flames lick hungrily at the fissure in the dam, but as he finished writing the sentence, he came back to the present, where he sat at the desk in the Field Room.

Scott shook his head violently, barely aware that Dick had run back into the Field Room to a computer, where he typed wildly.

I stay out of the Fever, Scott wrote. He felt himself focus, like he had adjusted a microscope. *I am fully capable of achieving the task at hand. I will teleport onto each Betan ship. I will place the bombs, and I will destroy all of the aliens to save the Earth.*

Scott continued to write strength into his body and mind. He felt himself growing stronger with each word. His heart beat rapidly with anticipation and adrenaline, and his eagerness to battle the Betans grew with every sentence he penned.

Eventually, he ran out of room on the scroll, but he didn't feel he needed more space. He felt stronger than he ever had. He felt nearly invincible.

"Are you ready, civilian?" Caspiz asked.

Scott turned and looked at her in surprise. He hadn't noticed that Shakespeare had returned with Caspiz, but she was in the Field Room, already dressed in the blue suit she had used for the previous mission. Only her helmet was off as she waited for Scott.

Shakespeare stood beside Caspiz, and Jules Verne, a man with silver hair and a short beard, stood next to them, holding two silver briefcases and Scott's suit.

"You look better," Shakespeare noted.

"I'm ready for this fight now," Scott said.

"Maybe you will be once you're outfitted," Caspiz said. "Get dressed."

"One of the Betan ships just fired!" Dick yelled.

"Anne, show us the drones," Shakespeare commanded.

The displays at the front of the room changed from the Imagination Field to a curved view of the Earth.

"That looks like the windows in the Command Ship," Scott said.

Shakespeare nodded. "That's where the video feed is coming from."

The Betan ship closest to the Earth was also the largest. Scott watched with bated breath as the missile it had fired neared the Earth. It drew closer and closer to the planet, and then...

And then it disappeared.

"Where did it go?" Dylan asked.

"Zoom in," Wells commanded.

The picture zoomed in closer than Scott would have thought possible, somehow staying focused the entire time. Scott could just make out the distorted remains of a black hole disappear, presumably taking the missile with it.

There was a collective sigh of relief as everyone in the Field Room started to breathe again.

"The Singularity Bombs work," Wells said in disbelief.

"The drones were in position just in time," Dick said. "They wouldn't have been there even two minutes ago. We're lucky."

"We can't keep relying on luck," Shakespeare said. He turned back to Scott. "Get dressed. We need you teleporting to the ships as soon as possible."

Scott grabbed the suit from Verne and began pulling it on over his clothes.

"You are lucky I had time to look at the files from the Betan ship before they arrived," Verne said. It took Scott a moment to process his words because his French accent was so thick. "And you are right; your plan to teleport to the centre of the tunnels and disable the force field should work."

Scott looked up from his spacesuit and at Verne as he zipped it up. "How do we disable the force field?"

"There's a switch on the side of the tunnel, inside of a compartment," Verne said. "Open the compartment and flip the switch. It is, surprisingly, not very difficult."

"It's not *that* surprising," Wells murmured.

"What's in the suitcases?" Scott asked. He grabbed a gravity gun from a desk to his right and strapped it into a large holster at his side.

Shakespeare looked down at the silver cases. "These suitcases carry three bombs each, one for each of you to place at the end of each tunnel, two for each ship." Verne placed the cases carefully on the table where Scott had been writing and unlatched one. Scott zipped up his suit, leaning over so that he could see clearly inside the case. Three cylinders were tucked into it, surrounded by thick grey foam to keep them safe. The outside shells of the bombs were black, but a green glow emanated from each.

"Will the bombs be deterred by the interior Betan shields?" Caspiz asked.

"Nothing stops these bombs," Verne said. "And even if, by some odd happenstance, the Betan shields *did* manage to stop the bombs from blowing them apart, everything inside of the ships will still be wiped out, which would, I believe, still solve the problem."

Verne took something out of the case, then closed it and locked it again. "Remember, you need to place a bomb at each end of each tunnel," he repeated. "You'll teleport to the middle of each tunnel and disable the shields."

"I want both of you to run to a separate end of the tunnel, place your bomb, meet back in the middle, and teleport to the next ship," Shakespeare said. "I'm asking you to meet back in the middle and escape together because Scott has to be a part of this story, and I don't want anyone left behind. Understood?" He waited for both Scott and Caspiz to nod. "When you've placed all of the bombs on all three ships, teleport to the Command Ship and use the detonator."

Verne held out the black and grey bar he had taken from the suitcase. Scott took it carefully.

"This bar is separated into three sections," Verne explained. "Turn the two outside sections away from you twice and turn the middle section toward you once. This will detonate the Particle Bombs. Just make sure you don't detonate the bombs before you teleport to the Command Ship."

Scott nodded and took the detonator. Verne handed one suitcase to Scott and one to Caspiz as Shakespeare turned to look at Scott.

"Are you ready, Scott?" he asked quietly.

Scott took a deep breath. He knew he was prepared for this fight... but his father had thought he had been prepared to go into his battle, too, and maybe he had been. But that didn't mean that he'd made it back.

"Does it matter?" Scott asked. "I have to do it anyway."

Shakespeare looked down briefly before meeting Scott's gaze. "You can do this, Scott."

Dylan and Wells walked up to them slowly from the bottom of the Field Room. Dylan handed one teleporter to Scott and one to Caspiz.

"You had better come back to me, little brother," Dylan said as he pressed the silver disk into Scott's gloved hands.

"I can't make any promises," Scott said. "I wish I could, but... Dad made promises, and he couldn't keep them. I won't do that to you."

Dylan embraced his little brother. "I know you'll come back."

Dylan released Scott and took a step back.

"Helmet on, civilian," Caspiz said. She fit her helmet over her head, and Scott heard air hiss as the helmet sealed to her suit.

"We'll have Curtis here when you get back, just in case," Shakespeare reassured him. "Good luck, Scott."

Scott ignored him and focused on Dylan. His helmet obstructed his vision as he put it over his head. He closed his eyes briefly as his helmet sealed to his suit, then looked at Dylan one last time before Caspiz grabbed Scott's arm.

"Let's move out," Caspiz said.

Scott took a deep breath and activated the first teleporter.

CHAPTER TWENTY-EIGHT

Scott materialized in a heap on the floor, more disoriented and ill than he had the first time he'd used a teleporter. He was fairly certain all of him had rematerialized, but he couldn't keep track of his body. Everything was spinning, and no matter what Scott did, he couldn't manage to stand up.

"What's happening?" Scott yelled. "Where are we?"

"The tunnel," Caspiz said breathlessly. "We're in the tunnel."

Scott tried to focus his eyes enough to make out what was around him. His surroundings were a blur, but he could see that he was encased by silver walls and threads of green light. He hung his head and tried to force himself to focus on one spot below him. It didn't do much good; the ground was spinning.

"Is the tunnel moving?" Scott asked.

"Yes," Caspiz said. "It's rotating in circles."

"How are we going to disable the force field if we're spinning like this?" Scott asked. He pursed his lips as he struggled to zip his teleporter into his suit pocket before he lost it.

"I'm looking," Caspiz said. "Just stay away from the force field as best you can."

Scott swore as he scrambled out of the way of a green laser. He could feel the heat surging from the light and knew that if he touched it it would burn through his suit, and possibly through him.

"There's the compartment," Caspiz murmured.

Scott looked up. Caspiz had managed to gain her footing and had a compartment open.

"I really hope this works," Caspiz said. She took a deep breath, and the green lights disappeared.

Scott let out a whoop of relief, especially since he had almost slid into another laser. His relief turned into confusion as he tumbled around in the tunnel.

"How am I supposed to place the bombs?" Scott asked. "I can't even stand up."

"Just get on your hands and knees, civilian," Caspiz said. "Start there."

Scott slid forward and turned, forcing himself into a crawling position.

"Keep moving, or you'll flip over again," Caspiz warned.

Scott crawled quickly, gaining more and more speed until he was keeping up with the tunnel.

"Stand up and run," Caspiz said.

"How am I supposed to do that?" Scott asked. "I can barely crawl."

"Just keep moving, Scott!" Caspiz snapped. "We don't have a lot of time."

Scott finally managed to stand. He stumbled but ran forward. He had to run diagonally to stay on the ground instead of running up the sides of the tunnel.

"Let's go," Caspiz said. She pointed to Scott's left. "Keep running that direction, and I'll run the other way."

"Who designed this thing?" Scott complained as he ran.

"You were supposed to have." Wells's voice came through over the headset. "The Reality Field just came up with something as ridiculous as the rest of your book."

"Wells, leave them alone," Dylan's voice barked. "Sorry, guys."

"We're tracking your progress," Dick's voice said. "We can see everything you see and hear everything you hear through your helmets, plus we're looking at the plans of the ship. Keep running. You should reach the end of the tunnel in another hundred and fifty yards."

"I know Caspiz can handle the physical activity," Wells said. "I just hope you wrote yourself a whole lot of stamina and speed, Scott."

"How am I supposed to place the bomb safely in a moving tunnel?" Scott panted, ignoring Wells and silently hoping that what he had written would suffice, even though he hadn't written specifically about running.

"Carefully?" Dylan's voice suggested.

"They won't go off until you detonate them," Dick said. "But it still wouldn't hurt to put them in a compartment of some sort. We'll see if we can find one in the plans."

Scott tried to focus on running forward without falling over, but it was difficult to concentrate. He was curious, and he wanted to look around, but he knew that if he did, he'd lose his balance. It would be just his luck to trip, accidentally open the case, and lose all three bombs down the spinning tunnel. They didn't have time for anything like that to happen.

Still, Scott couldn't help but notice the unearthly beauty of the spinning silver tunnel. It reminded him of the black hole in his room. The way it spun was almost… hypnotizing.

"Scott!" Dylan yelled.

Scott snapped back to reality as he fell from the side of the tunnel.

"What happened?" Scott asked.

"The spinning must have hypnotized you somehow," Dick said.

"I felt the draw too," Caspiz said. "Just stay focused on where you're going and stop looking at the scenery."

Scott struggled to get on his hands and knees to crawl again, when he noticed that he no longer had hold of the case.

"Where are the bombs?" Scott shouted.

"Are you *serious*?" Caspiz demanded.

Scott looked around frantically, his hands feeling out in front of him before he finally noticed the case bumping around the spinning tunnel another several feet behind him.

"I see it," Scott said. "I'll have to backtrack to get it."

"For hell's sake," Wells muttered over the headset.

Scott managed to rise to his feet and run toward the case. "Your snide comments aren't helping," he panted to Wells. "I need to focus. You can make fun of me when I get back."

"Promise?" Wells asked.

"Stop it!" Dylan shouted. "Caspiz, look out ahead of you. Based on our scanners, three Betans are entering the tunnel ten paces ahead of you on your left."

"I'm on it," Caspiz said.

"Will you be okay?" Scott said. He had just reached the case. He jogged in place to stay upright and grabbed the case as it fell from the spinning wall.

"Just focus on your part of the mission," Caspiz said. "I'm fine."

Scott switched off his concern, which he found wasn't incredibly difficult to do, and ran up the side of the wall, jumping over a black panel covered in buttons so he could turn back around. He was surprised when the move actually worked.

"I love being a writer," he muttered.

He continued to run.

"Scott," Dylan said, "you have two Betans approaching from a side tunnel to your right. Five yards."

Scott lifted his gun from his suit holster and shot the tall, scaly Betans as they appeared. He silently praised his writing again when he hit both targets in the head. They exploded, and the alien corpses dropped. Scott jumped over the Betan bodies as they spun around the tunnel, but he managed to continue running forward.

"Caspiz, you have a compartment coming up in about fifteen yards on your right," Dick's voice said. "I'm not sure how you'll open it with the tunnel spinning, but try to do it and put the bomb inside."

"Then, miraculously close the compartment, close your case without losing more bombs, run back to Scott, and get out of there. And also, don't die."

"Wells, if you don't stop with all of the negativity, I will take your headset," Dylan said.

"You may be good with computers, but you're not my mother," Wells said. "I can keep my headset if I want to."

"Stop it!" Dick yelled. Scott cringed against the sudden blaring in his headset caused by Dick's shouting. The high-pitched feedback made his ears ring.

"Okay, Scott," Dick said more quietly after the feedback ceased. "You have a compartment coming up on your right... well, it's currently on your right, I don't know where it will be when you get there... that's close enough to the end of the tunnel. Get your bomb into the compartment and run back to Caspiz."

"How far away?" Scott asked.

"Twenty yards," Dick said.

Scott was silent for a moment as he ran down the spiralling tube.

"I have no idea how to measure how far away that is," he admitted after a moment.

"We'll tell you when you're close," Dick said.

"The bomb is in position," Caspiz said. "I'm running back toward you, Scott."

"You've almost reached your compartment," Dick said. "Be on the lookout."

Scott warily allowed himself to look at the sides again, searching for some sign of the compartment. He felt his focus blur as a result of the spinning, but he clenched his teeth and forced himself to look for the cupboard that would hold his bomb.

"You're almost there," Dylan said. "You're coming right up on it."

"I don't see it," Scott said.

And then he tripped.

He tumbled to the ground and felt himself start to slide up the wall with the moving tunnel. His face heated with embarrassment, but he at least managed to hold on to the suitcase.

"What happened?" Dylan asked.

Scott looked up as he struggled to regain his footing. He noticed a handle indented in a cabinet, which was spinning up from the floor.

"I found the compartment," Scott said.

"Did you *trip* over it?" Wells asked in disbelief.

Scott felt his stomach twist. "Of course not," he lied. "The important thing is that I found the cabinet."

He scrambled to his feet, and, jogging in place, opened his case. He snagged a black cylinder and snapped the case shut, then looked up at the cabinet. It was on the ceiling now. Scott jumped up and grabbed the indented handle with the hand holding the suitcase. His weight pulled the cabinet open, and he was relieved when he managed to keep hold of the suitcase as well.

Scott grunted as he held on to the compartment door. He lifted himself up and threw the bomb inside. As the cabinet spun to the side of the tunnel, he pushed it shut and ran back toward Caspiz.

"You're about seventy-five yards away from each other," Dick said. "Scott, can you see Caspiz?"

Scott focused ahead of him and squinted. Caspiz sprinted toward him, a constant speck of blue in the spinning sea of grey. She was being tailed by two Betans. It didn't look like they had weapons, but then again, the massive, strong aliens didn't necessarily need them if they wanted to kill something.

Scott swallowed. "Yes."

"Do you see what's behind her?" Dick asked.

"What's behind me?" Caspiz asked.

"Just keep running," Scott said as he lifted his gravity gun. "I can handle it." He barely aimed before he casually fired two shots, hitting the two aliens squarely in the chest.

Caspiz jumped and stumbled but managed to keep her footing and continue to run. "It is uncanny that you're that accurate of a shot now," she said.

"Just keep running," Dick said. "Based on the scanners in your helmets, we can see movement outside the tunnel. You're going to have company in about five seconds, and you probably won't be able to shoot them all."

Scott pushed himself to run faster. He could see Caspiz picking up speed as well.

"Hurry up!" Dylan yelled.

"We're almost there," Caspiz said.

Scott unzipped his suit pocket and grabbed the teleporter.

"Duck, Scott!" Caspiz yelled.

He dove forward just as Caspiz did, and they clasped hands as they skidded across the tunnel to each other.

"Go!" Dick shouted.

Scott hit the teleporter as he heard gurgling and screaming from behind him. He would have breathed in relief if he'd still had lungs, but for the moment they were gone. He idly wondered how he was still able to think if his brain was separated into particles, but he didn't have long to ponder it before he and Caspiz found themselves in the centre of another spinning tunnel.

"Why do they all spin?" Caspiz yelled.

They unclasped hands and scrambled to their feet. Scott was able to catch his balance much faster this time around. He put the teleporter back in his pocket and jumped out of the way of a green laser from the tube's shield.

"Sorry to interrupt," Yang's voice said. "But I need you guys to hurry. Our drones are doing a great job protecting the Earth, but not so great a job of protecting themselves."

"What do you mean?" Scott asked as Caspiz scrambled toward a compartment that was currently above her head.

"Isn't it obvious?" Yin snapped. "We're losing drones."

"You've got to hurry," Yang said.

"We're *trying*," Scott said.

Caspiz leapt up, grabbed a handle, and the compartment opened. She managed to keep a hold on the door and reach inside to flip the switch. The green lights disappeared. Caspiz didn't pause as she let go of the compartment and dashed toward one end of the tunnel. Scott ran in the other direction.

"Haste is essential, especially now that one ship discovered you in their engineering tunnel," Dick said. "They may have notified the rest of the Betans. You're not as safe as you were before."

"They were safe before?" Dylan asked.

"The Betans are still distracted by our firing at them," Yang said. "We're not completely out of luck."

"Stop being so positive and admit what's happening out there," Yin said. "We just lost two more drones."

The pilots quieted. For a while, all Scott could hear was his own strained breathing as he ran down the endless, spinning silver tube. Then he heard Dylan swear under his breath.

"I hope your writing skills really worked the way you wanted them to, Scott," Dick said. "You have five Betans approaching you from a side tunnel."

"Which side?" Scott asked.

"It was on your left, but now…"

Scott crashed to the ground as Betans dropped on top of him from an opening in the ceiling. He grunted in pain at their weight.

"Scott!" Dylan cried out.

"Are you alright?" Caspiz asked.

"Worry… about yourself…" Scott said as he struggled to push a Betan off of him. "I'm fine."

The Betan on top of him seemed to smile, its pointy teeth grinning at him. Scott lifted the suitcase in his left hand and bludgeoned the alien's head in with it. Green blood oozed onto his helmet. The Betan's body weight fell on him, and Scott used its corpse to wipe its blood away from his visor.

Another Betan lifted its comrade off of Scott and threw the body to the side. Scott scrambled away just in time to avoid the Betan's grasping arms. Oddly, while these Betans were carrying weapons, they didn't have them drawn.

"Come on, Scott," Dylan's voice whispered.

Scott lifted his gun from around his neck and shot at the Betan. His bullet hit the alien's holstered gun, and it ruptured, spraying hot plasma in multiple directions. Scott rolled out of the way, narrowly avoiding an enormous glob of it.

Most of the plasma hit the Betan holding the gun. It was enough to melt a hole in its chest, and it fell backward, dead. The other three Betans screeched as plasma hit them, but unfortunately, the damage was not enough to kill them.

But it was enough to distract them.

Scott fired his gun again, exploding the head of one of the Betans. He scrambled to his feet and ran toward the last two Betans as the other alien's flesh ripped apart.

The Betans turned to Scott, screeched loudly, and jumped toward him. Scott waited until the two aliens were lined up just right, and fired. The force of gravity was enough to rupture both of their hearts. Scott twisted his mouth in distaste.

"I've placed my bomb!" Caspiz said.

Scott shook his head, confused. "What? How did you get there so quickly?"

"She didn't have to fight anyone," Dick said. "I know you're exhausted, but you've got to keep going. Run, Scott."

Scott shook bits of Betan flesh off of his suitcase and gun, then regained his balance and ran toward his end of the tunnel.

"Scott," Dylan's voice said softly after a moment. "How did you do all of that?"

Scott frowned. Dylan sounded almost… scared. Scott didn't ever want Dylan to be scared. Especially of him.

"I wrote myself to be better," Scott said. He panted with exertion as he forced himself forward. "It came true."

"But you killed so easily," Dylan said. "It was like you'd been doing it for years. How? How is that possible?"

Scott furrowed his brow. "It was either this or be defenseless on this mission. Do you want me to die like Dad did?"

"Of course not," Dylan said hurriedly, "but Scott, I've never seen anything like…"

Dick cut him off. "You have a compartment coming up."

"Try not to trip over it this time," Wells said.

Scott glanced around him. It was difficult to see through his visor because of the gore, but he managed to spot an indented handle to his right. "I see it," he said.

He leapt to the handle and tugged. It opened easily.

"You might want to get the bomb out first," Wells said.

"Shut *up*, Wells," Dylan said.

Scott released the compartment handle and opened the suitcase. He stumbled slightly as the tunnel turned but kept his footing as he grabbed a bomb and shut the suitcase.

The open compartment was now on the other side of the tunnel. Scott sighed and ran toward it, dropped the bomb inside, and shut the compartment, barely backing out of the way before it slid underneath him.

"Got it," Scott panted.

"Get back to Caspiz," Dick directed. "We were right. You have more company on the way."

Scott ran back toward Caspiz.

"I've passed the halfway point, I think," Caspiz said.

"You have," Wells confirmed.

"Good," Scott said. "I'm really tired of running."

"You have another tunnel to go," Dick reminded them, "so don't get complacent."

Scott groaned. "I know."

"That's weird," Dylan muttered.

"What?" Scott asked.

"We're getting some sort of message from Yin and Yang," Dylan answered.

"We're getting it from two of the Betan ships," Yang said. "They're the two that haven't fired yet; I think they're letting the biggest ship take the lead. Can you translate the message?"

"I'm working on it!" Scott heard Tolkien yell from the background.

"I'll go help him," Dylan said. "It might be important."

"Does it really matter right now?" Scott asked.

"You see me, Scott?" Caspiz asked, distracting him.

Scott looked up, blinked sweat out of his eyes, and squinted. He and Caspiz were close.

"You'd better get that teleporter out," Wells said. "You're not going to have time to do it in a minute."

Scott reached into his pocket and grabbed the teleporter just as he and Caspiz reached each other. Caspiz grabbed his shoulder, and Scott teleported them onto the last ship.

And straight into the constricting arms of an enormous Betan.

CHAPTER TWENTY-NINE

S cott kicked and struggled against the strong arms that circled his chest, but he couldn't get free. He looked up at the Betan who held him and felt his breath desert him in fear.

"Dygavery," he whispered.

The Betan king pulled his arms tighter against Scott. Scott felt a few of his ribs crack as Dygavery laughed. Scott grunted in pain but couldn't manage much more, because Dygavery was crushing him. At least he didn't have to worry about the force field this time; the Betans seemed to have already disabled it.

"Let him go," Caspiz shouted. Scott cringed. Her voice sounded loud to him through the headset. Dygavery didn't seem affected by the volume.

He opened his mouth and spoke. His language was guttural and gurgly. It sounded familiar to Scott, but he couldn't decipher anything.

"Let us go," Scott managed to breathe out.

The Betan king snarled down at him. As Scott looked into his dark eyes, he noted vaguely that the tunnel was not spinning, like it had on the other two ships.

"You don't speak Betan," Dygavery noted. He sounded surprised.

"You speak English," Scott replied.

Dygavery squinted at Scott. "You are not as mighty as I expected," he said. "I won't feel quite as victorious as I had hoped when I kill you."

"Then don't kill us," Caspiz said.

Scott heard her groan as a Betan hit her. He wished he could see her. He wished he could get his gun and shoot the Betans, but it had clattered to the ground at some point when he'd reassembled right into Dygavery's arms. He wished he could get out of Dygavery's grasp and do anything at all.

"I have to," Dygavery said.

"Why?" Caspiz said. "Why did you come to Earth? Didn't your alien friends kill enough of us?"

Dygavery stared down at Scott. "Religion," he said simply.

Scott furrowed his brow. They always fought for religion, but this was different. Dygavery had named himself a deity. Something was wrong, and Scott hated that he didn't know what it was.

"Scott," Dylan's voice whispered. "Keep him talking."

Scott gazed into Dygavery's dark eyes, but the king didn't seem to hear Dylan's voice.

"I have a plan," Dylan said. "But you have to distract the Betans so Caspiz can move."

Scott wished he could ask Dylan for more information, but he couldn't give any indication that he could hear his brother through his helmet. Scott knew that this plan, whatever it was, would only work if Dygavery remained ignorant of the one advantage Scott and Caspiz had.

"What religion?" Scott asked the king.

Dygavery growled. "Like you don't know," he hissed. His voice was low and threatening, but loud enough to cover any sound of Dylan's voice from reaching the king's pointed ears.

"Caspiz, close to your left foot there's a switch," Dylan was whispering. "It took Verne a while to find it. You have to find a way to turn it on."

"But I don't know anything about your religion," Scott lied to the king. "If you're going to kill me, at least don't let me die ignorant."

"Why?" Dygavery snarled. "Any knowledge in that little brain of yours is about to be snuffed out. It's a waste of time to explain anything to you."

The king squeezed Scott again, and he felt his cracked ribs fracture. He managed to scream this time.

"I love that sound," Dygavery said as he licked his thin, papery lips. "I wonder what it would sound like without that ridiculous bubble on your head."

"Hurry, Caspiz," Dylan said desperately.

Scott tried to move his head back to avoid Dygavery's hands, but it wasn't the king's hands he had to worry about.

Another set of strong Betan hands reached around his neck and twisted. The helmet whistled as it began to unseal itself. Scott took a deep breath, ignoring the pain from his ribs, and held it. It might be the last opportunity he had to fill his lungs.

"Caspiz!" Dylan shouted.

"What was that?" Dygavery demanded. The other Betan stopped twisting Scott's helmet, but it continued to hiss as oxygen escaped.

"Got it!" Caspiz yelled, and she flipped a switch with a flick of her foot.

The tunnel started spinning.

Dygavery lost his balance and dropped Scott, who fell backward into the other Betan, who had also lost his balance.

Ignoring the stabbing pain in his side from his broken ribs, Scott darted away from the Betan and sealed his helmet shut against his suit again. He breathed deeply in relief but quickly regretted it as his side screamed in protest.

"Hurry," Dylan said. "They won't stay off balance for long."

Scott scrambled on the ground, looking for his gun. He slid past the legs of an unbalanced Betan and spotted it. He crawled toward it, barely snagging it as it slid down a rotating wall. Scott grasped the handle of the gravity gun tightly and, groaning in pain, managed to stand. He turned around, gritting his teeth, and saw that Dygavery was already rising to his feet. Scott, jogging in place to keep his balance, turned his head around quickly and saw his case. It was close to Caspiz, who was just regaining her balance and had her own case.

"Take my case and place both bombs," Scott said to Caspiz through the headset. He glanced back to Dygavery, who snarled at him and limped forward.

"But—" Caspiz began.

"I can't run with my ribs broken," Scott panted. He lifted his gun and shot at a Betan behind Dygavery who had reached for his plasma gun. "Our best shot is for you to run, and for me to stay as still as possible and shoot the Betans."

Scott stumbled backward, felt his case with his foot, and kicked it toward Caspiz as he kept his eyes locked on Dygavery. He hoped his case had made it to Caspiz and not to another Betan.

"I've got it," Caspiz said after a brief moment.

"Run," Scott commanded, his eyes on the advancing Betan king.

"I have two Betans on my tail, and I can't carry both cases and shoot," Caspiz panted quickly. "I need you to cover me, Scott. Hurry!"

Scott swore and turned away from Dygavery. He took quick aim and managed to shoot both of the Betans running after Caspiz before Dygavery tackled him to the spinning tunnel floor. Scott felt tears slide down his face from the impact of the fall on his ribs.

"I don't know what's inside the silly silver cases," Dygavery sneered. "And I don't care. I'll kill you, and then I'll kill your friend."

Scott set his jaw and shifted his shoulders desperately. He managed to free one arm from Dygavery's grip and hit the Betan in the jaw. He was relieved and pleased to see the king's head tilt back.

They were briefly lifted onto the wall of the tunnel before the simulated gravity of the ship forced them down, separating Scott and Dygavery again. Scott cried out as his fractured ribs jostled around inside of his torso. Grunting, he managed to turn around, only to see Dygavery towering above him. Scott didn't have time to react before the Betan king grabbed him around the throat and lifted him into the air.

"I will destroy you," Dygavery spat. "And then I will obliterate this planet. There will be nothing left."

Scott kicked his legs, trying to hit Dygavery, but the Betan's arms were long enough that Scott wasn't close enough to reach him. He only managed to scrape against a button on his chest.

Scott watched in horror as blood spurted from the alien's chest and covered him. Soon, the blood seeped into the alien armor, and Dygavery no longer stood there.

He had shape-shifted into General Davis. Instead of a tall Betan, Scott saw a short but strong, balding Air Force general in a black uniform snarling at him. The transfigured Betan king dropped Scott to the ground, but before Scott could try to scurry away, the king put his armoured foot against Scott's throat and shoved down.

Scott felt his vision begin to darken.

"Fight him, Scott," Dylan shouted. "Please, Scott. Fight."

Scott listened to his brother's voice as he glared at Dygavery. If Dylan's voice was the last thing he ever heard, he would be alright as he died. But he was going to stare down the Betan king as he perished. Scott was not going to show any sign of weakness. Dimly, Scott was aware that his body was growing warmer. This seemed odd to him. For some reason, he'd figured his body would grow colder as he died. But it didn't.

He grew hot.

Terribly hot. If he could have screamed, he would have.

He was burning.

He opened his mouth, trying to scream, or to say goodbye to Dylan, or make some sort of final last noise, when a terrible screeching echoed around the tunnel.

Scott's darkening eyes found Dygavery again.

General Davis was the one making the horrible noise.

The Betan king was screaming.

Dygavery stumbled away from Scott as if he could feel the heat emanating from his body. Scott gasped as he finally, finally drew breath again. It hurt his ribs to breathe, but he didn't care. He just wanted oxygen back in his lungs.

"What's happening?" Dick demanded.

Scott tried to answer, but he still couldn't speak. He just shook his head in wonder.

Dygavery was backing away from Scott, still screaming.

"Why is he screaming?" Caspiz asked.

"I... don't... know," Scott managed to say. His voice was raw and weak, but he was relieved to be able to speak again. "And I... don't... care."

Scott lifted his gun and fired. The gravity force missed Dygavery's retreating figure.

"Wait, Scott!" Caspiz shouted. "It's General Davis!"

Scott aimed again. This time he hit the Betan King's hand, but it wasn't enough to kill him. Still, Dygavery dropped to the ground, his human arm bleeding.

"Scott!" Caspiz yelled.

Scott leaned his head back against a rotating tunnel wall and gasped. He was so tired and so weak, and he couldn't fight the spinning tunnel. He shut his eyes as the tunnel spun upward. He wasn't sure he could survive falling from the ceiling.

"It's not… Davis," Scott managed to say. "It's Dygavery. Remember… he's not… human."

The tunnel stopped spinning, and Scott slid down the wall as it settled. He opened his eyes and looked up. Caspiz stood over him. She no longer held the silver cases in her hands. She appeared to have abandoned them at some point. Instead, she carried the last bomb in her left hand. Her other hand held a particle gun, but it wasn't pointed at Dygavery.

It was pointed at Scott.

"What did you do to him?" Caspiz asked.

Scott shook his head. He slowly rose to his feet, grabbing his gun from the floor and ignoring the flaming heat in his body and the pain in his side. Scott aimed at the Betan king, then looked back at Caspiz.

"I don't know," Scott said softly. "And it doesn't matter."

"Stop, Scott," Caspiz said. Her eyes were wide, desperate. Scott had never seen her look so… vulnerable. "Stop, or I will shoot you."

Scott shook his head at the colonel in pity. "That's not General Davis. General Davis is in a different dimension. That's Dygavery."

"I'm warning you, civilian…"

"Caspiz, even if that really were General Davis, he's a traitor to the human race," Scott said. "That squirming, snivelling creature is trying to destroy the Earth. Stand down and let me do my job. Do your duty, soldier."

Caspiz's chin trembled, but she didn't lower her gun. "Please, Scott," she said again. "Don't."

Scott turned back toward Dygavery. "You may want to look away," he said as he aimed carefully through the site of the gravity gun. He was determined not the miss again. He clearly saw General Davis's head, even though the king had tried to crawl away from Caspiz and Scott.

Scott saw Dygavery mouth a word, but he couldn't tell what it was. Still, it sent a dagger of heat up his spine. He didn't know why, and he didn't care.

All he cared about was killing the Betan king who had threatened his brother and his planet.

Scott smiled.

He aimed.

"Please, Scott!" Caspiz yelled.

Scott fired.

CHAPTER THIRTY

Dygavery's head exploded, and bits of him splattered across the tunnel. Scott didn't even flinch when green blood hit his helmet. In fact, he rather enjoyed it this time. As Dygavery's body fell, he returned to his old form, and General Davis was gone.

It took Scott a moment to stop reveling in his kill and register the sound of Caspiz's soft sniffling. Scott turned back to her. Tears rolled down her face. Her gun was still pointed at Scott, but she stared with wide, watery eyes at Dygavery's body, where moments before, General Davis, her foster father, had waited for death.

"Lower your gun," Scott commanded.

Caspiz didn't respond.

"Jane," Scott said more gently. Caspiz shakily lowered her gun and hung her head, finally looking away from Dygavery's body.

"Let's place the final bomb and go," Caspiz said in a small voice.

"You have more Betans on the way," Dick said. "You should hurry."

"Can you walk, Scott?" Dylan's worried voice asked. "How badly are you hurt?"

Scott grunted as he made his way next to Caspiz and awkwardly patted her shoulder.

"I can walk," he said. "But Caspiz, you might still want to run if we have more hostiles on the way."

Caspiz glanced up at Scott, released a held breath, and nodded. Scott noticed that she didn't quite meet his eyes, and when she ran forward, she didn't look at Dygavery's body. Scott followed behind at a slower pace, trying his best not to upset his broken ribs.

"Why the hell didn't you tell us there was a switch to turn off the spinning in the other tunnels?" Scott asked, trying to distract himself from the pain in his side and the betrayed look on Caspiz's face.

Dylan laughed. It was a breathy laugh, full of stress and worry. "We didn't notice it before. We're lucky we noticed it in this tunnel. Otherwise…" he trailed off.

"Otherwise I'd be dead," Scott said. "But I'm coming back to you, Dylan. I'm not going to abandon you like Dad abandoned me."

"The bomb's in position," Caspiz said.

Scott looked up, surprised. "Already?" he asked.

"It's remarkably easy when the tunnel isn't spinning," Caspiz said. Her voice sounded dead.

"You might want to go even faster," Dick said. "Scott, there are more Betans approaching. Look behind you."

Scott stopped and turned around. He lifted his gun.

"They'll be there in about five seconds."

"I'm almost to you, Scott," Caspiz said.

Scott kept his gun up with one hand and used his other to reach for his teleporter.

It wasn't there.

"Um…."

"What?" Caspiz asked.

Scott looked up. The Betans were already there, staring wide-eyed at their dead king. There were only five of them. Scott lifted his gun and helped Caspiz kill all of them. It was easy compared to killing Dygavery.

Scott swallowed as he lowered his gun. "I don't have my teleporter," he admitted.

"What?" Dylan's strangled voice asked.

"I didn't have time to put it back in my pocket," Scott said. "I was busy being crushed by an enormous alien god."

"I still have mine," Caspiz said. "Cover me while I get it out."

Scott lifted his gun to his shoulder just as Betans poured into the tunnel in front of him. He swore as he fired rapidly at the alien horde.

"I've almost reached you," Caspiz said.

Scott didn't have time to look around for her. He just kept firing, ignoring the dark green blood and the falling bodies.

"Hurry," Dylan yelled. "More are pouring in!"

"Gotcha!" Caspiz said. He felt her arms close around his tender ribs, and he dropped his gun in shock at the pain.

Then they disappeared.

They materialized on the command ship. An alarm was blaring. Scott wasn't sure if it was going off because they'd teleported aboard or for another reason.

"Don't shoot it!" Yin yelled as Caspiz released Scott. She handed him the teleporter and stepped away from him. "What the hell is wrong with you?"

Scott looked around and saw that one of the screens on the wall had been blown apart.

"What happened to your screen?" he asked as he placed the teleporter in his pocket. He ignored the fact that Caspiz had stepped away from him so quickly and that she still had that utterly betrayed look on her face.

Yang laughed while Yin growled. Neither looked at him and Caspiz; they were far too focused on controlling the drones.

"*You* happened," Yang said. "You must have hit the trigger as you teleported, and the gravity force came through. Though I'm not sure where your gun is."

Scott looked down. "Sorry," he said. "I think I dropped my gun on the Betan ship, right before we teleported here."

"I think I've got it!" Scott heard Tolkien's voice say through the headset.

"How are you feeling, Scott?" Dylan asked, ignoring Tolkien. "How bad are you injured?"

Scott grimaced. "I think it's just my ribs. I don't think any organs have been damaged. I'll be alright."

"I'm glad you're safe and everything," Yang said. "But I, for one, would be even more glad if three certain alien ships exploded right about now. We're still losing drones fast here, guys."

Scott looked at the 360-degree view provided by the screens. He could see that Yang was right. There were barely any droids left, and they were darting around trying to fire enough Singularity Bombs to protect the planet from the missiles rapidly fired by the middle Betan ship. They wouldn't last much longer. The Betans needed to be destroyed, once and for all.

Scott took the detonator from his pocket and held it in front of him. He glanced at the Betan ships one more time and felt a small tinge of regret. He started to twist the left side when Dylan's urgent voice interrupted him.

"No, Scott!" he yelled through the helmet. "Don't!"

"Civilian, a good portion of our drones have been taken out," Caspiz argued. Her voice was cold. "You have to activate those bombs."

"Scott!" Dylan yelled. "Wait—"

"I'm not going to wait any longer." Scott interrupted his brother. "I have to protect you. The Earth is vulnerable."

"Scott, please, just listen—"

His voice was cut off when Caspiz unsealed Scott's helmet and lifted it over his head. Scott felt a moment of panic before he remembered that they were on the command ship and he could breathe.

Caspiz set Scott's helmet down on the floor and took hers off as well.

"You have to decide what to do," Caspiz said. "I understand that this is your story, and not mine, so I won't say more than this." She took a deep breath and gave Scott a pained look. "Those squirming, snivelling creatures are trying to destroy the Earth. Do your duty, soldier."

Caspiz folded her arms against her chest and turned away to stand by Yin, who was busy firing the Singularity Bombs from the remaining drones. Scott looked at Caspiz and Yin, side by side, both of them extraordinarily strong women who had seen so much in their lives and sacrificed their time and their existence to come to this moment to protect the Earth from the Betans.

Even Yang, who was more of a goofball and an optimist in general, was intense and focused on the battle around them. And then there was Paul, who would never come back, who would never drive them crazy with another alien theory. Paul, who was dead. Because of the Betans.

Scott lifted the detonator and twisted either end of it away from him. He took a deep breath, heedless of Dylan's muted voice yelling frantically from his detached helmet.

Scott exhaled.

And he detonated the bombs.

CHAPTER THIRTY-ONE

Three brilliant flashes of light nearly blinded him. Scott dropped the detonator and shielded his eyes against the blasts. It took him a moment to realize that the light came from the exploding ships. He had expected several enormous bangs, but of course, sound didn't travel in space. He could hear nothing but his own racing heartbeat. Impossibly fast, the blinding lights from the ships went out.

It was eerily quiet for several seconds.

And then the alarms went off.

"I'm not even touching the controls!" Scott said, raising his hands in defense.

"It's not you," Yang said. "Look at what's happening to the remains of the Betan ships."

Scott shook his head. "They exploded. It's what we expected."

"But none of us thought about what would happen to the ruins of the ships!" Yin yelled. "We're all idiots."

"What do you mean?" Scott asked.

Neither of the pilots answered. They were absorbed in what they were doing at the laser controls. The alarms continued to blare.

"What's happening?" Scott asked. "Why are the alarms going off? Why are Yin and Yang panicking?"

Caspiz walked away from Yin and came to stand by Scott, taking care not to touch him. "There must be some pieces of the ships that are on a path to collide with Earth."

Scott swerved his head to look at the display in front of Yin, which counted the number of droids still active.

"Can we protect the Earth with the Singularity Bombs?" Scott asked. "Do we have enough droids to cover it?"

Caspiz looked up at Scott for a moment, her hard eyes finally meeting his gaze. "No."

Scott looked back at Yin and Yang. His heart pounded and his breathing was shallow until, after what felt like hours but could only have been a minute or two, Yin leaned back and swore.

"What?" Scott asked.

"I've got the droids ready to fire the Singularity Bombs," she said. "And thanks to Yang, they're in position."

"So what's the problem?" Caspiz asked.

"There's not enough to capture the debris," Yin said. "The Command Ship will have to help... but with all of the ships that close together, they'll all be sucked into the black holes from the Singularity Bombs."

"So you're saying..." Scott began slowly.

Yin nodded. "We're not going to make it. The ship will most likely be torn apart in the black hole. We're dead."

Scott's stomach plummeted. It was the same as what had happened with his father. Everyone on this mission was going to die. Everyone.

Including him.

Yang's voice interrupted his panic. "Chill, Yin," Yang said. "You are so negative."

Scott stared at Yang as he pushed a few more buttons and jumped up.

"What are you doing?" Scott asked.

Yang forced his sister out of her seat. Yin struggled against him.

"Stop being such a martyr," Yang mumbled. Yin glared at him but finally allowed Yang to help her up. The twins ran up to Scott and Caspiz. She stared at them both, her brow furrowed as Scott gaped at them.

"What are you doing?" Scott repeated.

"Seriously?" Yang said. "You guys don't remember?"

"Remember what?" Scott shouted. He was frustrated, and he used his anger to hide his fear.

Yang rolled his eyes. "Activate autopilot," he commanded.

The laser chairs disappeared and the ship shot forward. Scott stumbled, but Yang caught him.

"You have a teleporter, right?" Yang asked.

Scott nodded and grabbed the teleporter from his pocket.

Yang smiled. "Let's go home."

Scott smiled nervously back.

And dropped the teleporter as the command ship rocketed forward again.

"Dammit, Creator!" Yang yelled.

Caspiz ran after the teleporter as Scott cursed himself for his clumsiness.

"Singularity Bombs launching in ten seconds," the computer said.

"Come on, Caspiz!" Yang yelled.

"Nine."

"We'll never make it," Yin muttered.

"Eight."

The teleporter slid away from Caspiz's extended arms.

"Seven."

Caspiz dove.

"Six."

Scott held his breath as the colonel slid toward the teleporter.

"Five."

Caspiz jumped up, holding the teleporter firmly in her grasp.

"Four."

She ran toward them.

"Three."

"Come on, come on, come on…" Yang muttered.

"Two."

She had almost reached them.

"One."

Yin, Yang, and Scott grabbed each other's shoulders as Caspiz drew closer.

"Fire."

CHAPTER THIRTY-TWO

There was a long moment of deafening silence. Scott's eyes were squeezed shut. Had he been taken somewhere else by the black hole?

He took a deep breath and slowly opened his eyes. He was in a large theatre-type room full of desks and computers. His face broke into a grin as he recognized the Field Room. He could have cried with joy. He had never been so happy to be at the Immortal Writers Castle.

"We made it," Scott muttered in disbelief.

Yin, Yang, Caspiz, and Scott separated from each other, each taking deep breaths. Caspiz handed Scott the teleporter, a tight, exhausted smile on her face. Scott put the teleporter back in his pocket again.

Yang started laughing. "We did it!" he yelled. He threw a fist up in the air and let out a whoop.

Yin and even Caspiz smiled in relief. Scott surprised himself by high-fiving Yang as he laughed.

Scott turned around to find Dylan, and his smile disappeared.

Dylan, Wells, Dick, Shakespeare, Verne, and Tolkien were gathered around a computer. Tolkien and Dick stared at the monitors in front of them with shocked faces, while Dylan, Shakespeare, and Wells stared at Scott. Verne bit his lip and focused on the floor. Curtis, who was there, Scott assumed, in case there had been a medical emergency, leaned against a wall, chewing his cheek. Dylan looked horrified.

"What's wrong?" Scott asked.

Dylan opened his mouth, but he said nothing.

Wells twisted his lips into a frown and turned back to the computer. He hit a few buttons, and the Imagination Field disappeared from the large screens at the front of the room and was replaced by lines of the Betan language.

Scott looked at the screen, shaking his head. "I don't understand," he said. He could barely hear himself over Yang and Yin's cheering.

Tolkien hit a few keys, and the symbols up on the screen started to change, translated into the English alphabet Scott had provided.

Scott felt heat pierce his head, but he ignored it. He didn't have time for a Fever attack right now. Something was clearly wrong... he just didn't know what it was yet.

The words on the screen continued to change, one letter at a time, until they were all in nonsensical English.

But then Tolkien pressed a few more buttons, and the words rearranged themselves on the screen until Scott could read them.

At first he felt the heat consume him as he read.

We came to destroy your world, the words read, *but when we realized what had happened, we came to see him.*

Scott's heart raced as his image flashed up on the screen.

We're on your side, the Betans had transmitted to them. *The War Ship is the only one that isn't. Dygavery has gone mad. But the rest of us...*

Scott swallowed hard as he remembered that the Betans on the first two ships hadn't fired on him and Caspiz. On the first ship, they hadn't even been armed.

We just want to meet our Creator.

Caspiz walked up beside Scott, staring up at the screen with horror on her face. Yin and Yang were still celebrating and hadn't noticed what was happening.

Cease firing, the Betans had pleaded. *We just want to meet our Creator.*

There was a break in the text as Scott's image flashed again on-screen.

Cease firing, the words repeated. *We just want to meet our Creator.*

Scott felt the world start to fade away. Everything seemed surreal as he was swallowed up in the heat of the Fever.

We just want to meet our Creator.

Scott closed his eyes.

And he was back on the red star. He was consumed by it, by the heat, by the power.

He looked out into space.

He saw everywhere—solar systems, galaxies, universes.

He saw into the past.

He saw everything—everything that had happened to him, all of the secrets that had been kept, all of the lies that had been buried with Kent Beck's body.

And Scott understood. He finally, finally, understood.

Everyone in the Field Room was oblivious when the barrier in his mind broke on the red star.

No one noticed the heat turn to cold, furious ice.

No one noticed him return to his body.

And no one realized that it wasn't Scott in his body anymore. At least, not the Scott they all knew.

"We finally broke the translation code while you were up there fighting," Tolkien was saying softly. His elbows were on the desk and his hands held him up by his white hair. "I started reading through some of the entries from the computer… something about finding their creator, but having to be careful because Dygavery would kill them all… and then this came and I… I just wasn't fast enough."

Scott ignored them all as he turned slowly to look at Caspiz.

"You did the best you could," Dick muttered. He patted Tolkien's shoulder comfortingly.

Caspiz didn't feel Scott pull the particle gun from her holster.

"But how did Scott's picture get on that database?" Wells asked. He, and everyone else, was oblivious to Scott's actions. "How did they know?"

Scott lifted the gun and pointed it at Tolkien.

"Scott?" Dylan asked. "What are you doing?"

Everyone finally noticed that Scott was armed. They all froze.

Scott smiled, shifted…

And aimed the gun at Shakespeare.

CHAPTER THIRTY-THREE

"You did this," Scott said. His voice boomed around the room in the sudden silence.

He pulled the trigger.

Scott was a perfect shot, since he'd written himself as an expert, but Caspiz knocked his hand to the side as he fired. It ended up being fortunate that his aim wasn't accurate, however, because Dylan foolishly leapt in front of Shakespeare to protect him.

But Caspiz didn't stop Scott's particle bullet from hitting Dylan.

"Dylan!" Scott shouted. He tried to run to Dylan as he fell backward, but Caspiz tackled him to the ground.

"Get off me!" Scott yelled. He swung at Caspiz and felt his fist connect with her jaw, but her hold around him only tightened. He wriggled in her grasp, ignoring the pain in his gut from his broken ribs, but then Yin and Yang were both on top of Scott too, crushing him firmly onto the floor.

"Curtis, attend to him," Shakespeare commanded. He couldn't see the bard, but Scott felt his anger boil. That bullet had been meant for Shakespeare, not for Dylan. But once again, Shakespeare was safe, out of harm's way, while everyone around him suffered.

Scott heard footsteps running into the room. He tried to look up to see who had come in, but every time he tried to lift his head, or any other part of his body, his characters forced him back down.

"Is he alive?" Scott yelled. With what he knew now, he probably shouldn't have cared, but he did. He couldn't erase what Dylan had meant to him for so long. "Is Dylan alive?" Scott repeated desperately.

Curtis was the one who spoke up. "He's alive."

"Barely," Wells said. He sounded angry.

"Why did you shoot Dylan?" Shakespeare asked.

Scott fought against his captors as his anger rose. "I was aiming for *you*!" he screamed.

"Why?" Shakespeare asked again. His voice was calm, and that infuriated Scott further.

"You did this," Scott said. "You made me kill all of the Betans. And everything before that... all of it was *your* fault! Kent Beck did what he did because of *you*!"

"What are you talking about?" Wells asked.

"Your father's death was not—" Shakespeare began, but Scott cut him off.

"No," he growled. "Not his death. Everything else. Everything that's happened to *me*."

"Scott, I don't know what you mean," Shakespeare said. "But I didn't force you to detonate those bombs. We *all* were responsible, including you. We all thought that the Betans were here to destroy Earth. By all accounts, they should have been."

"If anything, it's your fault," Wells said. Scott yelled in frustration and tried again to get up. One of his arms managed to escape, and he punched Yang. Yang stumbled back, holding his nose, and Scott pushed himself up onto his hands and knees before Yin and Caspiz had him again. Still, he managed to keep himself upright against the two women, and he stared at Wells.

"How is any of this *my* fault?" Scott snarled.

"You're the writer," Wells said. "You should know the Betans better than anyone. How did you not know? How did you even end up becoming an Immortal Writer in the first place?"

Scott laughed. Wells didn't know, then. None of them did. It shouldn't have surprised him. Kent had been clever; not even Scott had realized the truth until the barrier in his mind had collapsed.

Scott's laughter ceased as suddenly as it had come when he finally caught a glimpse of Dylan's still figure on the floor. Curtis was attending to him, but Dylan's left arm and part of his left side was missing.

Scott's anger flared.

And Yin, Yang, and Caspiz were all focused on Dylan now instead of him, their eyes drawn to the injured man by Scott's own attention. Their hold on him was lighter now that they were distracted.

Scott thrust out both of his arms and jumped forward. He managed to break his captors' clutches, and he darted toward the gun that had been knocked from his hands a few minutes before.

"Scott, no!" Dick yelled.

Scott could hear Yang, Yin, and Caspiz behind him, but he reached the gun first—

And then he froze midstride, inches from the weapon.

He tried to look around, but he wasn't in control of his body anymore. He could only barely move his head and his limbs a few inches at a time. Scott gritted his teeth. It was the first time the *real* Scott had been in his body for years, and now his power was gone.

Slowly, without his consent, his body turned toward Curtis and Dylan... and Liz. She must have run into the room; hers must have been the footsteps he'd heard, though how she had known to be there, Scott didn't know. He suddenly remembered her holding Caspiz with nothing but her magic only a short time before.

Liz's hands were in the air, and she peered at Scott through squinted eyes. "You've changed," she said. "I can't access your mind anymore, but I can feel it. The dam has broken, hasn't it, Scott?"

"Stay out of my head, witch," Scott said.

"What happened here?" Liz asked.

For a brief moment, Scott considered telling her. She had been good to him and had tried to befriend him... but it didn't really matter. She was one of *them*. She would never understand.

But he couldn't fight her, either. Scott had to admit to himself that he couldn't defeat her. Or the other Immortal Writers.

Not yet.

"Just let me take my brother, and I'll leave," Scott said. "I don't want any trouble."

"But clearly you do," Liz said. "You shot Dylan."

"I was aiming for Shakespeare," Scott snapped back. "I never would have hurt Dylan."

"But you did," Liz said. She slowly stepped forward, drawing closer to Scott. "Why did you try to shoot Shakespeare?"

Everyone turned and looked at Scott, but Scott only had eyes for Shakespeare, the man who had destroyed his life; Dylan, who had taken care of Scott for years even though he hadn't known anything; and Liz, the current threat who held him captive.

Scott stared into Liz's eyes and smiled.

He inched his arm back as much as he could, but he was careful to do it slowly so that no one would notice.

"You can defeat me now," Scott said. "I acknowledge that. I mean, how could you not? You've got me trapped in your Spirit Magic. I can't even move."

He reached his pocket and slowly put his hand inside. "But I won't be this defenseless forever," he promised. "In the end, you will all beg for mercy, but it won't matter. I'll slaughter all of you, just like I killed the Betans."

"You have no chance of ever defeating any of us," Liz said. "And I still don't know why you want to. Tell me."

"You wouldn't understand," Scott said.

"Then let me into your mind so that I can see," Liz said.

Scott just smiled again. "It's already too late," he said.

Liz frowned. "What—"

But her words were cut off as Scott hit the teleporter in his pocket, and he disappeared from the Immortal Writers Castle for the last time.

EPILOGUE

Scott—the *real* Scott, the *free* Scott—leaned back in his chair and grinned. He was in his own castle now at the top of the Earth, where he could always see the sun. And he was so much more powerful than he had been three years before, when he'd left the Immortal Writers Castle. But he wasn't powerful enough to take on the Immortal Writers... not yet.

But he had a plan.

Scott stared at the computer in front of him. It had taken him some time to figure out the intricacies of the machine, even with all of the knowledge that had returned to him the fateful day that he had shot Dylan.

Scott rubbed his stubbly chin. Dylan wouldn't recognize him now. He wouldn't know what to do with him. But Scott knew what he had to do to Dylan. Oh, he wouldn't hurt his brother outright, but Dylan had chosen to stay with the Immortal Writers, and if he became collateral damage... well, that was just a chance Scott had to take.

And he was ready to take it.

Scott took a deep breath and placed his fingers on the keyboard in front of him. Writing computer code was surprisingly similar to writing stories, at least to Scott. And he had discovered that, somehow, miraculously, it had the same effect on the Imagination Field. Or it could, if the programmer did it right.

Which Scott did.

He typed in the last few lines of code. He just had to fix a few bugs and send it off into the Imagination Field. It would hurt the Immortal Writers soon enough.

And he knew just who to target first. He'd studied the prisoners in the dungeon beneath the Writers Castle during his three-year exile, so he knew who would wreak the most havoc on the Castle while still going unnoticed. He just had to break him free.

Scott smiled and hit *Enter.*

He swirled around in his chair and watched his own screen of the Imagination Field shudder as the new information poured into it.

And then the Imagination Field began to change, and the Reality Field writhed with excitement at what was about to come through.

Scott smirked.

There was no way the Immortal Writers would survive what was coming.

IMMORTAL SUSPECTS SNEAK PEEK

Nowhere else in the Castle was ever quite as cold as the dungeon. Maren wasn't sure why. Considering who and what was down here, it would be more logical for the massive prison to be unbearably hot. After all, the dungeon was meant to be the Immortal Writers' equivalent of hell.

Yet Maren forced herself to trudge down to the dungeon at least once a month. It certainly wasn't for the scenery—she had tired of the spiralling stone staircase lined with flaming sconces that led down from the library after about the fourth time she descended into purgatory. Even the various cages where the prisoners were kept ceased to amaze her after a while. Nothing surprised her anymore. The writers all tended to handle their guilt one of two ways: they either put all of the blame on their villains and tortured them for the rest of eternity, or they felt guilty and tried to make them as comfortable as possible while they lived eternally, alone in a cage.

Maren was the only one she knew of who visited her villain. She felt that it was important to remind herself that she was partially responsible for all of the carnage. Visiting the Yeti was her own form of punishment. He disgusted her, but she always forced herself to watch what happened in his cell. It was the only time she really allowed herself to feel anything anymore.

Maren reached the bottom of the stairs, rubbing her arms for warmth while her hazel eyes adjusted to the dim, flickering light from Benjamin Beddome's endless flames. A shudder wracked Maren's body as her eyes grew used to the light. No matter how many layers of clothing she wore down here, the cold seeped through her clothes, her skin, and into her blood. Maren gritted her teeth to keep them from chattering and reached up, wrapping her hand around a metal sconce and pulling the torch down to light her path.

She stood in the entryway for the stairs, which was one of six arms that stretched from a large circle that served as a main lounge area for the prison. Not that it was much of a *lounge*, really. There were places to sit around a large pit of fire in the centre of the room, but they were only stone benches, and Maren knew that, despite being so close to the flames, sitting on them only made her colder. It was no use drawing any closer to the fire at all. It did nothing for the kind of cold that prevailed here.

Maren watched her breath briefly colour the air with its heat and mentally steeled herself for going to see *him*. She had to do this every time she came. There was no getting used to being around him, or being in this place at all. Just because it no longer impressed her didn't mean that she wasn't downright terrified of it regardless.

Her footsteps echoed across the stone as she walked to the third hallway to her right. Each hallway looked the same from the inside of the circle, but the villains were separated into different categories. The Yeti was with all of the other serial killers in Hall Three. She hadn't really explored the other hallways; it was too miserable down here to spend more time than she felt was necessary. But she knew that some of the other halls held aliens, sentient monsters, wizards, and other villains. Maren had tried to talk Shakespeare into putting annoying characters that everyone agreed never should have been written into a seventh hallway, but no one had been very keen on that idea, for some reason.

Maren started down Hall Three, taking careful looks into each cell as she passed it. Some of them were large and luxurious, well lit with couches, pillows, beds, and blankets, the villains lounging about and resting. Other cells were cramped and dark. There was barely any room to breathe in them, much less live for years on end. Some villains were tortured; Maren had to resist the urge to cover her ears to block the screaming. Then again, some villains were given books and televisions and virtual reality systems, and while they had to live alone, they could have some semblance of happiness while they did it.

The writer always had the right to choose how to punish their villains. Some writers just killed them; others locked them up here however they saw fit. Maren personally couldn't justify killing the Yeti, nor could she hurt him. Instead, she kept him locked in a cell the size of a small apartment. It was full of books, weights, self-replenishing food, and adorable stuffed elephants. The Yeti hated it, especially the elephants. No matter how many he destroyed, more appeared.

Maren grinned as she reached his bright cell. She could clearly see into it; the force field walls were transparent and allowed her to see everything. She couldn't currently see him, however. He must have gone on a killing rampage against the poor defenseless elephants. An enormous mound of them took up most of the cell, and even with his massive bulk, the Yeti was nowhere to be seen.

Maren took a deep breath through her nose, the chill biting at her lungs, and opened her mouth to speak.

"Yeti," Maren called.

Her voice echoed down Hall Three, and then silence fell. Even the screaming inmates quieted at the sound of Maren's voice. They all liked to hear what happened when she came to visit.

It was because of the silence that Maren was able to hear him.

"You have to leave," the Yeti said in a gruff whisper. "She's here."

Maren frowned. Had he finally gone mad? It was impossible for there to be anyone else inside of his cell.

"Soon, Yeti," a voice said. Maren's breath caught. She didn't recognize that voice.

And that was impossible.

"How soon?" the Yeti hissed.

"Soon." The voice sounded like it belonged to a young man. "Very, very soon."

Maren stalked up to the cell and placed her hand on the force field. It flickered blue once, and the mound of elephants disappeared as the shield turned transparent again. Maren thought she saw a strange grey shape disappear, but she wasn't sure. It might have just been the elephants.

The Yeti was sitting, hunched and alone, in the centre of his prison. No one was anywhere near him, unless you counted the five elephants that surrounded him, now fully intact, at least until the Yeti decided to tear them apart again and bury himself in another mountain of stuffed animals.

"Have you been practicing impressions?" Maren asked.

The Yeti growled and stood up, his shoulders still hunched in toward himself. His bald head glistened from the light of his cell as he turned around to look at his creator.

"Why are you here?" the Yeti asked.

"You ask me that every time I visit," Maren said.

"And you never answer," the Yeti snapped.

"True." Maren stepped back from the cell so she could get a better look at the Yeti. He was tall—very tall. They'd had to raise the height of the ceiling in Hall Three just to fit him into the prison. A loose black shirt and blue suit jacket with a red flower in the left pocket covered his massive torso. The clothes used to fit tighter, but the Yeti hadn't kept up on his trademark strength. He'd given up on exercising after the first five years in the dungeon and had started to get a little flabby instead of insanely muscular.

He'd also given up on wearing pants, though, thankfully, his shirt and jacket were long enough to keep Maren from breaking down and being sick when she came to visit. It did nothing to help her disgust, however, and even less to quell her fear.

"I see your pants," Maren said. She pointed to a dark heap in the back of the cell. "They look warm. Why don't you wear them?"

"You ask me that every time you visit," the Yeti mocked.

"And I'll never stop," Maren said. "You're disgusting."

The Yeti grinned, thin lips pulling tightly against a strong, stubbled jaw. "I don't know why you're surprised. I haven't worn pants in... how long have I been down here, now?"

"Twenty-nine years," Maren said.

"Twenty-nine years." The Yeti sat cross-legged on the floor, facing Maren. She quickly averted her eyes and focused on the man's face. His eyes seemed to grow darker as he looked at one of the grey elephants at his side. "It's been twenty-nine years since you've let me kill anyone. But what a spree that was, thirty years ago!"

Maren pursed her lips and worked to control her breathing.

"Do you remember the look on your face when you realized where I'd been that whole time?" The Yeti laughed. "You were like a puppy following a trail of treats... except I left you a path of corpses." He laughed quietly. "Thirty years apart. I've never had to wait so long before between roads."

Maren frowned. "What did you just say?"

The Yeti licked his lips, his eyes refocusing as his gaze found Maren's.

"You don't usually interrupt, little authoress," the Yeti said.

"I'm not little," Maren murmured.

The Yeti sneered. "I know it's been thirty years, but you're the same as I am. Neither of us will ever change. You'll be stuck as a seventeen-year-old forever, and that includes being trapped in that tiny body, in that tiny mind."

Maren exhaled loudly. "At least I'm not trapped in a cage."

"Aren't you?" The Yeti licked his lips again. "You always come back to visit me. You never miss an appointment. Sometimes you even come for extra visits. You *are* caged, Maren Armstrong. Your prison is just bigger than mine."

Maren felt the cold rip through her again, and she shuddered violently.

"Are you cold, authoress?" The Yeti grinned.

"How are you *not*?" Maren snarled. "You're not even wearing pants."

The Yeti shrugged. "I have fond memories of warmth. Do you know how warm blood is when it spills out onto you? Oh, but I forget—you *do*. But you don't know what it's like mixed with the heat of adrenaline when you know that you're the one who spilled it."

Maren's throat burned and her stomach twisted. It was nearly time to go. She'd felt quite enough for today.

"Tell me again," Maren said.

"Tell you what?" the Yeti asked.

She glared at him. "The same thing I have you tell me at the end of every meeting. Tell me why you did it."

The Yeti smiled and leaned toward the force field that separated him from his writer.

"Because of you," he breathed. "You wrote me to do it. You may not have known what you were doing, but somewhere inside of that little adolescent head, you knew, and you wanted me to. So I did. I did it for you, my little authoress. Because you made me to kill."

Maren shuddered as the cold gnawed at her.

"The real question is, why did *you* do it?"

Maren could only look into his dark eyes for a moment. He'd never asked her that before. "I... I don't know."

"And you'll keep coming back here until you do," the Yeti said.

"I'll always come back," Maren disagreed. "I'll always deserve it."

The Yeti lifted his long arms up to the ceiling. Maren looked away as he yawned and stretched. "No," he disagreed. "Soon you'll take my place. You'll be the one in this cage, authoress."

Maren furrowed her brow. He kept saying strange things tonight.

"What do you mean?" she asked.

Laughter reverberated from the cells surrounding them. Maren felt her heart race at the sound.

"What do you mean?" Maren yelled over the laughter.

Too soon, a voice whispered from the Yeti's cell. *Don't give it away. Too soon.*

"Who's in there?" Maren demanded.

The laughter died down, and the whispering disappeared.

The Yeti lowered his arms and cocked his head at Maren. "What are you talking about?" he asked.

Maren's shoulders tensed as she heard more chuckling from the prison inmates.

"Nothing," Maren whispered. "We're done here."

The Yeti stood up and leaned closer to Maren from his cell. Maren had never been so grateful that a force field was between them.

"Be careful, authoress," the Yeti said. "I think your cage might be closing in."

AUTHOR'S NOTE

Dear Reader,

Welcome to the world of the Immortal Writers! I'd like to personally thank you for joining me in this adventure. I hope you enjoyed your stay in the Writers' Castle, and that while you watched the Immortal Writers learn to fight their villains, you learned to fend off your own.

The *Immortal Writers* world is a place where anything can happen. Every story you've ever loved has the potential to live here eternally. It is my hope that as you read and get to know authors—some from my own personal Imagination Field, and others who have actually lived and created beautiful stories—that you will feel encouraged to read, to write, and to live. I hope that when you read this book, and settle down to read the rest of the series, that you will get a taste for the magic of stories, and for how the Land of Story can save us all in unexpected but truly phenomenal ways. Remember that our imaginations are powerful… even powerful enough to defeat our own personal demons.

I also hope that you have fun! Think about what kind of Immortal Writer you would want to be, or what characters you'd like to meet, or what worlds you'd like to explore in the Imagination Room. Would you ride a pegasus? Would you fight dragons? What fictional character would you fall in love with?

I encourage you to reach out to me at any time via my website www.immortalauthor.com with questions about reading or writing, or comments about the "Immortal Writers" series. I would love to hear from you and to see what secrets you have discovered in the Writers' Castle. And Shakespeare would like to hear from you, too… he never tires of hearing from his fans (it comes from being the greatest writer in the world, I suppose).

Thank you again for joining the Immortal Writers. Welcome to our ranks!

ABOUT JILL BOWERS

Jill Bowers is a technical writer by day and a fantasy author by night. She is one of two composers-in-residence for the Westminster Bell Choirs and has a great love for all music. She used to be the writer and host for the award-winning radio show Olde Tyme Radio on the Aggie Radio Station at USU and has dabbled in stage play writing as well.

Jill enjoys attending Utah's Comic Con and Fantasy Con and has an unhealthy attachment to Netflix. She lives in Utah and has a lovely dachshund that needs to lose weight because she probably doesn't get enough walks and is too cute not to feed. Jill attended Utah State University for their creative writing program, where she actually specialized in creative nonfiction rather than fiction. However, she loves delving into different worlds in fantasy and sci-fi novels and is excited to have people enter the worlds she has created.

Visit Jill online:

Blog: http://www.immortalauthor.com/

Facebook: www.facebook.com/immortalauthorjill

Pinterest: https://www.pinterest.com/jilliard08/

Twitter: https://twitter.com/Jilliard08

Goodreads: https://www.goodreads.com/user/show/2509616-jill-bowers

Instagram: https://instagram.com/jilliard08/

Youtube: https://www.youtube.com/channel/UC4FH9bS51qVga7rPot7awTw

BOOK CLUB GUIDE

1. Immortal Creators mostly takes place in the sci-fi wing, whereas we only saw the fantasy wing in Immortal Writers. In which wing of the Writers Castle would you most like to stay? Where else in the castle would you like to go that you've seen so far in the series?

2. What weapon from Immortal Creators would you want to try out?

3. If you could use the teleporter to go anywhere in the world, where would you go?

4. If you could use a fake version of anyone as a target in the Imagination Room, who would you choose?

5. If you could do what Scott does in the story and make yourself a master of any skill, what skill would you choose? Why?

6 . Do you feel that Scott is a reliable narrator when it comes to Lilly? Do you think the romance author is really as silly as Scott makes her out to be, or do you suspect there might be more to her than Scott realizes?

7. Do you relate to Scott's Writing Fever in any way, such as when you're daydreaming or when you read and write? How so, or how not?

8. Do you think Scott is correct in thinking that the Immortal Writers, especially Shakespeare, are responsible for Kent Beck's death? Why or why not?

9. Is Caspiz's belief that all of the Betans should be executed justified? If it is justified, does that mean that it's right? Why or why not?

10. What are your theories about Scott's connection to the Imagination Field?

WRITE FOR US

We love discovering new voices and welcome submissions. Please read the following carefully before preparing your work for submission to us. Our publishing house does accept unsolicited manuscripts but we want to receive a proposal first, and if interested we will solicit the manuscript.

We are looking for solid writing—present an idea with originality and we will be very interested in reading your work.

As you can appreciate, we give each proposal careful consideration so it can take up to six weeks for us to respond, depending on the amount of proposals we have received. If it takes longer to hear back, your proposal could still be under consideration and may simply have been given to a second editor for their opinion. We can't publish all books sent to us but each book is given consideration based on its individual merits along with a set of criteria we use when considering proposals for publication.

THANK YOU FOR READING IMMORTAL CREATORS

If you enjoyed *Immortal Creators* by Jill Bowers, check out these exciting young adult titles from Blue Moon Publishers!

The Battledoors Series by Brian Wilkinson
Battledoors: The Golden Slate
Battledoors: The Black Spyre

The Deadish Chronicles by Brian Wilkinson
Paramnesia
Hypomnesia
Hypermnesia

The Hit the Ground Running Series by Mark Burley
Hit the Ground Running
Flow Like Water

The Nefertari Hughes Mystery Series by Bethany Myers
Asp of Ascension
Diadem of Death
Medallion of Murder
Relic of Revenge

Fall In One Day by Craig Terlson

NemeSIS by Susan Marshall

And don't miss the next book in the Immortal Writers series: *Immortal Suspects*!

BlueM)on
PUBLISHERS